Also by the same author

Relative Dating
ISBN: 978184386456 1 (Vanguard Press)

Born in Carlisle in the footprints of the Romans, Thelma became fascinated by history at an early age. The past as well as the present has always enthralled her, particularly the interweaving of both together. She always wanted to share more of her love of history, and especially the quiet corner of her heart that still lives in Hadrian's country.

Marrying a sailor meant a nomadic lifestyle, something she still embraces. Her occupation has ranged from teaching in Derbyshire, to a steam-engine fireman in Wales, to nursing gunshot wounds in New Zealand. North Wales is her current home.

Tree Dimensional

Thelma Hancock

Tree Dimensional

Vanguard Press

A CIP catalogue record for this title is
available from the British Library.

ISBN 978 184386 512 4

*Vanguard Press is an imprint of
Pegasus Elliot MacKenzie Publishers Ltd.*
www.pegasuspublishers.com

First Published in 2009

**Vanguard Press
Sheraton House Castle Park
Cambridge England**
Printed & Bound in Great Britain

DISCLAIMER

While historical details are believed to be accurate all the characters in this book have no existence outside the imagination of the author, and have no relation whatsoever to anyone bearing the same name or names. They have not even distinctly inspired by any individual known or unknown to the author and all the incidents are pure invention.

1

He looked down on the remains of what had once been a man, nausea swirling in his stomach as the stink of excrement and urine stung his nostrils. He gently turned the elderly face towards the light from the window, examining the swollen tongue and bulging blue eyes, barely repressing a shudder at the still warm and malleable flesh.

"Rigor not set in yet Jonesy?"

"No, only been dead half an hour, hour at the most." The speaker was an older man, grey haired and grey eyed. Bob looked at them now, noting the dark and serious look with his own deep brown ones.

"Why would anyone want to kill a poor bloody cripple?"

"You tell me; you're the detective. What's your best bet at a motive? Burglary gone wrong?"

"Well, we'll find out soon enough. All done with him for now?"

Dr Ryan Jones nodded. "Yes," he sighed, "you can take your pictures and take him away; I'll notify the coroner and get the autopsy arranged." The police surgeon removed his blue, latex gloves and stowed them in an evidence bag, turning to pick up his big black and silver metal case. "I'll let you have the report as soon as I can but there's no doubt it's murder; the poor man didn't put his own hands round his throat and squeeze tight. That I'm sure of."

"Sure it was manual?"

"Yes. No ligature marks, and you can see the indentations where the thumbs pressed against the carotids. Poor bugger didn't stand a chance; whoever did this knew just where to press." He looked across the body at McInnis, "We'll find the hyoid's crushed too. I'd stake my reputation on it."

Then a small satisfied smile shot into his eyes and he nodded at the hands of the corpse which were bagged and tapped. "Got something under the nails though; the old boy did his best. Your murderer is likely to be carrying a few scratches!"

Robert McInnis signalled the photographer forward and stepped away from the body as the man got busy with flashlights and angles. He walked across the carpeted floor, careful not to scuff the pile, and stood next to the door of the quiet room.

A wooden three drawer filing cabinet standing next to the desk was closed, but the key was sitting in the top lock. He'd need to see if anything had gone from that and if the key was usually left accessible. The desk in the corner jarred slightly with its keyboards and modern computer screens sitting back to back, the latter a blank grey revealing no clue as to what had happened less than an hour ago.

This was an old fashioned room with an easy chair next to the old gas fire opposite the door, the small oval table next to the chair lent an air of comfort and tranquillity for a studious evening of winter quiet in the book lined room. These books were an eclectic mixture of old, sturdily bound tomes mixed with yellow paperback editions, both filled with erudite literature explaining the development of mankind. The overall impression was of a world of culture and learning before the intrusion of computing.

A fly bumped and buzzed against the closed window and the early morning sun, pouring through the panes, illuminated the scene in graphic detail. Bold shadows and bright patches showed the pitiful remains for what they were, no longer a man of study but to be studied as part of a crime scene.

Bob gave another quiet sigh and turned towards the young constable standing at the door. "Where's the witness?"

"In the kitchen, Inspector. She's pretty shook up. She's his research assistant and always arrives about half eight in a morning. Found the body as you see, says she didn't touch anything."

"Right, thanks." Bob McInnis nodded. "Stay put for now."

He turned his back on the busy scene and walked along the short, dark, panelled passageway to the kitchen at the back of the house, noting as he did so the absence of clutter. That, he thought, would be because of the wheelchair he'd seen in the study. It was lying on its side at present, like a large friendly dog guarding its master's body.

McInnis pushed through the swing door and entered a rather dark room. The sun, this May morning, wasn't high enough in the sky to lighten the gloom at the back of the house. The kitchen might not be well lit but it appeared well appointed. Against the back wall there was an abundance of melamine work surfaces either side of a double sink, with gleaming white-ware and a very modern range, all set low, he assumed, for wheelchair access. There was a faint aroma of bleach on the air, mixed with something else indefinable. McInnis sniffed gently, noting it for future investigation.

The only occupant of the room sat at a big old-fashioned table, its surface scrubbed white. It was set squarely in the centre of the kitchen and the young woman sitting at it, nursing a mug of tea, looked composed to Bob's eyes until, that was, she raised her eyes to look at him. Stark misery, mixed with dull horror, met his compassionate ones.

Bob nodded at the WPC standing by the door. "Thanks Constable; would you assist next door and let me know when Inspector Bell arrives please?"

She nodded her understanding and left the room, closing the door quietly behind her. Inspector McInnis came over and sat down at the table, pulling a notepad out of his inside pocket and opening it to a clean page.

"My name's McInnis; I'm going to be in charge of the case. My partner will be with us shortly. I understand you found the body."

For a brief moment animation flared on the alabaster skin. "It's not a body; his name was Professor Peter Neville!" She glared at him.

McInnis examined her face as she returned her gaze to the mug she held. "Well, well!" he thought. She looked to be in her mid twenties, neatly dressed in a grey dress whose colour was deceptive, the long sleeves fastened with white cuffs to match the 'peter pan' collar. It should have washed all the colour away from her features but instead it enhanced the ebony pageboy bob that swung around her jaw line and covered the white forehead.

"Yes Miss, and who might you be?"

"My name is Elizabeth Fielding."

"Can you tell me how you came to find the Professor this morning?"

Elizabeth Fielding continued to look down into her mug, gripping it tightly as she started to speak. "I'm Peter's research assistant; since the car accident he's been stuck in his wheelchair. He was coping really well but he couldn't get out and do the research. A lot of the older libraries aren't wheelchair friendly yet." There was a fine tremble going over her, he noted, showing itself in the hands gripping the mug.

"Even allowing for the 'net' he still needed to access some old books. I come in most days and he instructs me as to what he wants me to find out." She finally raised those haunted eyes to the Inspector's. "I come in between eight and eight thirty unless he wants me to go somewhere special."

She stopped speaking and he saw her knuckles turning white where they gripped the sides of the mug as she peered into the depths of the murky liquid. Bob McInnis waited patiently for her to continue, neither prompting nor fidgeting.

"When I came in this morning everything seemed as usual; I used my key to open the front door, as I always do. Dumped my bag on the little hall table next to the front door and went into the study where Peter nearly always was. He's..." She faltered. "He was an early riser. He copes..." she stopped again. "He coped very well, especially since the house has been adapted for his wheelchair." McInnis noted the changing tenses as her brain accustomed itself to the reality of the death.

A very faint smile appeared and disappeared on her face. "He loved showing off how much he'd improved; his latest trick was to stand and swing himself from the wheelchair to the seat near the fire. He was boasting of how he'd be ready for the Olympics soon!" She stopped again, raising eyes almost black, and filled with emotion she obviously wasn't about to release in front of him.

"That's very clear so far Miss Fielding. Now what did you do when you entered the study?"

"I found him on the floor. I could see he was dead as soon as I went through the door, his face was..." Her voice hitched slightly and her face twitched, remembering the grotesque mask, but aside from that she kept her demeanour impassive.

McInnis waited a beat or two and when it became obvious she wasn't going to add anything, mentally shrugged and asked, "Then what did you do Miss?"

"I don't honestly know Inspector; my head was buzzing, shock I suppose, I just stood there with my hand on the door knob. I don't know for how long. Eventually I crossed the room and used the phone on the desk to call the police and just waited for someone to arrive."

"Did you stay in the room Miss?"

"Yes, I couldn't leave him," she looked somewhat piteously at McInnis, " but I couldn't look at poor Peter's face either, so I turned my back and looked at the bookshelves. I remember thinking, I hadn't realised he'd got so many German books for children on his shelves. It's really strange that..." She stared into space.

"Why is it strange Miss?"

Elizabeth shook her head as if coming awake, "Pardon Inspector?"

"Why shouldn't the Professor have children's books?"

"Oh! He was a bachelor."

"Maybe they belonged to a niece or nephew."

"He hadn't got any living relatives that I know about Inspector." Elizabeth shook her head sadly. "The only people I ever saw visiting were professors like himself."

"What else can you tell me about Professor Neville? How did the accident happen? You did say it was a car accident?"

"Yes, about two years ago now. A hit and run. They never did catch the person responsible. The Professor was using a crossing and the car didn't stop. It shattered the bones in one leg and crushed the other foot. They said, the doctors, that his age was against him." She looked up briefly, "He'd got osteoporosis and that stopped things healing properly."

"How old was he Miss?"

For the first time he saw a puzzled expression cross her face. "You know Inspector, I really don't know. In his eighties I think."

"And he was a Professor of history?"

"Yes, Cambridge."

"And you don't think he had any immediate family?"

"I've only worked for him since his accident, a matter of eighteen months. No-one visited much."

"Thank you Miss. Now while you waited for the police, where did you stand, and what did you touch?" Bob McInnis, having circled round, returned to the main points of his enquiry.

Give her, her due; he thought, she was holding up remarkably well. She took a small sip of what must, by now, be cold tea and after a small pause said, "I faced the bookcase opposite the door with my back to it. I only touched the telephone on the desk, nothing else." She paused as, after the briefest of taps, a tall man, his original brown hair now turning a silver grey, entered the room, closing the door quietly after him, and approached the two at the table.

McInnis looked across at the older man. "This is Inspector Bell. He'll be assisting me during this investigation."

Bell held out a warm hand as he murmured a greeting. "Miss Fielding? Don't worry; we'll find out how the poor man was murdered." He had a faint Scots accent and a pair of the gentlest brown eyes that Elizabeth Fielding had ever seen. She relaxed her grip on the mug to offer her own hand and McInnis watched some of the tension leave her face. He hid the smile that wanted to cross his face; he'd watched Sandy in paternal mode before and wished he knew how the trick was done.

"I'll just sit here and catch up with the notes for a minute Miss, and then I might have a question or two for you." He pulled out a kitchen chair, sat, slipped a pair of wire rimmed glasses over his ears, then scanned the rough notes Bob had been making while Elizabeth talked.

The other two waited in silence. Bob was aware of her breathing; his eyes rested briefly on the gentle rise and fall of her bust, becoming aware of the soft noise as she exhaled. He shifted his eyes and took in the rest of her features, high forehead, fine deep brown eyes, aquiline nose, and at any other time, probably a very kissable mouth. He stopped that train of thought as he felt the warmth stealing into his cheeks.

Elizabeth's attention was on Sandy Bell. Looking at the grizzled grey hair and the smooth shaven cheeks he reminded her of her father and she unconsciously relaxed.

Bob was grateful for Sandy's quiet cough as he laid down the notebook and drew her attention towards him. "Right Miss, you came in as usual, went into the study, found the Professor's body and rang the police. Is that correct so far?"

"Yes Inspector."

"You say you used your key as usual. The door was locked then?"

"Yes Inspector."

"And who else has a key Miss?"

"Well Tracy does, she comes and cleans and does the Professor's washing once a week."

"Anyone else Miss?"

"I don't think so. Peter had his, and there's a spare set in the desk."

Sandy looked at the notes in front of him; Bob McInnis had underlined 'no forced entry'. He now scribbled 'desk' and drew a key next to the notation. "Now Miss, was the wheelchair on its side then?"

"Yes. I told this man," she nodded at Bob McInnis, "I didn't touch anything."

"Yes Miss, we just like to cover all the bases." Sandy Bell spoke soothingly, pulling off his glasses and smiling quietly at her.

"And can you tell me if the wheels were moving on the wheelchair?"

Elizabeth paused, closing her eyes as she brought the scene she'd been desperately trying to get out of her mind, back into it. She stood up abruptly and headed for the sink. Sandy was the quicker of the two men, standing and moving across the room. He patted her back as she lost her breakfast, then ran the tap on the resultant mess, before rinsing a clean tea towel and handing it to her. "OK sweetheart, sit you down again." He led the now visibly trembling girl back to the table, an arm around her shoulders, helping her into her chair and going to fetch a glass of cold water.

Elizabeth wiped her face. "Sorry." Bell handed her the glass and she took a sip and then rolled the glass between her hands as she looked up at him. "I'm sorry Inspector. The answer to your question is no, the wheels weren't moving."

"Thank you Miss. Now just you relax for a minute, take your time." Sandy looked her over. "I'm sorry, but we need to ask these questions now while things are fresh in your mind. Do you want anything fetching? Your handbag?"

Bob McInnis pushed back his chair. "Would you like a doctor Miss?"

"No Inspector. I'll be alright." Elizabeth pushed the fringe back from her brow with a slightly unsteady hand. "I just want this to be over, and the sooner the better. What else do you need to know?"

Sandy gave her a cautious look and, apparently satisfied, went and sat in his former seat, taking up his pen and glasses again. "Well now, just one or two other things occur to me. For a start did the Professor speak German?"

Elizabeth looked startled. "I have no idea Inspector Bell; why do you want to know?"

"You said the children's books were in German. How did you know? I wondered if you spoke German with the Professor?"

"No, I did it at school, 'O' level standard. Which is how I came to recognise the words. I suppose Peter might have. He was especially interested in the First World War; a lot of documents about that are in German. I found some research articles in that language but I put them through 'Babel' before I passed them on to him."

McInnis exchanged a look with Bell. Neither man was about to admit they didn't know what 'Babel' was.

"Right Miss. Now do you know if anything has been taken? It could be he surprised a burglar."

"I don't know Inspector Bell, I haven't looked. The constable who came first asked me to wait in here. I haven't checked around the premises."

"Well perhaps you could do that for us in a moment or two. The other thing I'd like to know is what he was busy with just now. What were you researching for him?"

For the first time a note of caution entered Elizabeth's voice. "Why do you need to know that?"

"I was just wondering if his murder might have anything to do with the work he was engaged in at the moment. That's all Miss Fielding."

Elizabeth looked at the two men thoughtfully. "I don't suppose it matters now. He was looking into the issues surrounding deserters on the Western Front. That's over eighty years ago Inspector. I shouldn't think anything he turned up would be worth killing him for."

"No Miss, nor would I." McInnis shrugged. "We'd appreciate it if you could let us have a list of those he's been in contact with, and why. Just to get a general picture of where he's been and what he's been engaged on." He gave another tiny shrug, "We have to start somewhere."

"But why would anyone want to kill him? He was just a defenceless old man; he didn't go anywhere anymore. He e-mailed people, and he phoned, and occasionally someone nearly as old as him came to visit, but this all seems so senseless."

Elizabeth Fielding was finally alone. The two Inspectors had gone about their business, leaving her in the kitchen. She sat hunched on the kitchen chair, finally giving way to the tears that she'd been swallowing throughout the interview. She cried silently, big, fat tears rolling down her pale cheeks, her fist jammed against her mouth in an effort to suppress any noise escaping to the still busy constabulary on the other side of the door.

Inspector McInnis, coming soft footed into the room hesitated just a fraction too long. He would have withdrawn and left her to cope with her grief; he didn't feel he was any good with weeping females, but she caught the movement from the corner of her eye.

"I'm sorry." He came around the table, patting her awkwardly on the shoulder, offering a clean handkerchief the size of a young tablecloth from his navy blue suit pocket. "I didn't mean to intrude."

She shook her head, tears dripping off her chin and trying hard to glare at him.

She wasn't pretty when she cried, he thought; her face was blotchy and her eyes red-rimmed, but there was no doubting her sadness and all the blotchiness in the world couldn't disguise the dewy softness on the cheek his hand had just brushed. It was a good thing to know she grieved because he had to eliminate her, and she was one of the few who had a key to the door. He was also aware that even murderers could cry over their victims.

She hiccupped and muttered, "What did you want Inspector?"

23

McInnis looked at her blankly for a second; what had he wanted? Oh yes, the computer.

"We can't seem to get into the computer. It's obviously got a password. Could you give us it?" He sought security in his official role.

She used his hanky, mopping her face, and, making a determined effort to calm herself, she took several deep breaths. "I'll come and do it for you." She stood up, swung round, and took one step and stopped, standing still as a statue. A cold sweat broke out on her brow and McInnis watched as she shuddered slightly. He thought he knew what was troubling her.

"It's OK. They've taken the Professor away."

She was standing directly in front of him and he could smell the faintly exotic perfume she wore. Ah! That was the source of that scent he encountered when he entered the kitchen the first time. He watched as her shoulders relaxed slightly. She raised eyes still awash in tears to his. "I'm sorry, I'm being a wimp."

He admired the bravery of the ghost of a smile offered, while he spoke gently to her. "We're all entitled to be a wimp sometimes." He gently and fleetingly touched the nearest shoulder, then stood back to allow her to precede him from the room.

There were only two men in the study when she cautiously opened the door, a young man dressed in a white nylon suit, zipped over a superb body, the hood pushed back to reveal bright, short, guinea gold hair which rioted about an almost pretty face, and Inspector Bell. The latter shot a curious look at McInnis as the policeman followed her into the room.

Elizabeth went to the computer, stretching out a hand to the keyboard, then drew back nervously. "Don't you have to dust it for fingerprints or something?"

The young man answered. "Nah! I've done that. My name's Mark Forester." He held out a hand and grinned down at her from his lanky six foot.

Elizabeth offered a hand, murmuring her name. She turned towards McInnis who found himself relieved that she'd been just as cool with the police 'Lothario' as himself. She paused, looking at the Inspector after she'd booted up the machine. "Inspector," she recalled his wandering thoughts, "what exactly did you want to read on the computer?"

McInnis was unaccustomed to being distracted and shook himself mentally. "Er! Let's start with his e-mails; there might be a clue as to who he's been in contact with over the last few days. Then if you could show me how to get into the current research project that would be most helpful Miss."

Elizabeth sighed gently. "Whatever you say Inspector."

McInnis was aware that Inspector Bell was looking at him curiously, but he couldn't help that. He looked at the screen as she accessed the e-mails, noting that there were over a dozen just for that day alone. He sighed to himself. He hated modern technology. He'd never really got to grips with it; he could use it if he had to, but he preferred a pen and paper any day. His digi-box had nearly driven him demented. He had a feeling this was going to be a difficult murder investigation.

Sandy Bell drew his attention, "Have you got anything pressing on your desk I can handle when I get back?"

"Not really Sandy."

Bell lowered his voice, "I've got the keys by the way, I fished them out of the desk and Jonesy left the effects from his pockets bagged. There's plenty of money in the wallet and a nice pricy wristwatch. A signet ring and gold chain with a wedding ring on it.

So it doesn't look like a burglary, unless she arrived too quickly for whoever... But I don't think so; she said the wheels had stopped."

Mark packed away the tools of his trade and flirted with Elizabeth. McInnis was conscious of the conversation going on even as he talked to Sandy.

"So how long have you worked for the Prof, then Elizabeth?"

"About eighteen months. Peter offered me the job right after I graduated."

"Oh yeah, what uni' did you go to? I'm an Edinburgh man myself." McInnis found he was grinding his teeth and had to ask Sandy to repeat himself.

"I said," repeated Sandy patiently, "that I'll go back to the station and set up the investigation team if you want to sort out the computer."

Bob nodded his agreement even as he listened for Elizabeth's reply.

"I was down at Bristol, but I transferred to one of the Cambridge schools. That's how Peter came to hear about me."

"Want to go for a drink and compare notes about college?"

McInnis frowned; he might be a Grammar school boy but he'd never made it as far as University. Elizabeth shook her head and McInnis watched as the black cap of hair swirled and settled obediently back to its frame around her face. He found he was grinning and caught an extraordinary expression flit across Sandy's face. "What?"

Sandy in turn shook his head. "Never mind lad. I'll take our young Don Juan away with me and leave you to compare notes. He's done the forensics in here," he grinned, "you're safe to touch things."

26

Bob cast a startled look at Sandy Bell and then frowned fiercely at him.

"...on the computer." Sandy gave a bark of a laugh, quickly suppressed, and swept the young forensic man in front of him, leaving Bob McInnis to battle with a computer and an inferiority complex he hadn't know existed until that moment.

The next hour was spent identifying the various names, cute and curious, that had been adopted by some very serious sounding professors. There were e-mails from the Imperial War Museum, one from some group dealing with deserters and another for those shot at dawn. There was a long e-mail from someone in a genealogical society with some details about a census form for 1901. McInnis sighed; he didn't think he was going to find the murderer among this lot.

Elizabeth Fielding had pulled herself together. She answered his questions with reasonable patience, even though she thought the man was mad. "As I told you before Inspector, they're all nearly as old as Peter was. I think the man he was in communication with in that last group was a bit younger, but he still must be the wrong side of fifty."

She shifted slightly in her seat; she'd pulled her chair round to Peter's computer earlier, and now found she was not entirely comfortable with the intimacy of their positions while they shared the same small screen. She was conscious of the warmth of his body through the thin white shirt, and the faint smell of soap and aftershave as he moved in the chair near her.

"Can I have a look at the research now?"

She stretched her right arm across the keyboard and Bob McInnis winced slightly as that elusive scent was wafted under his nose again. "Just tell me what files to open Miss." It came out more harshly than he'd intended and he felt her stiffen next to him.

"Certainly Inspector. You need to access these four here and this one here." She clicked buttons rapidly and he blinked, horrified as files popped onto the screen and layered over each other. Elizabeth caught the slightly dazed look on his face before he managed to cover it, and hid her smile. Serve him right, she thought.

Bob moved the cursor and clicked the mouse on the first file, revealing a tangle of dates and names.

"Hmm!" He tried to sound as though he knew exactly what he was looking at while he was wishing frantically that he'd left this bit to Sandy.

He clicked randomly on various other files bringing up some in French and German as well as English. Elizabeth watched his antics for a few minutes then took pity on him. "If you just open that file there," she nudged his hand, placing hers over it, and moved the cursor, "you'll be able to collate most of the information you're looking at now."

McInnis privately doubted it, and who the hell used the word collate in normal conversation. He was beginning to sweat slightly and he didn't think it was the heat of the sun now streaming through the double glazing. "Yes Miss." He twitched his hand and she removed hers.

He settled down to read the new file and she quietly got up and went into the kitchen, filling the kettle and preparing a tray. If she didn't think too much it would be just like any other Monday. She'd go back through and there would be Peter sitting typing two fingered as he pulled together all the information he was accumulating.

She could hear the police still busy upstairs, doing whatever policemen did in these circumstances. She shivered. Only it wasn't a normal Monday, and she'd never come in to find him working again. She sighed, rubbing her hands over her face. She was going to miss him; he'd been not just a mentor and employer but

28

something like a grandfather too. He'd teased her about her non-existent boyfriends and her passion for what he called chick books. God knows where he'd got that phrase from. Oh! Well, better get back to that policeman before he wiped Peter's files for her.

"You're right Miss Fielding." Bob McInnis looked up at her entry, pushing back his chair to stand up and come for the tray. Elizabeth was too quick for him. As she set the tray down on the corner of the desk she refrained from saying 'I told you so!', but only just.

"This isn't going to help me find a murderer, but it's fascinating stuff. I've lived in this area all my life and I didn't know half of this had happened." Bob sat down again, covering his embarrassment with conversation. The younger cops were always teasing him about his manners; they said women didn't like being treated differently, but he couldn't shake the habits his mother had clouted into him.

"I thought you might like a drink Inspector. It's gone lunch time."

"That's very kind of you Miss Fielding."

For some reason she found herself irritated. "For God's sake call me Elizabeth!"

Bob McInnis looked up at the girl standing next to him. It seemed his colleagues might be right, but no, he couldn't call her Elizabeth; he was having to resist her subtle and totally unconscious allure as it was.

He nodded noncommittally and for some way to fill the silence said, "Will you be dealing with the funeral or do you know who will?"

Elizabeth drew a breath. "I should think I will. As I said, I don't know who else would. Part of this research was to find out if Peter had any relatives. I'm not privy to all his notes though Inspector."

McInnis nodded. There she went again; 'privy', heavens but he felt a klutz. He shrugged it off, concentrating on the murder and its ramifications. "Have you any idea who his solicitor was?"

"Oh, yes," she nodded. "They're a Carlisle firm. I'll get you the address." She moved round the desk and pulled open the bottom draw on her side, extracting a black book and running a pink tipped finger down the list inside. "Here you are Inspector." McInnis watched the finger and found he was licking his lips.

He took the book and made a note of the address. "Thank you M…" He nearly swallowed his tongue in an effort not to say Miss again. He stood up abruptly. "I need to look at this a bit more but I must er, go er, and do things." He found he was almost backing away from her. What the hell was wrong with him?

Elizabeth watched his retreat with some surprise and, she had to admit, a certain degree of hurt. He gathered speed as he crossed the floor of the study and all but flung himself through the door.

She stood looking rather puzzled, first at the closed door and then at the neglected tea things, then shrugged. She had things to do too. She had a funeral to arrange, elderly friends of the Professor to contact, and a new job to find. But the last could wait a little while.

She poured herself a cup of tea and sat down at the computer, looking at the cursor as it blinked beside the start of a sentence. She hadn't seen this bit of work. Peter wasn't exactly secretive about his work but he did like to get his ideas straight before he showed them to her. The sounds of activity outside the study faded away as she became absorbed in the words in front of her.

Meanwhile a slightly frazzled Bob McInnis was sitting behind the desk in his office, holding a head that ached slightly and staring sightlessly at the ubiquitous PC on his desk, the 'Windows' logo bouncing around. He picked up a mug of steaming tea with both hands and wondered what the hell was the matter with him.

Sandy found him there five minutes later. He came over and, pushing aside several plastic folders teetering on the top of the in-tray, placed more on top of them.

"I've organised the troops Bob. The Super's given us a nice little band to go and knock on doors in the area, the Coroner is even now hard at work, and forensics are keen to solve our murder for us. There are also little green men dancing outside your window."

"Eh!" Bob shook his head, glancing at the window where a wilting plant slowly expired in the heat of the afternoon sunshine.

"Nothing." Sandy grinned in a slightly evil way. "So how did you get on with the research? Will it give us any clues do you think?"

"God knows Sandy. I don't think so, it's all ancient history." He shook off whatever was distracting him. "I would like to get some information as to the cause of the accident that put him in that wheelchair though."

"Oh, that's your tack is it?"

"Well it's certainly an idea; do you think it could have been a first botched attempt?"

"Maybe. In which case we need to go back to what he was doing then, rather than what he was busy with now."

"Yeah, that's what I thought." Bob sighed, "I hate working with computers Sandy." He cocked his head. "I don't suppose you…"

"Not bloody likely!" Sandy backed away from the desk. "I can't even set up the ring tone on my mobile, or rather I can't get rid of the blasted jingle the kids have put on it." He backed away a bit more. "I'll ring the hospital and see if I can get his old notes." He reached the door and opened it. "I'll even get the London Police to dig out the old accident notes, but I'm too old and too smart to get

31

tangled with that young woman." He winked and closed the door smartly on the obscene word his partner called him, reflecting that he couldn't be one of those; he'd seen his parents' marriage certificate.

Bob McInnis sat still for a few moments after the precipitate exit of Sandy Bell, a faint smile on his face, then pulled forward the files littering his desk. There was a nasty rash of burglaries happening; it all looked like opportunistic stuff but there might be a 'Mr Big' out there somewhere. He would get things organised here then go back to the house and try to make some sense of all that research. 'That young woman' couldn't stay there for ever.

Elizabeth Fielding was totally absorbed in her former boss' work. She thought he was doing work on the deserters, that's what Peter had told her, but this sounded more like a novel and one she wanted to read. She loved history; it had, after all, been her chosen subject at university.

She sat scrolling down the page, her tea neglected and her grief subsumed by a greater tragedy that Peter was revealing through his story.

"Oh God!" He spoke softly, but his own words would have been lost anyway, as he approached the towering mass of twisted metal. The heat hit him like a physical blow as he edged nearer to the train carriage. That was followed by other sensations; the normally comforting smell of wood smoke assailed his nostrils, overlaid by the greasy aroma of burning meat. He swallowed, his Adam's apple bobbing in his throat as he prevented the bile from rising.

As his breathing eased from the frantic dash from Gretna Green to Quintinshill signal box, his ears began again to register noise. The clear sound of a lark rising above the shouts, whimpers, groans, which were all beginning to be drowned out by the cheerful crackle of the flames, like some malevolent beast mocking the efforts of the puny humans to destroy it. Then an explosion shook the ground near him, knocking him sideways onto hot metal and, adding to the noise were the terrified screams of those whose fate had now been sealed.

He threw off his jacket, tossing it on a fence post and, with shirt sleeves rolled up, began the gruesome task. Before many minutes the sweat was dripping from his face. The men for the most part worked silently, conserving their strength as they pulled bodies from the burning wreckage of what had been three trains. The old wooden frames of the carriages in the troop train hadn't stood a chance when the Glasgow express had ploughed into them, and neither had the men inside.

Everyone worked, hour after hour. The Royal Scots who had escaped in the first instance now aided their companions in arms, pulling hot stanchions away, carrying bodies to the side of the field, joking quietly with men who had lost limbs and laying hands, gentle as women, on eyes that now stared sightlessly at the blue sky of the hot spring day.

Peter finally had to move away from the burning pyre; exhaustion was making his head swim. He staggered drunkenly away. "Here lad, catch hold."

A sweaty arm was put round his waist and he was half carried, half stumbled, away from the carnage and sat down on the grass.

"Take a swig frae the bottle laddie."

He lifted his eyes, following the heavy brown skirt upwards to the thick greeny blue bottle held out to him. "Thanks Missus."

He drank deeply of the spring water, its faintly peaty tang helping to quench his thirst, then lay down on the grass, allowing the swirling sensation in his head to ease. Opening his eyes he was amazed to see the sun shining high in the sky. "What time is it?"

The woman spoke, her accent country thick, like a hearty soup, and just as comforting. "It'll be nigh to two now." She too gazed up at the sky. "Sik a braw fine day it is too."

"Have you anything to eat missus?"

"I can find ye a bitte if you'll bide a minute."

He sat up as she walked away, and looked around the farmer's field. While he'd been busy, so had others. He could see mattresses and sheets spread around. One man was gathering the remains of weapons, piling broken butts and bent barrels in an untidy heap. Peter, mentally calculating the number of weapons, was horrified all over again at the loss of young lives.

A car parked in the centre of the field was being used as a supply depot for bandages and splints. An old crone was seated on the ground, her long black skirts spread out like a fan around her while she rolled torn sheets against her knee, forming fat sausages of material into usable bandages.

The woman returned with a hunk of bread and a small piece of cheese. "Here ye are lad."

He accepted it gratefully and she sank down on the ground next to him, sighing heavily and pressing a hand to her back. As she leaned back he saw that she was heavily pregnant. She noted his glance. "My man is over to the side there helping with the bodies. He said I should go home again but I canna leave while I can help. It's no as if it's my first bairn." She offered a grim smile. "The other five are with their granny. I can keep this one safe a bit longer."

Peter nodded, chewing industriously. The bread was tough and he sipped at the water to ease its passage down his throat. He swallowed. "It's kind of you to share, with such a large family to feed."

"We a' do what we can to serve the country laddie."

"Have you sons at the front then?"

"Not now." She stopped speaking and he looked away, sorry he'd asked.

Then she sighed deeply. *"He shouldn't have gone. He was only sixteen ma bonnie lad. He died last Christmas Eve some place in Belgium. They said as how the War would be over by then, but it wasn't and it isn't."* She stopped speaking again, her body going still with suppressed grief.

Peter found he had no appetite, and no idea how to comfort her. He stood up, relieved to find his head had cleared. *"I'd best get back to it. Thanks for the food."*

"Aye lad, save a few more to get shot!" She spoke quietly and bitterly, and he didn't know how to answer that either.

He worked long into the evening, only stopping when it became obvious that heavy moving equipment was going to be needed to separate the towering pile of burning embers. They hadn't found any more bodies for quite some while and the voices that had been heard occasionally from underneath had ceased.

He shivered as the evening dew settled on his already damp shirt, and looked absently and without much hope for his jacket. It still hung on the fence where he'd tossed it so carelessly many hours before. Another man came up to him, offering a cigarette from a battered packet of Camels. *"We canna do more, the noo. 'T brigade will ha' finished soon."* They stood in companionable silence drawing tobacco smoke into their lungs.

The older man turned away, eventually saying, *"I dinna want to go but 'a canna stay any longer."* He walked away across the field. Peter knew exactly how the man felt. He was most reluctant to leave while there was any chance he might be needed, but what he desperately wanted was to get the stench of burning flesh out of his nostrils and the sight of blood away from his eyes.

He resolutely turned his back on the fire, now muted to a soft crackle and gentle rustle as it settled on the Scottish landscape. It had been one hell of a day he thought, as he headed for his temporary lodgings.

He stripped down and washed his body piecemeal at the stone sink in the scullery, scrubbing his arms with the heavy lye soap supplied by his landlady. He kept discovering small burns which stung like bees, and was amazed to find a vicious and deep scratch on his chest which bled sluggishly as he scrubbed the grime away.

"Here lad," his landlady was stout and motherly, "you'll want a dab o' iodine on that." A surprisingly elegant hand offered the brown ribbed bottle and a piece of rag. He accepted with a muttered "Thank you."

She stood in the doorway watching him apply the stinging liquid and observing the handsome man who was her lodger. He was well set she thought, with a deep chest, narrow hips, and long muscled legs. The hands moved gingerly over the gash and she hid a smile at a man who could accept the pain of the gash and wince at the sting of the iodine. "We'll be ower flowing wi' folks on the morrow. They've been coming out from Carlisle all the day gawking over the fence at the crash. Folks like to reassure their selves they're alive, ye ken."

Peter lifted his head from his task to look at her from piercing blue eyes. "Yes I know." He paused at his self-imposed task. "I didn't notice the crowds."

"Aye, well ye were busy. Will ye eat lad?"

He nodded his head, blond hair flopping over his forehead, returning to his ablutions and setting the bottle carefully on the draining board. Her skirts whisked away from the door jamb and she disappeared towards the black lead stove in the kitchen. A heady aroma of lamb broth issued from a blackened pot to mingle

with oil lamp fumes and wood smoke as he came through, and he
knew he was glad to be alive too.

Elizabeth raised her head as she became aware that the young constable left at the door was speaking to her.

"Excuse me Miss Fielding but the Inspector's on the phone. He'd like a word if convenient." Elizabeth felt the heat rising in her cheeks as she nodded. She'd been ignoring its imperative ringing, since the police invading the house seemed to be using it for their business. Now she picked it up from the desk. She was astonished at the sudden surge of disappointment she felt when the Scottish accent of Inspector Bell spoke in her ear instead of the Cumbrian tones she had been expecting, but answered him politely.

"What can I do for you now Inspector Bell?"

"We've got the reports of the accident to the Professor. I wondered if you could add anything to it. Did he discuss it with you at all? Is there anything he might have told you since?"

"It happened down in London Inspector."

Elizabeth was plainly puzzled by the questions. Bell could hear the question in her voice.

"We think the two incidents might be connected."

"Oh no, surely not!"

"Did he speak about it at all?"

"Only to say it was no-one's fault. Apparently he'd been caught up in a crowd of tourists waiting to cross a road and the surge had caught and pushed him onto the crossing before the traffic had stopped. I think he'd been on his way to the Imperial War Museum at the time."

Bell scribbled frantically at the end of the line.

"Inspector?"

"Yes Miss Fielding, I'm still listening. Was he going there in connection with the research you were helping him with, or for some other project?"

"I don't really know." Elizabeth shook her head at her reflection in the window.

"Can you give me the name of the person he was going to see?"

"You've already got it Inspector. It was on the list of e-mails I gave to the other Inspector."

"Ah yes." Bell cast an eye over Bob's neatly written notes of names and associated places. "That's most helpful Miss Fielding. Thank you. Now..." He paused. "Have you had a chance to look around yet? Do you know if anything has gone missing or if anything has been disturbed?"

"I'm sorry Inspector, I haven't looked yet. I'll do that right away and get back to you if I may."

"Thank you again Miss Fielding; I'm aware how distressing this must be for you."

Sandy Bell put the phone down and picked up the directory to find the Imperial War Museum in London.

Elizabeth, replacing the receiver, looked blankly at the screen. There was nothing in the story she'd been reading so far that could bring about the death of an old man. All this information was a matter of public record. The Quintinshill Railway Disaster of 1915 was well documented. She knew, she'd been doing the research on it for Peter Neville. Granted the Scottish Records Office wasn't quite as free with their information, but so many people had been present that not a lot was hidden from the public. Peter had made it live, put flesh and blood on the bare bones of the disaster, but it wasn't a state secret.

She closed the file and, pulling Peter's personal phone book forward, mentally prepared for a few harrowing minutes as she let people know that their old colleague had died in somewhat distressing circumstances. She'd look around soon, but she wanted to get the phone calls done while she still had a bit of control left. Looking through Peter's stuff wasn't, she felt, calculated to sooth her frayed emotions.

2

It had been a long and tiring day; Elizabeth had spoken to elderly men who had been shocked, and frankly puzzled, at the sudden death of Peter Neville. She had looked round in a cursory sort of way downstairs, but nothing was out of place as far as she could see. The place was liberally scattered with grey and black dust where the fingerprint experts had been at work. Some of the furniture had been moved slightly in Peter's bedroom; she assumed also by the police. Now she felt she could do no more, and just wanted to go home and grieve in peace.

"Good afternoon Constable." She closed the door behind her, leaving the young man on duty to admire her legs as she walked away, not that she was aware of that. She stopped at the curb waiting for a gap in the traffic. School children raced past her on their way to freedom and, despite her tiredness and sorrow, she found a smile rising to her face at their sheer enjoyment and energy. She was admiring a young man on a skateboard, cap placed backwards and his blazer flapping in his own slipstream, when she felt herself pushed roughly from behind.

The squeal of brakes assaulted her ears, and the sting of petrol invaded her nostrils as she lay shaking on the ground. She opened her eyes to see a black tyre barely six inches from her head. She lay still, dazed and disorientated.

"Miss, Miss! Are you alright?" The young constable she'd last seen standing outside the door was bending over her, his face as white as she imagined hers must be.

She lay a minute more, doing a mental inventory of her limbs. "I think so Officer, though I expect I shall begin to ache in a little while." She attempted to rise, but found herself held firmly down by a large, if somewhat shaky, hand on her shoulder. "Stay still Miss Fielding. I'll radio for an ambulance, then we can get you checked out."

"I'm perfectly alright Officer."

"Nevertheless." He spoke into his RT, asking for backup and an ambulance, while keeping a wary eye on the crowd that was forming and the woman under his hand.

A squad car was singing in the distance, its siren rising in volume and pitch as it approached. Elizabeth lay still. She had little choice; some Good Samaritan had brought a blanket from their car and covered her. But the constable still kept a hand resting on her; as if he feared she'd make a run for it she thought, with a slightly hysterical giggle. She didn't think she could hobble. Parts of her anatomy she usually didn't dwell on were beginning to make their presence felt.

The ambulance crew were brisk and efficient, running firm hands over her limbs and asking pertinent questions. Satisfied that it was the stumble that had landed her on the ground, and not the car that had struck her, they gave her suitable advice. She refused the offer of a trip to the infirmary. "I'm just a bit shaken thanks. I'm sure I'll have a few bruises in the morning but there are no limbs broken."

They left her somewhat reluctantly. The driver was equally adamant in refusing to go to hospital. He was a big florid looking man wearing his fifty odd years, and business suit, well. He sported a moustache that would have done an RAF colonel proud, and the black eyebrow that dominated his forehead stretched from one side of his eyes to the other. He had been inclined to bluster about people not looking where they were going initially, but suddenly seemed to realise how close he had come to running her over in his Range Rover Sport. He'd begun to look a trifle sick and had eventually sat back in his car and closed his eyes.

41

Elizabeth watched with some sympathy as the police took charge. "Just blow into the bag sir."

"I've already told you I've had a drink Officer, I've just come from a business meeting. I've had a whisky and soda."

"Yes sir, but we still need to go through the test."

He sighed but complied.

Elizabeth wasn't surprised to see the crystals change colour.

One of the police from the squad car approach as she turned away. "Do you feel able to give me a statement Miss?"

She nodded then wished she hadn't; her head had come into contact with the tarmac with some force and felt as though it wasn't entirely secure on her neck.

"If you'd just get into the back of the car for a minute Miss?"

Elizabeth climbed in and waited as the Officer got in beside her. "Now Miss if you could just give us an account of who you are, and what happened." He paused, biro held at the ready.

The personal details dealt with, Elizabeth continued, "I'm not absolutely sure of what happened. I was waiting to cross and watching the kids come out of school heading for the centre of town and I think …" She paused trying to bring the sequence of events together. "I think one of them must have knocked against me in the crush. The next thing I knew I was lying on the ground, smelling petrol and wondering if this was it."

She looked at the scratches on her slightly shaky hands. "The driver did well to pull up. He can't even have been doing the speed limit to have stopped so quickly."

"Quite so." He looked out of the window as the man was ushered into another squad car and driven away. "Would you like someone to take you home Ms Fielding? We'll probably have to come and take a fuller statement later but for now..." He stopped.

Elizabeth tried a smile and found it a painful process. "It would be nice not to have to do battle with the bus out to the suburbs."

"Right Ms Fielding. I'll whistle up a car for you."

She was slightly astonished to hear him do exactly that, stepping out of the squad car and uttering a piercing whistle, causing onlookers to start in alarm. However it was obvious his partner was used to this form of communication as he came striding over. "What's up Alan?"

"Get us a car for the lady, John."

"Sure thing."

She was bundled efficiently into another car and decanted neatly onto her own doorstep within half an hour. By seven that night she was soaking in the big bath at the back of the house, bubbles tickling her nose, her eyes closed and a mug of sweet tea steaming on the side.

Inspectors Bell and McInnis were not in such a relaxed state when the news finally filtered through to them as they sat with their evening mugs of tea in the office.

"And you say she took no harm?"

"Aside from a few bruises, and being a bit shook up, no sir." Constable Higgs was doing a bit of shaking on his own account as he looked at the brace of Inspectors.

Bell cocked his head on one side, looking the man over, shaking his head slightly. Either he was getting old or they were recruiting in the junior school these days.

43

"Another man was left on duty as per protocol, sir, at the scene." Higgs fixed his eyes on the older Inspector's face, not caring for the expression on Inspector McInnis'.

"When you returned to your post had anything been disturbed?" McInnis voiced the question politely, but Higgs shivered in his regulation boots.

"The front door was still locked, sir."

"That wasn't what I asked you Constable. Had anything been disturbed while you where dealing with the accident?"

"I don't think so sir."

"You're not paid to think man. You're paid to do your job." McInnis snarled.

Sandy held up a hand for peace. "Look lad, we know you had to respond to the accident. We're not blaming you for that. What we need to know is if anyone took the opportunity to have a look around the crime scene while you were busy?"

"I...I didn't check sir. I'm sorry."

"OK, you'll know to check next time. Dismiss!"

The pair waited until a pair of quivering legs in official police blue had taken the constable from their sight. "I don't like it Sandy. If she interrupted whoever it was this morning, a diversion would have given them a good chance to take another look. The question is, was it just a look or a double whammy. Get rid of her and look round." McInnis stood up as he finished speaking.

"We'd best get over there and check out the scene ourselves. Not that we'll be able to tell if anything is missing or not. We really need that young woman there, but I'm a wee bit reluctant. She's had a hell of a day so far." Sandy Bell was swinging his jacket round his shoulders and stuffing his arm into the sleeve as they headed for the door.

44

Bob McInnis nodded his head in agreement as they both exited.

The sun had already shut up shop and gone home by the time they arrived at the late Professor's door. The constable on duty, an older man, gave a sketchy salute as they walked up the garden path, and stepped to the side as they used the confiscated keys found in the desk to let themselves in.

The house seemed chilly to McInnis as he stood in the dark front lobby waiting for Sandy to find the light switch. "She didn't ring back did she?"

Sandy feigned innocence. "Who Bob?"

"Miss Fielding, she didn't phone back to say if anything was missing?" McInnis sounded testy.

"No, but then being tossed into the path of a vehicle might have made her a trifle absent minded." Sandy gave a quiet grunt and the hall filled with light. "Right, let's see if we can spot anything out of place."

"I'll take the upstairs. She wasn't tossed in front of a car until after she left the house Sandy." He raised an eyebrow at his colleague and headed towards the openwork staircase and laid a hand on the polished wood of the newel post. He turned his head and looked down at his friend and colleague. "Do you think I should do an OU course?"

Sandy Bell looked at him in silent astonishment for a moment. "What the hell for? You're working your way up the ladder fine without a lot of letters after your name. Open University would just give you even more paperwork to juggle lad."

"I just wondered. These young lads coming through now are always on about 'up-skilling', even after they've got their degrees, and sometimes I feel a bit..." He shrugged.

Sandy frowned. He knew Bob McInnis had a fine brain; they'd been partners since the man left the beat and joined the CID. "They might have letters after their names lad, but most of them haven't got the street savvy you have. That can't be learnt in a book. If you want to study, fine, but don't let boys like Mark Forester force you into it." He turned away and went through the slightly open door of the study.

Bob McInnis felt his cheeks grow red and turned away, making his way upstairs. Sometimes Sandy could see through him too damn clearly. Flicking on the switch at the top of the landing, he looked around at the four doors confronting him; only one was ajar. It didn't look as though the Professor used the upstairs rooms any longer, despite the stair lift he could see neatly stowed against the landing wall.

As he opened the first door, a joint toilet and bathroom which had a faintly musty odour, he wondered absently where the man had slept. A reasonable sized bedroom was next, with furniture from the 1950s. Bob admired the old fashioned dressing table with its crochet doilies as he pulled out drawers and found them lined with old newspapers but otherwise empty.

The wardrobe, of massive size and good quality oak, was likewise practically empty. It made him think of 'Narnia' films. He cautiously opened it to find nothing but a few coat hangers swinging on a bar across the top, and a pair of very old slippers lurking in the dust at the bottom.

He glanced at the bed draped under a fat eiderdown and gave it an experimental prod; it squeaked. He wouldn't have liked to sleep in that he thought; he pictured his own comfortable, and silent, divan style bed and smiled.

The second bedroom was, or rather had been, the master bedroom. Another very large wardrobe was filled to bursting with suits, all of them of a rather sombre hue but, as Bob could feel, of

46

excellent quality. The aroma of mothballs was almost overwhelming; he shut the door hastily on the silently hanging suits. There was a full length drawer at the bottom and this contained a shoebox stuffed with photos. Bob pulled the box out and set it on the bottom of the bed for further investigation.

The dressing table, another period piece, but the period this time was 1920s he thought, had a matching washstand and appeared to have been made from mahogany. He cautiously opened the door under the tiled top of the washstand to reveal a bowl and jug. Someone, McInnis thought, would certainly benefit when the old guy's assets were sold off. The furniture in this room was very nearly antique status and he suspected was very desirable in the right quarters. However, judging from the thin film of deer velvet dust on everything, nothing had been disturbed up here in weeks.

He left and went to the one remaining room. It lived up to its name; it really was a box room. There were enough boxes in here to re-equip Pickford's removals. He stood at the door looking at the floor, where one set of shoe prints in the thick dust were revealed by the single bulb overhead; they went in, stopped at the window, and retraced their steps out. He cocked his head, in unconscious imitation of Sandy Bell, and stared at them. "Hmm!"

With a detour to gather up the shoebox, Bob headed back downstairs. Sandy greeted him in the hall. "Impossible to tell. It all seems just as it should, smells of furniture polish in the bedroom down here. The kitchen has state of the art equipment tucked away in the cupboards, there's enough sharp knives to perform open heart surgery; the study doesn't look any different to this morning except that Miss Fielding has obviously removed the fingerprint dust."

"I found a shoebox of photos and, as he was paying someone to clean up she should be sacked. But, like you say, Sandy, nothing seems out of place."

The two men stood a minute considering. Sandy glanced at his watch. "I think I'm going home. My wife has hardly seen me this last week, what with burglars and muggings. How about you Bob? Do you want to come back for a meal? There's always plenty."

"No," Bob spoke slowly, "I think I'll have another go at the computer. I'll see you in the morning Sandy. We need to interview the cleaner, Tracy I think her name was. Do you want to set that up for sometime tomorrow?"

"Aye lad, I'll see to it." Sandy with a flicked salute left, closing the door quietly behind him. Bob caught his soft "Night Constable" before it shut.

He went into the study, surprised to see not only the main light, but several smaller wall lights, switched on. He walked across the carpet and set the box down on a convenient chair. He then turned to the computer he'd accessed that morning, settling down in front of it. Having managed to turn it on and remembered the password he struggled to bring up the right files.

He found he had a light sweat on his forehead, despite the chill of early evening, by the time he'd worked his way back to the research file that Elizabeth Fielding had clicked to so easily that morning. He sat back with a big grin on his face. He could do this he thought, as long as no-one rushed him. Now where had he got to before he'd gone back to the station?

He rolled the cursor and stopped at the section on the railway disaster. Was this fiction or fact? He puzzled over the description of the area for a minute; well he knew where Gretna Green was, everyone did, didn't they? His parents had gone there to celebrate their silver wedding anniversary by renewing their vows over the anvil only a few years ago.

But Quintinshill? Where the hell was that? Bob frowned at the screen. He tried to go back through the files to see if that would help, but ended up with something on bagpipes. He found he was muttering to himself as he read off the screen, "The Camelon Pipe Band. Oh, for heaven's sake!" He shocked himself as he heard his own impatient words spoken out loud. He was going to have to ask; and he really, really, didn't want to ask Elizabeth Fielding for help.

He stretched out a hand for the phone then withdrew it; a cunning look coming into his eyes. Maybe he could nip across the border tomorrow. There'd been a nasty fatality on the A74 over the weekend. All the road works were making life difficult. He could just pop over the border and do a bit of on the spot inspection. If he happened to find himself in the vicinity of Gretna Green there was no harm in asking a few questions was there? Satisfied with his reasoning, and story of checking out a Road Traffic Accident, Bob McInnis shut down the computer, leaving several files open on the way and the box of photos on the chair.

Another RTA was being discussed in several houses in the town. Several school children, asked for their eyewitness accounts by the police, had been noisily thrilled.

The officers in charge hadn't been so enthusiastic; the information given ranged from the scarcely believable to a rehash of the latest TV plot. Among the dross they felt there must be a nugget of truth, but how to find it was another matter. More reliable reports from slightly less excited, but equally thrilled, and more upstanding citizens were helping, but not a lot.

One of those reports had come from Tracy Cavendish, late cleaner to the Professor. She was now telling her husband all about it as she served him sausage and mash liberally coated with onion gravy. She was tall and well built, with only the slightest glimmer of black shining through her blonde hair at the roots. Her eyes were brown and set in a sea of mascara; the lush lips, well painted with Max Factor's No. Seven brand, gleamed in the overhead light as she talked at her husband.

"I was just coming back from The Lanes. It was on the corner near the 'Tec, you know that crossroad bit at Victoria Place. She was really lucky not to be hurt badly." She sat down next to him and wrapped her hands round a mug of tea. Her husband continued to watch the TV, ignoring her as he viewed Sky Sport which was showing the latest football match. He wanted to see if Beckham would live up to his enormous price tag.

"I suppose I'll have to get another job now. I liked working for the old man; he wasn't always hanging about watching what I was doing." Her husband grunted, scooping up the last of the mash and gravy with his knife as he followed the play on the screen.

"He was a gent too, unlike some I could mention; he gave us that lovely Christmas box last year too; and all under the table."

Tom Cavendish pushed his plate away and picked up his own mug, transferring his attention to his wife as the adverts rolled on screen. "Who wasn't hurt?" He took a gulp of instant coffee, made a face, and spooned in sugar with a liberal hand, stirring vigorously.

"Eh?"

"You said 'she was lucky not to be hurt.' Who?"

"I told you. That secretary girl that works for the Professor; she got knocked down this afternoon."

"No you didn't."

"I did."

He shrugged. "Anyway, why have you got to get another job. Has he sacked you?" He drank more coffee, holding the spoon to the side of the mug with his thumb, and nodded his head in satisfaction at the taste.

His wife uttered a long-suffering sigh. "I told you! The coppers are asking questions 'cos he was found dead this morning."

Her husband snagged her hand, setting the mug down with a thump. "Hey!" She pulled her arm away and smoothed down the new blouse she hoped he hadn't noticed yet.

"How did he die and when?"

"I dunno. They haven't talked to me yet, and nobody seems to know what really happened. It might be on the nine o'clock news."

"You be careful what you say to them! I'm still on the social, and you aren't supposed to have a job."

"Yeah, I know, but they won't be interested in that."

"The coppers are interested in every bloody thing! Always looking for an excuse to stick their noses in other people's business."

"Oh Tom!" She looked at him scowling at her, and wondered what she had been thinking about to marry him. She shrugged in her turn, turning her head away to look at the TV. "Change the channel, then we can catch the news."

It only made the local news and came second to a Northern councillor's bigamous affair. Tracy stood up and cleared the table. Speaking as she walked through to the small kitchenette at the back of the room, she said, "See, I told you he was murdered."

"They didn't tell us much on there; you'll have to tell me all about it after they talk to you."

Tracy felt flattered; her husband didn't normally show that much interest in her or her affairs. "Are you coming down the pub in a bit? I've got a bit of ironing to do and then I'm going out with Janie."

"Nah. I want to see the rest of the match." Her husband watched her clearing away and taking the dishes through. He admired her large breasts, encased as they were in the polyester satin blouse. He hadn't missed the newest purchase, but didn't think it was worth arguing about; she'd only bitch or cry and he couldn't be bothered with either at the moment. He had something else on his mind.

"Leave the ironing; you haven't got a job to go to; you can do it tomorrow. Give Janie a call." Tracy frowned suspiciously across at her husband as she neatly stacked sauce bottles on the room divider. He was slouched on the comfortable leather settee, his eyes focused on the football again.

"No, I like to do it while it's damp."

"Suit yerself. Get us a can before you start will you?"

Tracy relaxed and pulled a can of 'Iron Bru' out of the fridge door, walking through and shoving his trainers aside to dump it on the low coffee table next to him. Her husband continued to watch, occasionally shouting at the commentator with such inventive invective as occurred to him, as she ironed shirts and blouses.

She finally took everything away upstairs and her husband looked around cautiously; he had a phone call to make and didn't want her overhearing it. He looked at his watch and decided that the few minutes until she went out wouldn't matter, but he sidled over to the door and listened up the stairs. Hearing the shower running and the rather overpowering smell of her chosen body wash, he turned away and picked up her handbag.

Tom Cavendish, with an eye on the stairs, rummaged around in his wife's capacious handbag, abstracting her key ring and her mobile. He checked over the first, slipping a key back on, then, still watching the stairs, switched the mobile on and checked her calls. He knew Janie's number and her parents; she'd been texting Susan too. He flicked to see what she had to say to her big sister, but it was all girl chat.

He hastily stuffed both items back in her bag as he heard the shower switch off, shoving the bag back under the settee. He was going into the kitchen as she came down with a towel wrapped around her head and a blue dressing gown wrapped around her voluptuous person.

She hadn't fastened the gown, just looped the sash, and he was treated to a sight of her figure totally unrestrained by Lycra. She rubbed her hair vigorously as she came into the room, making various outlying portions of her anatomy jiggle suggestively. "Are you sure you won't come out Tom? Or would you like me to stay in?"

"For God sake! No. And fasten your clothes; what if someone came to the door?"

Tracy shrugged and pouted a little, "You'd have to get off your backside and answer them, wouldn't you."

Tom turned away, getting another can from the fridge. He waited in silence, leaning against it as she used the hairdryer and went upstairs again to dress.

When she came down in a microscopic miniskirt and another new blouse he ignored her. She scrabbled under the settee, grabbing her bag and tipping all its contents into an even larger bag of a stunning shade of red to match her lipstick.

"I'm off, don't wait up." She tripped out and he sagged against the settee seat waiting for the thump of the front door. It wasn't that he didn't find her attractive still; it was just that she was in the way. He'd make it up to her he thought, when she got back from the Pub.

Mrs Sarah Bell and her husband were also enjoying their supper. The drop leaf table was laid with a nice white cloth and the brown teapot had a jaunty knitted cosy covering it. Sandy was debating the merit of a further slice of his wife's fruit cake, which he was very fond of, a large grin on his face as he looked across the tablecloth at his wife, whom he was more than fond of. "Well, you could have knocked me down with a feather. There he was gazing into thin air with his hands all sweaty. Poor lad, proper smitten by her, and all of a heap too."

"Sandy." His wife was comfortable with her middle age and her rounded figure; her fifty summers sat lightly on her but she frowned, showing lines as she looked at her husband, her tone reproving. She reached across and sliced him another piece of cake as she continued, "How do you know he was smitten anyway?" She put the slice on his plate, pushed it in front of him and watched him tuck in with enjoyment; she liked to see him enjoy her food.

"Well you know Bob. Sharp as a tack that boy. But today, he kept drifting away, and what's more he wants to do a degree!" Sandy looked a bit scandalised.

"Well why shouldn't he? Nothing wrong with the lad's brain."

"No Sarah, but it's the reason behind it. Five minutes listening to her and Mark Forester talking and the little green god had got him."

"I mind when the little green god got to you too Sandy, and all because you saw Charlie Fisher kiss me behind the bike sheds. If you'd waited you would have seen me slap his face for him too." She settled comfortably at the table, drinking sweet tea from a large mug proclaiming, 'Stress! Deal with it' in red script. "Don't be nasty lad."

She sipped, "So tell me about the case."

Sandy raised an eyebrow. "I've told you most of it. The Professor was strangled by someone who either had a key, or he let in. We haven't found a motive yet, but I'm seeing the solicitors tomorrow. That might give us a clue about money and who gains. Blackmail, though we haven't turned up anything along those lines yet, he seemed a harmless old guy. Women, but he doesn't seem to have had one. I suppose he could have had a relationship with a man, which might give us jealousy too. He'd got a lot of kids' books and no kids, so I suppose he could be a paedophile and that might lead to either blackmail or murder; but I somehow doubt it." He drank tea, looking quizzically at her over his mug.

"You've got a strange mind Sandy."

He gave his wife a loving look, "What else? There's ambition, academic or otherwise. Elizabeth Fielding, the young woman who worked for him, managed to get it back together remarkably quickly after the initial shock." He grinned, "But I'm not sure Bob will ever be the same again."

"Sandy!" His wife twinkled across at him, her blue eyes crinkling up in mock reproof.

"OK. Where was I? Means, strangulation, motive, dunno, we'll know better maybe when we get a squint at the will. When, this morning but why now and not last week or next week, again dunno; list of suspects, legion if the e-mail list Bob brought back with him is anything to go by." He took a hefty bite of cake, and spoke rather thickly round it. "He was into history in a big way the Prof', but I don't think that's going to help us much and we couldn't see anything missing. But you never can tell."

He washed down cake with tea and smiled at his wife. "What have you been up to today then love?"

Major Madogan was also reflecting on the day's events, sipping whisky and soda in front of an unlit gas fire in his own sitting room. He was not a happy man. He hadn't enjoyed the three hours he'd been forced to spend down at the central police station, answering questions about his personal life in a small and rather claustrophobic room, windowless and containing hard wooden chairs to match the hard wooden table.

"Yes Officer I admit I'm a bit over the limit." The officer was looking at him cold eyed.

"More than a bit, sir."

"Look man I've cooperated. I've allowed you to take blood. I'm willing to sign a statement saying it wasn't anyone's fault. Can I go?" He glanced at the thick Rolex on his wrist. "I have an important meeting in half an hour."

"I'm afraid you won't be able to keep it sir, I'm very sorry." Alan, the constable who'd arrested him for drink-driving didn't look sorry. "Would you like to use the phone and make alternative arrangements?"

The Major eyed him bitterly. "No." It was said flatly, "I'd like to get out of here."

"Yes sir. If you could just give us your details?"

"I've given them once."

"Er yes but… they aren't totally accurate." Alan pushed the printout from the DVLA in front of the indignant Major's eyes. "As you can see the Driving Licensing Authority don't have your details unless this is you sir. Mr Madogan of The Oaks."

"I've found, Constable, that a title helps in the business world; it opens doors and I've served my time in the army." While he had been in the army he hadn't lasted much longer than training camp and six months of drilling in base camp, and certainly hadn't merited any rank above private. He conveniently forgot that he'd been told to quit before they threw him in the glass house.

Blasted girl! Now the police were looking a bit too closely at him. He'd already got six points on his licence, his belief that he'd only been a little over the odds as false as his title.

"Quite sir." The constable was very polite. "So if you'd like to confirm these fresh details sir."

Major Madogan flicked through the papers and scrawled his name at the bottom of the page. "Can I get my car now?"

"It will be available in the morning sir. SOCO need to finish with it." Alan Smith mentally added, 'and you might be sober then'.

The Major had been forced to shell out for a taxi to bring him home. He'd had to ring and cancel his appointment and would probably lose the contract and a great deal of money in consequence, and to top it off he'd endured a phone call from one of his less salubrious acquaintances. He believed he was entitled to a certain degree of respect, and all the man could do was laugh at him for getting caught.

He suddenly hurled the glass against the wall. It was all her fault, and by God she would pay for it. The expression on his face was vicious enough to shatter the glass without any need for contact with a wall.

Elizabeth stirred in the rapidly cooling water as she heard a tap at the door. "I'll be out in a minute Dad."

"Just so you don't fall asleep in there."

"No I'm fine."

"OK." Her father moved away down the landing and switched on the lights in her bedroom, going to the single bed, set facing the window. He put a mug on the walnut side table then fumbled under the duck egg blue duvet and clicked on the electric blanket.

He wasn't a young man anymore and he'd had a shock when his only daughter had come in slightly the worse for wear and told him about her day. Her employer had been his friend too. The traffic accident had set his rather erratic pulse jumping like frogs in a pond. But Elizabeth knew better than to try and hide things from him. He sat under the window, in the rocking chair she'd commandeered from downstairs, rocking gently almost as a means of comforting himself while he breathed in the mixed scents of lavender and her perfume.

Elizabeth, snugly wrapped up, came into the room a couple of minutes later. "It's time you were abed Dad. You know what the Doctor said, no later than nine thirty."

"I'm alright darling. More to the point is how are you feeling now? Are you sure you shouldn't have gone to the hospital?"

"I'm quite sure. I've got bruises on places I didn't know existed, but otherwise I'm fine." She came over, tilting his head and dropping a light kiss on top of the balding patch. His hands came forward and gripped hers fiercely. "I love you Beth, I couldn't bear to lose you." The eyes she'd inherited from him looked at her; a hint of his anguish, thinly hidden, showed.

"Goop!" She returned the pressure of his hands then stepped back and went over to the bed, crawling under the covers. "Mmm, thanks, that's nice and warm on my..." Her lips twitched and then blossomed into a grin.

"You'll take the car tomorrow, please."

"I was going to ask if you needed it anyway Dad."

"No I'm not planning on going out; I was going to work on the opus." He smiled at her.

"OK, now go to bed Dad, I love you too."

He stood up, an elderly academic, slightly stooped, and came across to the bed, dropping a kiss on her forehead before going out and shutting the door behind him. Her mother had died giving him this precious daughter. She'd been a special surprise to them after nearly twenty years; they'd never expected to be parents and then there'd just been him and the small squalling bundle.

He tried not to be overprotective. He thought he'd done well, encouraging her to go away to university, to have her own friends, but she said she wanted to live at home where she could be spoilt. They both knew she worried about his health but since she seemed genuinely happy here he hadn't argued very hard. She'd filled his life for so long now, today's accident had shocked him more than he'd let her know. He decided that an early night wouldn't do either of them any harm.

3

Bob McInnis had risen early, paid a token visit to the office to set things in motion for the day, and was now driving happily out of town and over the border into Scotland. Traffic was a bitch at this time of day but most of it seemed to be heading in the opposite direction to him. He flicked the radio on, unsurprised to hear that his murder had moved up to national status overnight. According to the BBC, Professor Peter Neville had been well known and respected by academia.

McInnis wondered if there was anyone down in Cambridge that hadn't been so keen on Neville; he'd heard these academics could fight dirty. However he also heard that the pen was mightier than the sword when academics fought; he wondered if a ruined reputation would be viewed as worse for a professor than loss of life.

He wasn't looking forward to getting to grips with men who made him feel uncomfortable; still he'd have to interview them soon. Easier though to wait for the funeral than take time out to go south if there was no compelling reason to meet them. Now where was the entrance to the blacksmith's shop? Ah down there.

He followed the road round, admiring a nice little group of red and shaggy highland cattle in a nearby field, and parked neatly in an almost deserted car park. He climbed out and looked around the area, the wind whipping at his hair and light jacket and bringing the odour of cows. His nostrils flared slightly as he took in the fresh country smells. He shoved his hands in his trousers pockets as a cloud covered the fitful sun.

He'd intended to walk to the forge and see if the local guides there could give him any more information. A plinth at the side of the path attracted his attention, mainly because it had a circle of poppies laid at its base. Poppy wreaths in November he was used to, but this was May. He strode over to get a closer look.

So it was true, he thought, bending over to read the inscription. It was dedicated to both The Royal Scots and passengers who died on that fateful day nearly 90 years ago. He nodded his head, turning his back on the memorial and looking out over the fields behind. Somewhere over there. He squinted into the near distance, tracking the modern train route by its overhead lines, then headed purposefully back to the car and the local map. Last night's quick look at the map had shown him the general area. Now he was going to be more precise.

Ten minutes later he was driving cautiously down a narrow lane looking for a place to stop. Spotting a turn off just before the railway bridge he swung the silver Peugeot into a field opening and slammed his foot down hard as he found a blue Megan parked in front of him.

He got out and looked around for the owner, thinking he would explain he was on police business. Elizabeth Fielding was just walking into the field entrance.

"Miss Fielding."

"Inspector McInnis!" She looked as surprised as he felt, rushing in with an explanation as if he'd accused her of something. "I came to see where Peter was talking about."

"So did I Miss Fielding." Bob McInnis felt the warmth stealing into his cheeks. He felt somehow as though he'd been caught prying into someone's private affairs without a good excuse.

"I couldn't quite visualise the area, even though I've done lots of research, and seen lots of pictures in books." She hurried on with her explanation. "If you go up to the bridge you can see where the original signal box was and get an idea of how the accident could happen."

"Thank you Miss." He swallowed pride. "Would you like to show me? I'm not at all sure I've understood what happened."

The pair turned and walked back along the lane until they stood on the stone railway bridge overlooking the line. McInnis looked at a small posy of flowers and a Canadian flag stuck into the side of the lichen covered wall. He'd lived on the Border for all of his thirty-three years and never knew about this tragedy and a Canadian did; he felt slightly ashamed. He brought his attention back to Elizabeth as she spoke to him, the wind stealing her words.

"If you look down the line Inspector you can see how it curves away. There was a double loop to allow passing trains. But that day the signalman filled both and then forgot about the troop train." She paused, brushing her hair out of her eyes. "He stopped it on the up line forgetting that the Glasgow Express had been passed through. There you have the makings of a tragedy." She waved an arm to the line and the quiet fields on either side.

McInnis stood looking at the area trying to make the story he'd been reading fit the geography in front of him. "That field there," he pointed midway between the curve and another bridge in the distance, "that would be where they laid the bodies?"

"I should think so." She turned from her contemplation of the field and looked at him, seeing the compassionate eyes and the firm lips. His attention was on a modern diesel just coming around the corner, its bright yellow livery rapidly approaching the bridge on which they stood.

"If it would help we could go round to the bridge on the other side of the curve and look back this way. I went there first this morning."

McInnis sighed. "No." He shook his head. "What I meant to say Miss Fielding is that yes, it probably would help me to understand the research, but it isn't going to help me find a murderer. This was just for my own understanding."

He stood a moment longer, absorbing the quiet that had descended after the passing of the train. He looked down the line towards the English border and listened to a robin singing in a nearby blackthorn which was just bursting into bud, the May blossom rich on the air. It would have been a day like this he thought, spring; with the sun shining, he remembered the story had said. Spring and youth and death. They didn't, shouldn't, be found together.

He turned away and began to walk back to the cars. Elizabeth turned with him. "It's sad isn't it? Not the fields, they don't seem to be haunted by anything, except maybe Friesian cows. But sad, thinking of all those young men killed before they could even get to the battlefront. It must have taken a lot of guts to get back on a train and go and fight in the Dardanelles. Or maybe they wanted to fight, for the sake of their comrades."

"Is that where they were going Miss Fielding?"

"Yes. Not many of them survived that either."

The pair arrived at the cars. Elizabeth stopped at her driver's door. "Will you need to speak to me again today Inspector?"

"Yes please Miss. I've got to go over the list of names you gave me yesterday and put faces and places to them. We're having trouble finding the man at the War Museum. You did say he had a meeting with Professor Neville the day he was knocked over down in London?" He looked at her standing in the breeze, her hair blowing, and remembered her accident. "I'm sorry; I should have asked how you were after your near miss yesterday."

"I'm fine, just a bit bruised Inspector." She looked at him curiously. "Inspector?" His face was blank.

He stopped looking through her and looked at her. "Sorry Miss just had an idea. You gave your statement to Constable Higgs?"

Elizabeth shook her head. "No I think the constable's name was Alan, Alan Smith. He said he was in traffic." She raised a quizzical eyebrow.

"Ah right Miss; I may need to talk to you again about it."

'Strange guy' she thought. "Right Inspector. I'll be at Peter's most of the day. I don't quite know what to do about his research, but I have to sort out his private papers for the solicitors."

"Ah, we'd prefer it if you didn't touch any of those until the solicitors are present Miss Fielding."

"That's perfectly alright Inspector. I locked his desk last night so nothing has been disturbed. Would you like the keys?"

Reflecting that as damage control went it was as good as shutting a bulkhead door on the Titanic, McInnis shook his head. "No Miss, that's fine. We'll look at things with you later today."

McInnis moved his car and Elizabeth Fielding backed out cautiously onto the narrow road and drove away. Bob McInnis pulled his mobile out and keyed in Sandy's number. "Sandy?"

"Yo."

"The man who nearly squashed our Miss Fielding, what do we know about him?"

"Haven't looked at the sheet yet. I'm swamped with e-mail names here." There was just a touch of resentment. "Where are you Bob?"

"I'm at Quintinshill."

"Where? Never mind, tell me later, what have you got in mind lad?"

"I'm wondering if our murderer is trying the same method on Miss Fielding as he did on her employer. It's a bit of a reach Sandy, because it was a very public accident, and the driver didn't actually hit her. Question is, was it the driver or the one who gave her the shove. But…"

"OK I'll see traffic and see what info I can get. Are you coming into the station?"

"Yes, give me an hour. I have to look at an RTA first, up on the A74; other crimes don't stop because the Professor got murdered."

"Oh that's what you're doing! Why didn't you say?" McInnis felt slightly guilty as he heard the tone change in Sandy's voice to one of sympathy. "See you later then."

McInnis flipped his mobile shut and started the car heading back to the main road. He viewed the stream of traffic with disgust; he'd be lucky if he made it back in the hour, given the constant thunder of trucks passing his exit. Still having used this as his excuse, albeit a genuine one, he'd better go and talk to some of the workmen who'd witnessed the fatality.

Sandy Bell was muttering to himself behind the tottering pile of paperwork. He enjoyed his partnership with Bob McInnis most of the time, except when he got stuck with the paperwork. He'd been partnered with Bob's father and, when Jim had died unexpectedly of a heart attack, had suggested the boy, a newly qualified sergeant in the CID, might like to be his partner for old time's sake. Mostly it worked well.

He waded through the list of names Bob had generated the day before and picked up the phone yet again.

"Yes sir, we are pursuing our enquiries, we understand you were in contact with Professor Neville in relation to his current research."

"Pardon?" The voice at the other end of the phone blared at him and he held the telephone away from his ear slightly, then repeated himself a few decibels louder.

"Yes, yes, you don't have to shout man. I'm not deaf." This was the third phone called he'd made to someone who 'wasn't deaf'. He thought he would be if he had them bellowing in his ear much more that day, and hoarse from shouting back at them.

He wouldn't mind so much if he had actually been making any progress, but he was getting the same song and dance from them all. They corresponded by e-mail. They hadn't seen the Professor for varying lengths of time, certainly not in the last six months. The winter months kept everyone indoors didn't it? Sandy shrugged as he put the phone down on yet another elderly man.

He thought he'd try to get through to the cleaner again for a change of pace. He waited patiently for the phone to pick up, idly taping his pencil against the list.

"Ah, Good Morning, you are Mrs Tracy Cavendish?"

The voice at the other end sounded both suspicious and sultry, an odd mixture thought Sandy.

"Who's asking?"

"I'm Inspector Bell. Would you like to ring back to the station and ask for me Madam? You can get me on ext 6 at the main police station."

"No," the voice changed, becoming all sultry. "Are you ringing about the Prof'? Poor man stuck in that chair and attacked like that."

66

"I would like an interview with you, today if possible Mrs Cavendish? We can come out to your home or you can come here to the station. Whichever you prefer."

"Oh, I'll come in; Tom wouldn't like you coming to the house." It was said rather naively and Sandy raised a mobile eyebrow at Bob who'd just come through the door bearing mugs. Sandy sniffed, and then grinned, coffee.

Bob moved a teetering pile to the side and set the mugs down, listening to Sandy in politically correct mode. "We wouldn't want to cause any embarrassment Mrs Cavendish; when can you come in? About an hour? That will be fine, thank you so much."

Bob removed a handful of ginger biscuits from his jacket pocket and laid them on the table. "Apologies."

Sandy replaced the receiver. "Oh yes! What you been up too?"

"Well I did go out to check up on the RTA but I got caught up in the Prof's research yesterday and wanted to see if it was fact or fiction. But I shouldn't have left you with the donkey work Sandy."

Sandy, his hands holding the coffee mug as if it was the elixir of life, shook his head, "Doesn't matter lad." He stretched an arm towards the ginger nuts and, setting down the mug, began to dunk them methodically as he filled Bob in on progress so far.

"We've got a lot of doddery old men who hardly ever leave the dubious safety of their own homes and have no reason to want the Professor dead. So I don't think professional jealousy is a motive at the moment." He crunched down on a biscuit. "There doesn't appear to be a woman but I've yet to go through his papers, and I've set up an interview with the solicitors for three, out at the house."

He pointed the remains of the biscuit. "He hadn't got a sheet, not even a speeding ticket. A very clean living old gent. I'm coming up blank Bob." He drank more coffee. "We still need the girl to tell us if anything is missing, and maybe the cleaner can fill in a few details there too."

McInnis drank coffee in the ensuing silence, and then asked, "So I gather the cleaner is coming in for a little talk; what do we know about her so far?"

"We know she was present when Miss Fielding had her accident yesterday. She was interviewed as a witness."

"Good grief! What else?"

"It seems she's being doing a bit of moonlighting, working for the Professor. Her name popped up as being married to Tomas Cavendish, he's on the fringes of the law. Been looked at a few times, nothing proved, but we think acts as a fence for Barker. Then there's been a bit of petty larceny which we couldn't make stick either. Interesting isn't it?"

The two men grinned. McInnis leaned back in the chair. "So who's going to see Mr Barker then?"

"Oh it's been a while. I think I'll pay him a visit; Gareth would like to visit Little Dennis again I'm sure." Sandy's lips twisted wryly.

Mr Barker was a polished man: his nearly bald head gleamed, his teeth had that ring of confidence or, if you were cynical, looked like tombstones in sunlight; they glowed like white marble. He wore handmade suits with just that touch of elegance about them achieved only by the very rich, or criminals.

He was a bookmaker officially, having several shops under his control. The police would dearly like to have seen his unofficial books. He was suspected of having a hand in the protection racket as well as fencing, and not the kind that kept the farm animals restrained.

At the time that Sandy Bell was speaking to Bob McInnis he was also talking, but to a much less receptive and intelligent audience however. The man he spoke to could have benefited from a bit of restraint; he certainly had something in common with the bovine breed, being singularly large and dense at times.

"Dennis, I want you to nip over to Longtown for me."

"Got that boss."

"You're to wait outside the museum and David will meet you and give you a parcel for me. Handle it carefully; it's some records I've acquired and they're a bit fragile."

"Meet David and get a parcel. OK."

"Bring it back and take it across to Cyril. He'll know what I want doing with it. Is all that clear?"

"Yes boss."

"Then I want you back here. I might have a little job for you this evening."

Dennis stood up. He was tall and very broad; his suits always looked as though they'd been bought one size too small, the cuffs revealing just a tad too much wrist, the trousers just a little too much boot. His face in repose could put one forcibly in mind of one of the great ape family, which was rather insulting to the great ape.

"Now have you any questions Dennis?"

"Er!"

"Yes?"

"Where's the museum boss?"

Frank Barker sighed, audibly. Then he shifted his bulk and pulled a piece of paper forward, hastily sketching the main road into Longtown and marking the small museum on the resultant map.

"Can you follow this Dennis?" He shoved the piece of paper over. "Show me how you're going to get there."

Dennis poked a stubby finger the size of a pork sausage along the line and worked it towards the cross.

"Good. Off you go."

Dennis moved across the floor to the door, his feet hardly disturbing the pile of the carpet. He had the agility of a boxer, for all his bulk, and that was why Frank Barker kept him around. He could fight dirtier than anyone else Frank knew, without leaving many obvious marks. In fact just having a visit from Dennis could reduce some of Barker's associates to a large grease spot on the rather nice Axminster on his office floor.

One of those associates was waiting to see him now. Tom Cavendish was pleased to see Dennis heading out the main door of the betting shop. It wasn't that he was frightened he assured himself; it was just that he wanted a private conversation with Frank Barker.

Barker came to the office door, all geniality and friendliness. "Come in Tom. How can I help?"

The two men walked towards the desk and Barker sat down, offering the younger man a seat.

Tom sat on the edge of the leather, his legs wrapped defensively round the front legs and his knees pressed together, "It's like this Mr Barker. It's about that key I got you last week."

"Yes?" Barker's face remained impassive but there was an implacable quality to his eyes that reminded Tom of a recent nature programme about snakes, cobras he thought they'd been. "I trust you haven't told anyone about that."

"No, no." Tom felt his palms sweating slightly. "I didn't know what you wanted it for." He lifted his head and looked the older

70

man in the eyes for a second. "Nor I don't want to know either. But the man's dead and I don't want no part of a murder."

"I don't know what you're talking about Tom. I haven't involved you in a murder." Barker smiled revealing his teeth.

"Well..." Tom could feel the sweat trickling down his back and under his arms even though the room was cool. "I just thought I'd let you know I don't know nothing. You can trust me."

"That's good to know Tom, because we'd both regret it if I couldn't..." He paused smiling thinly again, "Wouldn't we?"

Tom Cavendish nodded. He scraped back his chair and stood up. "Thank you for seeing me Mr Barker." He removed himself from the room with more haste than grace. His expression when he left wasn't quite so chastened and might possibly have given Frank Barker pause for thought. But not a lot of pause, and not a lot of thought. Barker tended to be a man of action; he believed it spoke louder than words.

Tomas Cavendish's wife was also using actions to speak; she was flirting, unsuccessfully, with the younger of the two detectives sitting across the table from her. He was rather cute she thought. He'd got a nice suit and tie and he'd stood up when she came into the room. She sat up a bit straighter in order to put her bust on more prominent display.

"Now Mrs Cavendish. We've got the basic details of where you live from Miss Fielding, but if you could just confirm them for us." McInnis read off the address and telephone number.

Tracy nodded, her curls bouncing and wafting a strong aroma of opium towards the two men, who barely refrained from wincing.

"Could you tell us when you started to work for the Professor and how you came to hear about the job in the first place."

"About eighteen months ago it would be. The poor man had come back from hospital. Down in London he was for ever such a long time. They can do wonders these days but he hadn't mended properly or something. Anyway, I saw the advert in the paper so I rang up." She paused, watching McInnis jotting down her words in shorthand. "Aren't you clever? I never could get my head round that stuff at school."

Sandy spoke, attracting her attention. "Did Professor Neville interview you himself?"

"Oh no, it was that nice Miss Fielding. She asked all sorts of questions. She told me I would have the freedom of the house so I had to be reliable and of good repute." She grinned at them, "Not that I knew what that meant but I guess I am 'cos she employed me."

"Did she oversee your work as well?"

"Eh?"

"Did she tell you what to do once you'd been employed?"

"Oh no. She told me what I'd got to do in a general way every week and sometimes she would ask me if I could do a special job, a bit different like. Like washing the curtains, or emptying out the cupboards. But she didn't stand over me."

"Were you responsible for cleaning upstairs too Mrs Cavendish?" Bob came back into the conversation.

"Well I was supposed to, but there wasn't time every week. And it's not as if he had visitors to stay." She looked boldly at him.

"And you had a key to let yourself in with?" Sandy took over again.

"Oh yeah, it's on my key ring, look." She pulled a black and glossy handbag the size of a small cabin trunk off the floor and began to haul objects out of it, dumping them on the desk in front of her, forming a small mountain over which she batted her mascara-bedaubed eyelashes. "Here you are!" She waved the keys at them.

"May I?" McInnis gathered up the large bundle. There actually weren't that many keys but what with a fuzzy pink elephant, a series of enamel charms, a silver pen and a small felt covered notebook, the whole thing was wrist breakingly heavy.

McInnis picked over the keys gingerly; he held the two Yale keys up by their rings, taking care not to touch them. "One of these is it?"

Tracy took the bundle back, making sure she squeezed his hand on the way. "It's this one. Do you want to keep it now?"

"Yes please." Sandy held out his hand as she detached it, also avoiding the key itself. "Has anyone else had access to these?"

"Oh no. I keep them in my bag. All the time."

"Now Mrs Cavendish, could you tell us where you were yesterday morning? It's just routine."

"Oh I has a lie in on Mondays, we go out Sunday nights. Well when I say we, Tom, that's my husband, he doesn't always go with me, but yesterday we had a lie in if you know what I mean." She grinned slyly at the two Inspectors.

"Hmm." McInnis ignored the innuendo as he looked up from his writing. "Now it would be helpful if you could come out to the Professor's house in the next day or so and just look over the areas you normally cleaned. We need to know if there's been anything taken or moved. Can you do that?"

"Of course, anything for you love. I can come over this afternoon if you want." She beamed at them both in turn. "Do you think the poor man was killed for his money then?"

"What money?" McInnis focused on her with gratifying attention.

"The money he kept in the safe in the study. He had some bits of silver I cleaned for him and some medals and some old badge things and some of those plastic bags from the bank with notes in. They were behind the books in the study." She beamed again. "I thought Miss Fielding would have shown you."

"Oh that! Yes. We'd like you to check that too." Not by so much as a blink of an eye did either detective let her know that this was the first they'd heard of a safe.

"I think that's all for now Mrs Cavendish except for a set of prints. It's just for elimination purposes." Sandy smiled across at her. "It's quite a simple process; there's an ident unit over there. You don't have to; it just makes it easier for us to eliminate you from our investigation."

He stood up and pointed out the small glowing pad connected to the computer in the corner of the room. Tracy looked somewhat doubtfully at the contraption. Sandy walked over, reciting Section 82 of the Criminal Justice Act as he went. "It's like this Mrs Cavendish, you give it, we eliminate you and then we destroy them."

"Oh." She stood up and sashayed her way across the room. "Well if you say so. What do I do?"

Sandy Bell competently placed her fingers on the pad and pressed buttons to process the fingers into the National Automated Fingerprint System.

"Now Mrs Cavendish if you could come out to the house about three thirty that would be most helpful."

Sandy Bell escorted her to the door, McInnis stood as she left, but remained firmly behind the desk as Sandy showed her out, leaving the door wide as he came back towards Bob.

"Phew. I don't know what's got into the female population at the moment lad. Have you changed your aftershave or something?"

Bob McInnis shook his head ruefully. "Don't be daft Sandy. She'd chase anything in trousers."

Sandy laughed. "Well she didn't all but drool over me lad!" He sat down opposite, in the chair lately occupied by the cleaner. "Well that seems like an unasked alibi for Cavendish but I mistrust those on principle." He frowned. "We'll look into it. What else? We have a safe and money. Yon lass never mentioned it yesterday. I think we'd better get out there and see if it's still got any contents."

McInnis looked a bit grim. "No she didn't mention it, and she didn't say anything when I saw her this morning either."

"When you saw her this morning?" He raised an eyebrow and pointed a finger at McInnis. "What you been up to lad?" he glanced at his watch, "but I think you'd better tell me on the way. We've got a solicitor to meet, and before that I want to look around the house again with Miss Fielding's assistance." His expression was grim as he grabbed his jacket from the back of his chair.

They walked in tandem towards the squad car where a patient Gareth ap Rhys waited, reading a cowboy story in the driver's seat. He'd been assigned to Bell as driver and told to report early with the comment of 'Get some decent wheels lad', from Sandy ringing in his ears.

"I met Miss Fielding out at Gretna Green and she gave me some ideas." Bob McInnis climbed in the back of the car after Sandy and they settled back for the short drive to the Professor's house.

"I thought I'd taught you better than to have ideas about witnesses, Bob? I'm too young and innocent to hear about such things." He grinned wickedly, "The lies you tell to be with a pretty girl!" He shook his head sadly, watching his partner going a dull brick red.

"I didn't mean that at all and you know it, I never, I didn't, I meant..." He stopped as he saw Sandy grinning at him. His further comment was unprintable. But he was grinning himself when he said it.

So was Gareth. He was a tall, dark haired and well muscled constable, whose bulk was increased by the heavy flak jacket bristling with pockets which he wore over his uniform. He'd worked with this pair before and admired both of them, Sandy Bell, because he was old school enough not to be politically correct when it suited him, Bob McInnis, because McInnis had come into plain clothes from the street and appreciated what the beat men had to put up with from the local population. As they arrived Sandy Bell spoke to him from the back seat.

"Gareth, cover for Higgs for a while would you? I want him to do a little job for me."

"Sure thing Chief." Gareth locked the squad car and nodded at Constable Ian Higgs, standing looking faintly bored at the door.

The two men had arrived at the house at the same time as Elizabeth Fielding was pulling up in her little blue Megan. She parked neatly behind them and they waited quietly for her to come to where they stood with PC ap Rhys.

"Afternoon Miss Fielding." Sandy Bell gave her a polite nod, Bob McInnis stood silently by, admiring today's ensemble of dark green skirt and jacket.

"Good afternoon Inspectors, Constables." She turned towards McInnis, "If you'd said I would have left yesterday when you did." She looked at McInnis, "You said to wait to look at the paperwork with you, so I didn't come over this morning. I didn't know I was doing anything wrong." She sounded a bit defensive.

76

McInnis said, "You don't owe us any explanations as to your movements Miss Fielding and we would have said if we wanted you to leave. We'd finished working in the study before I left."

Sandy opened the door and stood back to allow her to precede them into the hall way. He spoke quietly to Higgs, "Now Ian, I want you to pop down to the school. See the headmaster and ask him to show these photos to anyone who was a witness to the accident yesterday. Then come back here." Sandy paused, eyeing the very young constable. "You did well yesterday lad. Going to Miss Fielding's aid." Sandy was good at the pat/stroke routine. "Oh! And while you're at it lad see if you recognise any of them too. And cast your eye over the mug books when you get back to the station."

Elizabeth walked through into the study and stood just inside the door.

"Miss Fielding," McInnis had stopped abruptly, nearly colliding with her, and inhaling her scent unexpectedly.

"I'm sorry Inspector. It's just..." She took a deep breath, "I keep expecting Peter to be sitting there as usual, with some sly comment about boyfriends or shopping, and it's so empty." He heard her breath hitch slightly, and watched as she struggled to pull herself together.

She went forward and sat heavily in her own chair behind the desk. Bob McInnis was torn by a variety of emotions. He desperately wanted to ask her what she meant by boyfriends, had she got them by the score, or just one special one. He wanted to hold her tight and tell her to have a good cry if it would help, and he was angry with her for withholding information. Then again, because she had, he was suspicious. In fact for once in his life Bob McInnis' cage was being very firmly rattled, and he didn't like it one bit.

Sandy Bell cast a look at the conflicting emotions chasing across his colleague's face as he stepped into the room, and into the breach. He could sympathise with Bob, but now wasn't the time for the man to go to pieces on him.

"Well, we'll hope it isn't as empty as all that Miss Fielding. Perhaps you could give us the keys to the desk." He watched her looking inside a small black shoulder bag that matched her black leather court shoes. "And the ones for the safe."

Elizabeth looked up with a stunned expression on her face. "Oh! Good God, the safe, I'd forgotten all about it." She stood up dropping her handbag on the desk and headed for the bookcase with some speed.

McInnis, coming out of his brown study, halted her forward progress. "I think you'd better tell us rather than show us Miss." His expression was grim, and his grip on her forearm strong.

"But!"

"CSE should be here very shortly; they need to dust for prints Miss." Sandy shook his head at Bob McInnis and Bob abruptly let go of her.

"What's CSE?" She stood looking from one man to the other as if she expected to be clapped in irons on the instant, and couldn't understand why it hadn't happened already.

"If the safe's been tampered with we need to see if there are any prints on it. Yours might smudge them. CSE is the Crime Scene Examiner; like forensics on the TV." What McInnis didn't say was 'and they might be there already, unsmudged'. Elizabeth Fielding was nobody's fool however; she could read his unspoken thought.

As she glared at him a tall thin man of about sixty-five entered the room. He advanced across the carpet with one gloved hand held out and the other holding a very old leather briefcase, with a driving coat draped over his arm. "I'm Richards. I was Mr Neville's solicitor. You are the detectives dealing with his murder I understand." He had quite a plumy voice and smelled expensive.

Bell nodded. "Bell, and this is Inspector McInnis; he's in charge on this case."

"Ah! Right." Richards sat on one of the upright chairs in front of the old-fashioned fireplace, removing his right glove and hitching the knife edge creases of his charcoal pinstripe suit, settling his briefcase on his knee, beginning to open it and then pausing with his hand inside the bag. "Do you want to read the Will first or would you rather look through his papers?"

McInnis spoke slowly, "I think we'd better see to the papers first if you don't mind sir."

"No, no, that will be fine; I've cleared my desk for a good two hours this afternoon, so that I can be available to assist you gentlemen." He set the briefcase on the floor and brushed his light brown hair back, then resettled a pair of dark rimmed glasses on his nose.

"Perhaps we could go through the papers from the desk while we wait for forensics Miss." McInnis was regaining his calm. He didn't know what the hell was wrong with him, but he was aware he was letting Sandy Bell down by his behaviour.

They sat down around the desk with Elizabeth going to the Professor's side and unlocking the drawers. "Here you are gentlemen." As chilly tones went hers came straight from the freezer, with the door wide open. She pulled out bundles of bills fastened together with elastic bands, a sheaf of bank statements, and a small pile of obviously personal letters, placing them on the top of the desk.

Sandy exchanged a look with Bob McInnis and then divided the spoils equally between them. Silence reigned in the room save for the patter of spring rain as it began to hit the windows.

Elizabeth was calming down. She was woman enough to resent the implications of their actions, but sensible enough to recognise that they were only trying to save her from incriminating herself. She offered a small smile to the solicitor and sat down in the chair opposite to him. Resting her hands in her lap she watched the two men as they worked their way through the paperwork.

Sandy, dealing with bank statements, gave a brief grunt as he scanned down the lists of figures. There were regular direct debits for the house services, a standing order for a nice sum to Elizabeth Fielding's bank account, cash withdrawals once a month of a thousand pounds and nothing much else. He couldn't see any signs of large sums being withdrawn for blackmail and the man had a healthier bank balance than Sandy had ever had with two teenage children to put through college.

"Has he any other accounts Miss Fielding?"

"Not that I'm aware of Inspector." Elizabeth tried hard to sound conciliatory and must have succeeded since Sandy gave her a faint smile.

He looked enquiringly at the solicitor, who had been sitting apparently absorbed in his own thoughts. "Mr Richards, do you know if the Professor had any other sources of income?"

"I understand that he has gilt edged shares which he gambled with a little, his pension and a sum invested. He used the interest to live on. The account originally belonged to my father, Inspector Bell; I only took it over some two years ago when my father died. I'm afraid the only work I did for Professor Neville was to change his Will for him about six months ago and I advised him on a few points of the law."

"Thank you sir."

McInnis, half listening to the exchange, gave a cursory glance at the electric and water bills, and then turned to the private letters. There were only about six, and they were written in what he thought was German. The only letter in an envelope was dated nearly three years ago and addressed to Peter Neville from a Fraulien Smitt. He went to put it back in the envelope and found another slip of paper, but when he pulled this out he found it less comprehensible than the letter.

The other five letters were obviously much older and, while signed Peter, were addressed to a Hans. He puzzled over one for a few minutes then set them to the side, running his hand round the back of his neck. "Sandy," he passed the first over. "I can't read the date but they look oldish. He must have been in correspondence with this Hans. We need to see if we can find out who these two are. It proves he was fluent in German, but I don't see what relevance that has to his murder."

Sandy, after a swift glance at his face, looked at the paper. "Hmm, we'll have to get the interpreter to have a look at them." Elizabeth, coming over, glanced down then fastened on the letter held in his hand.

"I can try for you if you want." She spoke impulsively then regretted it as the two men exchanged a frowning look. "Er, we'll see Miss." Bob McInnis was still waging a private war; he wanted to believe her but whether for her sake or his own he didn't know. Could someone forget the existence of a safe? He supposed she might have in the stress of grief. Professional judgement wouldn't let him go with his gut though.

He was saved from any more comments by the entrance of Mark Forester; he lounged casually into the room. "What you got for us then?"

"We have become aware of the existence of a safe. We need it cleared before we open it." Sandy Bell stood up and everyone in the room became aware that he was a Senior Detective Inspector despite his easy going ways.

"Ah! Yes sir." Forester stood almost to attention as Sandy went across to the bookcase. "Behind here Miss?"

Elizabeth stood up and went cautiously forward. "It's behind those two dictionaries Inspector." She pointed out the books, careful to keep her hands from touching anything.

Mark, after a cautious look at Bell, put his case down, opened it and pulled out a pair of blue latex gloves. "Right sir, I'll just dust and then you can have a look."

Sandy Bell stood back, watching him work, and Elizabeth resumed her seat. Bob McInnis watched her sitting placidly down again and settling her skirt over long legs. He admired the face bent over her task and decided absently that a spurt of temper leant her cheeks a rather nice colour, then looked to where the forensics man was busy plying his trade.

"Got some prints and some smudges over them. It's an old safe, wouldn't take much to break in, but I can't see any scratch marks on the lock." He reached back for his camera, took some photos of the lock and the dust revealed prints. He carefully applied sticky plastic to the dust marks, flipping the top plastic over the results and printing on the date, time and place on the side, then stowing everything away in his case. "I'll process this and let you know sir."

"Don't be in such a hurry man." Sandy spoke sharply. "We haven't finished with you yet."

"Bob, you want to come and open her up?"

McInnis pulled latex gloves out of his pocket in his turn and, taking the keys from Elizabeth's desk, moved forward and opened the safe door. Mark watched him critically, pleased to note he left as little trace of his passing as possible. Sandy was watching Elizabeth. She displayed a lively interest in the proceedings, but no fear that he could detect.

He turned his head and looked at Richards as that man gave a small cough; he was watching the byplay with a lively interest too.

He swung back as McInnis gave a grunt. "Empty Sandy."

"What! But, but I've got the only key!" Elizabeth Fielding looked ready to collapse, the faint glow of remaining temper deserting her face to leave it milk white.

Richards sat calm as a Buddha; he glanced briefly at Elizabeth and then returned his gaze to the police as the two inspectors stared at her.

"Right Forester, get any prints from inside, then I want you to go upstairs. There's a set of footprints in the small room over the stairs; if you didn't collect them yesterday I want them run through both the Mark Intelligence Index and the National Footwear Reference Collection, and don't neglect the windowsill. There might be a few latents." McInnis nodded brief dismissal of the younger man and turned back to Elizabeth.

"I'd like you to tell us what was in that safe Miss, but first I want to know why you have the key and not the Professor?"

Elizabeth sat straighter in the chair, flicking back her hair; it was a nervous gesture he'd noticed her using the day before. He watched the midnight hair fall neatly back into place as she spoke. "I have the key because Peter couldn't get into the safe; he was in a wheelchair. He couldn't balance for long enough to stand and open it." She looked McInnis in the eye. "He trusted me Inspector."

McInnis said nothing to that; he just gave a brief nod as he reseated himself behind the desk in what was Elizabeth's chair. "And the contents of the safe?"

"There was always a tidy bit of money; he used to give me expenses in cash. He had some nice Georgian silverware, small stuff but pretty." She frowned. "There was a medal case. I don't know what the medal was, I never opened the box, but I recognised it because my dad has one the same colour."

McInnis waited while she paused, rubbing her hands down her skirt, "I don't think there was anything else."

"And when did you last open the safe Miss?"

She flushed, "I asked you to call me Elizabeth, and unless I'm a suspect I'd appreciate it if you would do so." She looked from him to Inspector Bell, who still stood by the open safe, and back with a certain degree of defiance. Forester chose that moment to disappear, but not before Sandy had caught his smirk. He thought he'd have to have a word with one man or the other before this case was over.

McInnis gave her a long look. "Very well, Elizabeth, when did you last have occasion to open the safe?"

"I believe it was last Thursday Inspector. Peter asked me to go up to Leith and photograph the memorial to the Royal Scots who died in the train disaster; a lot of them were buried there."

McInnis nodded his understanding and Sandy gave him a curious look.

"Oh and he asked me to go to Eastriggs, to the museum, as well. To get some information they'd got for him on the munitioneers." She placed hands that had been gesturing her words neatly back in her lap, then put her hand up to her mouth. "Oh that reminds me, there was a tray of O.W.S. badges in the safe too."

"O.W.S?"

Sandy smiled as it became Bob McInnis' turn to look slightly at sea. "'On War Service' badges Bob; my granddad had one. I'll tell you about it later." He turned back to Elizabeth Fielding. "Was there anything else Miss Fielding? It's really important."

The solicitor cleared his throat; he placed his elbows on the chair arms and steepled his fingers, looking at Bell over them. "He mentions both a wedding ring and a diamond engagement ring in his Will. I don't know their whereabouts."

Elizabeth was shaking her head, "No I didn't see anything like that in there. I can't think of anything else Inspector."

"That's OK Miss Fielding, if you'd let us know if you do?"

Bob McInnis was watching Forester who had sidled back into the room. "Have you finished Forester?"

At the other man's nod he indicated Elizabeth Fielding, then spoke to her directly over the desk, "Would you mind giving us your fingerprints?" He held up a hand as she opened her mouth. "It will help us eliminate you from our enquiries Elizabeth, but you don't legally have to do so." He looked back at Mark Forester, a steely look in his eye. He hadn't missed the smirk either.

Mark advanced, bag in hand, and Elizabeth, looking slightly apprehensive, rubbed her fingers on the front pleat of her skirt and moved to the desk again.

He pulled a large ink pad out and several sheets of paper from the side pocket of the bag. "Just roll your fingers over the pad like that." Mark wasn't slow when it came to holding her hand and moving her fingertips over the ink. "Now roll them onto the paper… that's it." He was near enough to note the faint dew of sweat on her upper lip and gave a small chuckle. "That's the way. We'll destroy them as soon as we've finished with them Elizabeth. You don't have to be nervous; you won't have a criminal record. These won't go on to NAFIS."

Elizabeth offered him a faint smile while he packed his equipment away. "Thank you. Do I need anything to get it off?" She looked at her inky fingers somewhat ruefully.

"Nah, just soap and water should do it. It'll be great when they get the hand held Lifescans, save a lot of mess and speed things up." Mark eyed the trio of men as he prepared to leave; he would dearly like to have asked her for a date, but given the battery of officialdom, decided he'd maybe catch her another time.

He left the study and had got as far as the front door when Tracy Cavendish was admitted. She gave him a somewhat predatory look, "Well hello handsome! Are you a policeman too?"

Mark Forester had spent time out on his father's boat; he could recognise barracuda when he saw it. He edged towards the door holding his large forensic bag in front of him as a shield. "Yes Miss, and if you'll excuse me I'm on official business." He was the one being given a smirk this time, but he couldn't blame Gareth for that. He was too busy escaping with his skin intact.

Tracy meanwhile, having watched his departure, followed the sound of voices and stood on the threshold of the study. "Hello again Inspector McInnis."

McInnis frowned fiercely. "Good afternoon Mrs Cavendish." He noted that she'd changed her skirt. This one was even shorter and he absently wondered how she moved in it; it seemed to him as if it might cut off the circulation a bit round the top of her thighs.

Sandy stood up from his seat behind the desk. "If you'd like to continue looking over the papers McInnis? I'll take Mrs Cavendish round and she can see if she notices anything missing."

"Thanks Sandy." He looked back at Elizabeth. "Would you like to go and wash your hands Elizabeth? Mr Richards and I can manage for a minute."

Elizabeth stood up with her hands held carefully in front. Bob moved and opened the door for her, watching as she walked away down the passageway to the kitchen.

He turned back as Richards stirred in his chair. "I take it you'll want to know the contents of the Will Inspector? Perhaps while that young lady is not present?"

McInnis nodded. Richards pulled three written pages from his brief case. The paper was thick and the colour of Devon cream.

"Aside from some bequests to various charities, and one or two gifts to acquaintances, much of the money goes to Miss Fielding, including the rings I mentioned. Professor Neville changed his will, as I said, some six months ago. This house is to be sold and the money invested to fund a scholarship at Cambridge. There are a few minor beneficiaries, but the bulk of the cash goes, as I said, to Miss Fielding and..." He stopped as she came through the doorway.

She had obviously heard him. She looked horrified. "Oh! God, I don't want his money."

"Nevertheless Miss Fielding you are the chief beneficiary, including all the research he was undertaking at this present time." He looked somewhat apologetically at McInnis.

Later describing the scene to Sandy he said, "She looked genuinely upset Sandy. I really don't think she had a clue as to how the Will was arranged." He shrugged and settled back behind his desk. "Still it gives her a hell of a motive. We need to check her finances."

"OK. I'll get a warrant for that. We've got some preliminary reports from the neighbours." He held up a sheaf of papers. "Now how about nipping down to the canteen for a mug of tea before we start lad. This case isn't going to be hurried." They strolled out together, shutting the door on the pile of paperwork.

Once established at a slightly sticky vinyl covered table with thick white mugs in front of them, Sandy sat back with a sigh. He looked about the nearly deserted canteen; most of the day shift had gone home long ago and the late shift hadn't arrived yet.

"You tell me what you know about 'Royal Scots' lad and I'll tell you all about O.W.S. badges." He raised an eyebrow.

Bob McInnis filled him in on the reading he'd done the day before, and his subsequent visit to the railway bridge that morning. "So you see Sandy, while the research is interesting I don't think it'll help us, I don't think the motive lies there. Unless it's an academic thing. Pinching ideas or being the first to tell the story maybe."

"No lad, I'm inclined to agree with you." Sandy pushed his empty mug away and sat back, making the chair creak. "So what other motives have we got?"

"We've got the money. Or rather we haven't got the money. But why didn't they take the wallet and watch he was wearing? Though we do know where the wedding band the solicitor mentioned is. That was with his effects wasn't it?"

"Yeah. No diamond ring though. He was a blameless old chap, so not blackmail."

"He didn't go anywhere so he didn't see anything worth killing him for."

"There's the Will in favour of Miss Fielding."

Now it was Bob's turn to shrug, "I dunno Sandy, we're getting nowhere with this."

"Give us a chance lad. You've only had the case thirty-six hours!"

They stood up, pushing back plastic chairs with a faint squeal of protest, as they headed back to McInnis' office. "So what's an O.W.S. badge then?"

Sandy nodded to himself. Bob might not be a graduate but he hung onto points like a terrier with a rat until he'd got all the answers. "'On War Service' badges. Like I said, my granddad had one. If you worked in a reserved profession you wore a badge so young women who should have known better, wouldn't give you a white feather and ask you why you weren't in the trenches getting shot."

They went into the office and Sandy closed the door, going to sit on one side of the desk. "My granddad was a left-handed riveter, in the Glasgow dockyards."

"A what! Never mind tell me in a minute." Giving a backhand wave McInnis sat down and leaned back in his seat. "Let me get this straight. I thought everyone rushed to enlist in the First World War? Your country needs you and all that."

Sandy shook his head. "No, they didn't. Some did, usually the wrong ones, the ones who couldn't be spared; they started conscripting late 1915 I think." He scratched his head then transferred the hand to a five o clock shadow and gave that a scratch too. "Wait a bit while I think."

McInnis waited patiently while the older man frowned into the past.

"Granddad had these O.W.S. badges tucked in with his medals. He'd been working in the dockyard until 1917, then even the under 18's and over 45's started getting called up, married men too. Granddad did escort duties in the North Sea after that, against the subs. But before that there were all these trades." He looked across at Bob, hands in his pockets and lent back in the wooden chair, resting his elbows on the arms.

"I thought submarines were the Second World War."

"You young fellas, don't know nuthin'! How do you think the Lusitania sank? Submarines go back to the American War Between the States."

"Good grief Sandy, how do you know that?"

Sandy looked faintly embarrassed, "I read it in a cowboy book, and I wanted to know if it was true or just a bit of plot." He grinned at Bob, "That's not for general consumption lad. Now where was I?" He rubbed a finger under his nose and thought while Bob just sat watching him.

"Oh yes, it's like this. A war's not just fought on the battle ground lad; you have to have a support network at home. A bit like 'the house Jack built'. You need mines to give coal, to keep the steel works going, to supply the ammunition factories. You need railways to move all those materials around. Dockyards, anyone in the docks was reserved 'cos you need battleships to fight with, and someone to build them."

Bob leaned back himself, swinging slightly in the office chair as Sandy continued.

"Then you have to feed all these people, so farmers and such like too. The women eventually filled in a lot of the jobs. But some men, well they'd been trained and were thought of as too important to be gun fodder." He shrugged, "Until they got desperate, then just about everyone got called up."

"OK I understand that much." Bob sat forward, nodding his head. "So these badges, were they like medals, worth a bit?"

"Nah, you can pick them up in junk shops for a few pounds, pence even. There must have been a reserve occupation just to make the things; there were millions of them, mostly just embossed metal. They started out as lapel pins but when the women got in on the act they became badges. It's a handy way of dating which professions lost men first to the women; women didn't have lapels." He raised an eyebrow and smiled slightly. "They were useless after the war though."

"So they wouldn't be stolen for their value."

"Not if someone knew what they were, certainly."

McInnis shrugged, "Ah well, bang goes another theory." He returned the faint smile before sighing heavily. "We'd better get started on these interviews Sandy, see if anyone in the neighbourhood saw anything."

They'd been reading for a couple of hours when Sandy, reaching out to put on the desk lamp, alerted McInnis to the time. He looked out of the window, a bit puzzled to see that the sky had gone dark blue and all the shadows had crept closer. "Go home Sandy." He looked at the older man. "We've put in a long day and the Professor can wait another day for justice."

Sandy smiled, lifting the corner of his mouth. "Your dad used to say that."

"Yeah I know. He never talked much about his cases Sandy, but sometimes, after I joined the force, he'd talk through a difficult one at home. He said the dead could always wait for justice. But the living they needed love."

"I'll see you in the morning lad." Sandy stood up, pulling on his suit jacket and carefully putting his glasses away in the inside pocket. "See you take your Dad's advice."

McInnis gave him a cautious look but refrained from comment. "Night Sandy."

After Sandy had gone, shutting the door behind him, Bob McInnis pushed the pile of papers untidily into their file and sat back; it was the first real chance he'd had to be alone that day. He was a cautious man who liked to weigh all the facts. He was incurably honest too, even with himself.

What was going on? Normally he could sum up the people he encountered on a case and decide the truly innocent straight away. Miss Elizabeth Fielding however wasn't easy to sum up.

To start with she had a lot of circumstantial evidence against her. She was the possessor of the keys that opened not just the door but the safe. She stood to gain a small fortune from the Professor's Will, which had been changed in her favour in the last few months. She'd been first on the scene. And finally, he admitted to himself, he was more than just physically attracted to her and that was clouding his judgement.

He stood up, scooping his discarded jacket from the back of his chair and leaning over to switch off the desk light. Maybe he needed to take Sandy's advice after all and go home.

4

Elizabeth Fielding was standing in the graveyard, shivering as the words of the funeral service were said over the final home of her former employer. It had been a week since she'd found the body; she was beginning to hate Monday mornings.

There was only a handful of old men around the grave, all of them huddling in thick black overcoats. She'd done her best to contact people but the weather had turned surprisingly nasty for the first week of June, with torrential downpours everyday for the last three days. Many of them couldn't, or wouldn't, venture north for the funeral.

She had been standing listening to the rain fall in a gentle patter on the coffin, but now became aware that it wasn't falling on her, and also that she could smell McInnis' aftershave. She looked up and back, to see him holding a large black umbrella over her.

He looked compassionately at her face, at the barely restrained tears which had been mixing with the rain. She'd lost weight this last week: her face thinner and paler. He tucked a firm, warm hand under her arm as the first pit-a-pat of soil hit the wooden lid and the grave diggers moved to their appointed tasks.

"Miss Fielding," she looked up at him, "Elizabeth, can I give you a lift anywhere? Do you have to look after people?"

"I've offered, but they came in a hired car and intend to travel back together, so no. And yes Inspector, you can give me a lift, but I'm going home so you may regret your offer." Elizabeth looked at him, brushing wet hair out of her face.

McInnis nodded to the couple of Detective Sergeants who'd accompanied him to the graveyard. They would do some quick and informal interviews in the church; he'd already spoken to the vicar about it, but looking over those present he didn't think the interviews would bear any fruit. "No I wouldn't have offered if I didn't mean it."

It was said simply and Elizabeth gave him a curious look as they walked out of the churchyard. She stood a minute while he unlocked the car, looking through the parting sheets of rain. "My mother's buried here. It's a lovely spot when the sun shines; you can see the hills all blue and purple of a summer evening. I never felt sad here when I visited before. But then I never knew my mother."

McInnis helped her into the car, wordlessly, then went round and settled himself in the driver's seat. He drove efficiently and carefully without asking for directions, allowing her time. What for she wasn't sure, she was just aware of his comforting presence.

She'd seen him briefly several times over the last week. He'd been to look over Peter Neville's work, on the computer. She'd found him poring over masses of hard copy of research when she'd gone in one day to check the mail. He'd been courteous, and kind. She could see that he didn't like working with the computer but she'd also seen his dogged determination to master what he needed to know, and admired him for it.

At first she'd been put off by that serious, verging on stern, face but she'd found him grinning at his partner one day and realised she trusted him. It had shocked her a bit; she didn't know if she liked him, but that trust was there anyway and she found it comforting.

When they pulled up outside her gate he came round and opened her door for her, holding the umbrella as she got out and then escorting her to the front door. "Are you coming in Inspector? I assume you didn't just come to the internment to hold an umbrella."

He inclined his head, flicking rain from his hair and giving her a faint smile.

"Well as to that Miss Fielding, yes and no."

He followed her into the hall and she took his fine wool coat and hung it next to her own, before turning and walking away from him. He followed and found himself in a very comfortable sitting room with a small coal fire burning in the hearth. "Hello darling." He heard the words as he entered the room and felt an unreasonable and uncharacteristic rush of jealousy, until he caught sight of the speaker.

Elizabeth swung round, "Inspector McInnis I'd like you to meet my father Noel Fielding. I'll put the kettle on Dad."

McInnis moved forward and shook hands, then sat down in the chair the older man pulled slightly forward. Elizabeth, after one warning look at him, left the room. Bob McInnis was puzzled by that look. He turned toward her father, not quite sure how to proceed; Fielding had a faint grin on his face.

"She's shielding me again, don't worry. I suppose you've come to ask her some more questions. Poor Peter, what a terrible way to die, but I suppose it was time for Atropos to cut the thread." He sat down opposite McInnis.

McInnis maintained his calm. "I suppose so sir."

"And do you serve Tisiphone?" McInnis was beginning to panic; was that what the warning look was all about? Was her father potty?

Elizabeth came in with a tea tray, as her father finished speaking, "Father he's a policeman, not a Greek scholar. He has other abilities."

Bob McInnis cast her a strange look; was she actually giving him a compliment?

Elizabeth gave him a half smile as he rose and took the tray from her, setting it on a small table at the side of the settee. "He's talking about the Fates and Furies Inspector, Tisiphone avenges murder."

"Then the answer is no, I don't serve her sir. I seek justice for the dead, not vengeance. That's not my province."

"Then you've never lost a personal friend, young man." Noel Fielding looked at him over a pair of glasses perched on the end of his nose.

The smile was grim as McInnis said, "No, perhaps not, but you are right; I do have to ask Miss Fielding some more questions."

Elizabeth set the teapot down with something of a snap. "Elizabeth, for God sake."

"Only if you call me Bob!"

"Does that mean I'm no longer a suspect?"

McInnis was cautious. "No, but I find I'm tired of being called Inspector in that rather precise voice of yours." He looked at the slim pencil thin skirt and white blouse, and thought she gave the impression of a strict school marm when she took that tone of voice.

Her father, observing the byplay, gave a faint chuckle, "She does rather make you feel like something nasty under a rock when she's mad at you doesn't she?" He smiled affectionately at his daughter.

He stood up, accepting the cup and saucer his daughter handed him. "I'm going to my study darling, play nicely." He patted her shoulder in passing and left the room.

McInnis watched his exit with both surprise and a certain amount of relief.

"You said yes and no."

Bob gathered his wandering thoughts, looking at Elizabeth. Her face had been in his dreams rather too often for his own comfort over the last week. It had distracted him from his work as well. He'd gone to the funeral that day in part to see if the attraction he'd felt was real, or just something he'd imagined. Now he saw her again, in her own setting, he realised it wasn't imagination. Well business first.

"A few questions then Elizabeth. Did anyone else have access to your keys?"

"Not that I'm aware of." She sat down in the chair her father had recently occupied, placing the cup and saucer at her feet and holding one hand out to the fire. She lifted her head and looked at Bob McInnis fearlessly. "I kept them in my handbag, whichever one I was using."

"OK, then did anyone have access to your handbag?"

"My father, I suppose, but that would be absurd." She shook her head and he watched the ebony hair glint in the firelight. "He rarely leaves the house; he's quite a sick man."

McInnis sighed. He wanted to believe she was innocent but forensics had come back with the information that the safe hadn't been picked, that only her fingerprints, Tracy Cavendish's and her employer's had been found on the safe. Hers on top of both Tracy's and his, smudged but still there.

"Are you sure no-one else had a key."

"No, I'm not one hundred percent certain, because I only worked for Peter for eighteen months. But I'm nearly certain." She picked up her cup and sipped tea, sitting very straight in the chair.

"Alright, leave that for now. Now, did you go upstairs at all, at any time?"

"No."

"Just no."

She sighed. "The last time I went up was..." she paused, looking out of the window at the rain. "Christmas last year I think. I had no reason to go upstairs." Her lips twisted a bit wryly. "Tracy didn't go up there much either. But then there really wasn't any reason for her either. Peter didn't exactly have visitors by the score."

Bob McInnis set his untouched tea down and rubbed his forehead. The cold rain had given him a headache; at least that was what he was going to blame it on.

"Can I ask a question?"

"I don't promise to answer, Elizabeth."

"Are you any nearer to finding out who killed him?"

He looked across and shook his head. "We're still sifting evidence but no, no we're not. I'm sorry."

She gave a small shudder. "I'm sorry too."

They both sat quietly for a few moments then McInnis said, "I didn't just come to ask you questions. I wanted to see you."

Elizabeth put her head on one side, reminding him of a small inquisitive starling listening for a worm. "Why?"

"I don't precisely know," Bob McInnis looked straight at her. "I shouldn't become involved with anyone who's part of a current case. But..." He shrugged again, "I think I'm attracted to you, and that's unusual enough for me to risk coming to see you for private reasons."

"Well," she turned rosy red, but tried for sang-froid, "that's honest." She set the cup down in its saucer. "What do you want me to say?"

McInnis was as pale as she was red. "I'm not generally lost for words when I ask questions but you see with you I am." He gave a soft sigh, "I'm a bit out of my depth. I should have known better.

What with your father talking Greek to me, and you going to university." He stood up. "I'll be going Miss Fielding; just concentrate on thinking about who else might have had some keys. I'll let myself out."

Elizabeth watched him head to the door then spoke softly. "I think I prefer Elizabeth; and you could always ask me out for a drink."

Bob McInnis stopped with his hand on the door knob and turned back to her slowly. She watched him as he flushed slightly and then straighten, "Would you care to come out for a drink Elizabeth?"

"Yes I'd like that. I'm available most nights."

"Tonight?"

"Yes."

"Sure?"

At her nod he said, "I'll call for you then." He smiled properly for the first time in front of her, and she realised that he was a very handsome man. Then he whisked out of the room, and had gone before she'd moved enough to see him out.

Sandy found him beaming like a lunatic at his desk an hour later. "Have we had a break through?"

"Oh yes."

"What?"

"She says she'll go out for a drink."

"Eh!" Sandy looked like a man hit unexpectedly with a wet fish. "Who?"

"Elizabeth of course."

"There's no of course about it; you've been hip deep in paperwork for a week with every second clue implicating her, and you've asked her out for a date!"

The smile left McInnis' face. "Yes."

Sandy sat down slowly. "Bob. Lad. You can't, you know you can't."

Bob McInnis firmed his lips, his face serious. "I can and I have." He looked at his partner; saw the compassion, the understanding, even the love that Sandy hid under banter and buffets. "Sandy, I've never felt like this before, but I need to find out what it's all about." He paused, pushing back an errant lock of hair. "You don't seriously think she murdered Peter Neville do you?"

Sandy sat still, absorbing the seriousness of the situation. "Not physically, no. She's neither strong enough nor, as far as we can find out, had the training. It was a skilled killing," he said slowly, "but she could be behind it." He held up a hand. "You know that Bob. We've got enough to hold and question on circumstantial at the moment."

Bob McInnis nodded his head slowly in acknowledgement. "Yeah I know, but I just don't believe it Sandy." He scrubbed his hands over his face. "What did you come through for anyway?" He gave another nod, this time directed at the papers in Sandy's hand.

Sandy opened his lips as if to speak, then closed them again. He gave Bob McInnis a long look then shrugged. "Alright lad. But be careful. Now," he laid the papers on the table, "we've finally got a translation of those letters and I've managed to contact Fraulein Smitt. I don't think it helps us much but at least we can cross them off our 'to do list'." He sniffed.

"It appears Fraulien Smitt is researching her family tree. She speaks excellent English, which makes it odd that she wrote to Peter Neville in German, howsoever that might be; she had found some letters which had been written by her uncle during the First World War."

"Good God! How old is she?"

Sandy looked puzzled, "I've no idea; anyway..." He waved a hand dismissing this interruption, "she'd got these letters and thought that our Peter must be a cousin of some sorts. The letter we have was only a covering one. We think that either there were others he got rid of, or they'd used e-mails."

"So he didn't write them?"

"No. That's what I'm telling you, don't keep interrupting." Sandy sounded testy. He shook his head. "Where was I?"

Bob assumed this was rhetorical and kept his mouth shut.

"OK, so these old letters, were written by Peter Neville's father to a cousin in Germany called Hans Erkel. They make interesting reading. It took the translator so long because they're written in gothic script and High German, a combination the police interpreter couldn't handle." He grinned across the desk. "And the other sheet of paper, with the bar code on. I thought I'd seen something like that before, on CSI."

Bob raised an eyebrow. The fact that his highly esteemed colleague watched the American forensic team series was a secret they both kept very quiet about. Sandy would never have heard the end of it in the police station.

"Hmm so what was it?"

"DNA."

"Eh!"

"DNA. It seems this Fraulien Smitt is very go ahead; she's been using DNA to track her ancestors."

"What, like in a paternity suit?"

"Well sort of. I didn't understand all the ins and outs Bob, but it seems you can say where your ancestors originally come from in the world, like China or Africa, or Europe, and you can tell if it's the mother's line or the father's that you're following. They lost me a bit there," he rubbed his nose, "something to do with XX and XY."

He shrugged, "So she'd been tracking hers and said she had thought the Professor was one of her paternal relatives, and did he want to see these letters. Also she thanked him for his DNA sample. Now this is where it gets interesting," he waved the sheaf of papers at McInnis smiling, "because these results show he was from the maternal line instead."

McInnis scratched his head. "Well it's kinda interesting, in an academic sort of way but I don't see how it helps us solve his murder."

Sandy sat back. "Yeah I know," his smile faded, "nor do I Bob. At least it's one less mystery to deal with though. What have you got?"

"Well the technical guys have been through his computer. He wasn't using any porn sites, he wasn't e-mailing small children and he didn't have young boys visiting. So I guess he just liked children's books, his father spoke German, maybe the books were his, not our *Corpus Delecti*. He wasn't a paedophile Sandy. I didn't think he was, but you have to look."

"Yeah I know."

"The neighbours aren't very observant, and they aren't in that much," Bob continued, "most of them work. They knew the Professor in a casual sort of way; they seem to agree that he was a nice quiet old chap who kept to himself most of the time. He used to go out quite a bit when he was able, held a sort of soiree for the people of the street at Christmas time, but that was the only real contact they had with him.

102

"He has masses of stuff on the computer about the First World War; they're going to print me some more hard copy of his research so I can see how he was tying it all together and, before you say it, I know that won't help us find out, but I'm interested."

Sandy Bell nodded agreement. "Have we got anything more on the first accident?"

"Elizabeth seemed to think it was a hit and run but I've looked through the stuff you got from the London Police. On the face of it, it was just an unfortunate accident. The Chelsea tractor that hit him contained a distraught mother and her children on the way home from school. I'm not surprised he came off second best from the encounter, but she didn't know him from a bar of soap. She wasn't speeding or drunk and only had a couple of parking tickets to her credit."

"Didn't anyone see anything?"

"Nope, nothing."

"Bummer. How about our Major?"

"Bit shady. The Army has promised to send us his record."

"Oh he was in the army then?"

"Yeah, he was in and then he was out, quick march. They didn't care for his attitude Sandy."

"Any of the school kids recognise any faces?"

"Couple saw Little Dennis in the vicinity, but before we get our hopes up, that was the vicinity of the school, not the accident."

"Oh yeah, what was he up to do you think?"

"Hard to speculate with Little Dennis, Bob. Could be drumming up a bit of custom for Barker. I'll get the drug team to have a little chat down at the school in any case." Sandy paused, thinking. "I only put his picture in on spec; I didn't expect it to bear fruit. I was expecting maybe Tom Cavendish's face to get a pop though."

"Nope, no reaction to that one."

"Hmm." Sandy sat turning a pen over as he assimilated facts and decided how to broach the next bit. "I have to ask Bob, have we got the warrant for Miss Fielding's financials?" Sandy looked apologetic.

Bob shrugged, "It's OK, and yes we've got it, on the circumstantial evidence. I've not had a look at it yet Sandy."

"Want me to do that one?"

Again Bob McInnis shrugged, then under Sandy's scrutiny nodded, "Yeah it feels a bit..." He shook his head, "Don't say it Sandy, I know what I'm doing," he paused again, "I hope."

"What next?"

"I've yet to follow up on Barker. It's a tenuous connection, but I can't ignore it."

"Not so tenuous with Dennis around. Take Gareth." He grinned. "Besides if Barker doesn't get a visit every few months he begins to feel neglected. I wouldn't want him unhappy." Sandy's grin became a little evil.

He looked at his watch. "I've got an appointment with a solicitor Bob. I'd best be off." He stood and gathered papers.

McInnis worked solidly on through the wet afternoon. The piles of paperwork moved from one side of the desk to the other as he waded his way through the tedium of interviews with neighbours, police traffic reports, and possible connections to his murder victim.

At the back of his mind he was thinking of the coming evening; he wondered if he was being a fool. Worse, risking his job and reputation for the sake of a woman. But when he thought of the woman concerned, the straight look she'd given him, he knew he had to go onward and be sure. He'd lived with caution too long, and if he was honest he was lonely sometimes.

Elizabeth Fielding was also doing some thinking; Bob McInnis wasn't the kind of man she'd normally accept a date from. She wondered what they'd find to talk about. Certainly not Greek goddesses! She recalled the swiftly concealed bafflement of that morning when her father had mentioned the Fates and Furies. She was slightly puzzled by her own agreement to go out, but they would see.

McInnis decided to take her over the border. It wouldn't do for other members of the constabulary to see them out together during an ongoing case, he was aware of that. He didn't want to have a lot of ribald comment thrown his way either. He'd picked her up outside the neat terraced house as the rain had stopped.

He silently approved the casual jeans and sky blue jumper; he admired even more the figure it outlined as he helped her into the car. He in turn was being scrutinised as he set the car in motion. Elizabeth wondered if he possessed jeans; he was in yet another conservative suit. Granted it made him look very, she searched for a word and came up with 'respectable', but it wasn't exactly casual.

"Where are we going, or is it a surprise?"

Bob turned his head and spared her a quick look, taking in the pretty profile and a whiff of scent. "I know of a nice pub, with a couple of fireplaces." He transferred his gaze back to the traffic. "If it gets cold again we can lounge by one of them, but if not they've got some rather lovely grounds to sit out in. It's on the outskirts of Gretna." He paused, changing gear and glancing in the mirror. "I didn't think you'd want anything too..." he waved a hand and put it back on the wheel, "with the funeral this morning."

"It's alright. I've said goodbye, now I'm getting on with life; that's what Peter used to say when some old friend died, and there were about four of his friends who died while I worked for him." She smiled sadly, "He said he'd nearly outlived his own generation."

Bob drove quietly for a while then shifted in his seat and glanced across at the silent girl beside him. Was she regretting this date already? Should he have waited longer before asking her? Impossible to tell, and too late now anyway. He spoke, keeping his eyes on the road, "Do you want some music? There's a pile of tapes in the glove compartment?"

"No, but it might be fun to see if we have the same taste in music."

He grinned suddenly, his gloomy thoughts lifting as he thought of the collection of tapes he'd currently got in the car. "Feel free." He waited with a wicked glint in his eye as she rummaged through them.

"If these are all yours I'm reconsidering this date."

"Which ones are you concerned about?"

"Well, 'the wheels on the bus' seems rather, er, juvenile."

"What else?"

"I can't help feeling Meat Loaf isn't your style either."

"You'd be surprised." He shot her another glance and she discovered that smile could be devastating when he was relaxed. "But one is the nephew's property, and the other my sister's. I forgot they were there until I told you to look." He gave a chuckle.

"So which are yours?"

"I'm fairly eclectic; it really depends on what mood I'm in. I like the classical stuff but I do like Meat Loaf sometimes too."

"Myself I like Chopin."

He swung the car through a pair of opened gates and up a short driveway. "I've heard all women like Chopin, especially in expensive stores." He flashed another grin at her groan.

"That's a terrible pun."

He parked under the shade of some Douglas firs. "Oh I thought it was punny myself." He dodged the gentle backhander, "Out or in?"

Elizabeth, waiting for him to lock the car, gave a slight shiver. "I think in. That sun's still a bit too watery for me."

He took her arm as they walked towards some rather imposing steps. "They use this place for marriages; it's one of the many original forges." He raised a mobile eyebrow.

Elizabeth was actually quite enchanted by the inside, even if it was a little over done with tartans and deer's heads. "I suppose it's good for the tourists."

"Do you mean like fly spray is good for flies?"

She caught herself grinning at him as he went to fetch her a port and lemonade and then realised that it was the first time she'd really smiled all week.

He came back and set his half lager on the table next to her drink. "Warm enough?" He sat down at her side and enjoyed the pleasant frisson of pleasure as she moved next to him to pick it up.

"So we might not have music in common. It's your turn to pick a topic."

McInnis turned to her, "Actually I'd like to pick your brains if it's not too painful." His face was serious. "I've been reading through the Professor's notes, and I'd like to know what's fiction and what's fact. But if you don't want to discuss it I'll quite understand." His face in repose had become quite stern and serious again she thought, but that earlier grin lingered in her mind.

"I don't mind. I take it you don't think his research has anything to do with his death now?"

McInnis shrugged slightly. "I don't see how it can."

"So what would you like to know?"

"This whole area was a munitions factory. Is that right? That's one of the reasons I brought you here. I thought you might like a drive later and you could show me the area it covered." He looked a bit apologetic and gently touched her arm.

"Don't keep apologising Bob, it's a fascinating subject, I know. I've researched it." She laid a hand on his as it rested on her arm. Hers was warm and soft like the smile she offered him. "Now where shall I start?"

"1915 would seem like a good place."

"Ah, now that was a busy year up here in the north of England, or rather the south of Scotland. The British government of the day was running out of munitions; they couldn't keep the guns fed on either front, but especially the Western front. So they decided to build a new factory." She sipped delicately and set the glass down again.

"It was a big factory; it covered nearly nine miles from here in Gretna to Annan. It was designed by the bloke who gave us the Nobel Peace Prize. He invented dynamite." She offered an ironic smile. "They didn't just build a factory, but three whole townships to service it; schools, churches, and a ballroom. It was an incredible achievement."

"So that bit is true." McInnis frowned. "I suppose you've read Professor Neville's stuff about it."

"Not all of it." She looked at him thoughtfully. "I thought he was writing some sort of treatise on the deserters. And then, like you, I read some of the story. It was good, but I can see your problem, fact or fiction. Faction I suppose." She paused, then offered, "I can go through it with you if you want."

Bob McInnis hesitated just a bit too long.

"Don't worry about it Bob."

He gave her a small smile, "I'm making a bit of a mess of this. No more shop talk, let's just enjoy finding out about each other. Deal?" He held out a capable hand and she put her smaller one in it.

They sat back with their drinks. "Tell me about the nephew that likes 'the wheels on the bus'."

She discovered that Bob McInnis was a nice man; he wasn't just charming and handsome but he obviously loved his nephews and nieces, of whom he had five. He loved his sister too; she could hear it in his voice when he spoke about her. His brother-in-law was in the services, and they were based down south. He obviously missed them.

He spoke about his father whom he also missed. "Sandy Bell became my father's partner when his old one retired, and Sandy took me on when I joined the CID; he's a good man Sandy." He thought about the concern on Sandy's face when he'd told him of the date earlier in the day. Then he put it to the back of his mind. This girl didn't murder anyone.

"Would you like another?" He held up her glass.

"No thanks. Let's go for that little drive and I'll point out what's left of the dispersal site." She stood up with a smile and held out a hand.

After a slight pause Bob McInnis put his hand in hers and they walked out together into early summer dusk.

"I love the Solway; I sometimes go bird watching on the other side."

"Yes." Elizabeth gently swung their hands as they walked towards the silver Peugeot. "I like that bit near the repeater station; there's a flock of greylag come in there. Noisy, but wonderful to watch in flight."

They climbed into the car and McInnis set off towards Annan.

McInnis was in his office next morning, studying the report from the army, when Sandy came in. Sandy eyed him carefully; he was dying to ask how the date had gone, but didn't quite know how to broach the subject. He'd endured a mild tongue lashing from his wife, Sarah, when he'd told her Bob had got himself a date with a suspect.

She'd told him he was a daft old fool and, worse, a mother hen not to trust Bob McInnis' judgement. Then told him there would be no cherry cake for those who didn't find out if the lad was OK, and all the details. He liked her cherry cake a lot, as his slightly tight waistband could testify.

"Hi Bob, what we got this morning then?"

"Army report on Madogan, Sandy, nasty piece of goods. Joined when he was 23, did about six months training, liked to fight and wasn't choosy who with. They thought if they could have got some discipline into him he'd have been a good candidate for the SAS; but the psych evaluations said he'd got..." McInnis looked at the paper, scanning down the sheet, "mild psychopathic and sociopathic tendencies."

"And he's wandering the streets?"

"Well he hasn't, as far as we know, committed a crime Sandy. We know where he was from Closed Circuit Cameras as he passed a couple of the big supermarkets and they've clocked him speeding, but his story checks out. He was at a luncheon, and he did have another meeting to go to. The second one was with slightly off white members of the public, and he was taking a funny route to get

110

to them. But that might have been for road works, or traffic, or any number of reasons. There's nothing we can pin on them either ..." McInnis laid the paper down. "He certainly has the ability, and sufficient training, to kill an old chap like the Prof' but we haven't turned up a connection to either him or Elizabeth."

"I supposed we'd better cross him off the list then." Sandy Bell sighed. "How about Cavendish?"

"Hmm, he's up to something Sandy. I've had an inconspicuous shadow on him for the last week. He's visited Barker at least twice. Cavendish spent a large wad on the horses both times he visited, more than a man on the social could have. And he wasn't winning."

"We'll keep checking." Sandy paused, swallowed, and then shrugged. "How was the date?"

Bob leaned back and swung the chair round to the small window, watching the sun pop out from behind a cloud, then swung back. He looked at Sandy, whose cheeks were an unaccustomed pink.

"Sarah gave me hell last night!"

Bob laughed, "The date was good." He smiled a singularly sweet smile. "She's a darling Sandy."

"Oh! Oh dear!" Sandy shook his head. "I think I need a mug of tea." He stood up as did Bob. "Tell me something to keep Sarah happy then."

"We went to the pub and then looked at dispersal mounds and we smelt ether."

"Right. Haven't I taught you better than that? Dispersal mounds! Ether!" he muttered in disgust. Then he looked sideways at the younger man as they walked the familiar beige and brown corridor. "What the hell is a dispersal mound anyway?"

Bob grinned across as they pushed open the door to the canteen. "It's the buffer between the storage, or place of manufacture, of two highly volatile substances." He continued to grin at the frustrated expression that settled on Sandy's face. "Sorry Sandy, couldn't resist, that's how I felt last night. Don't worry 'Dad' will tell you all about it." He accepted the punch on his arm as forgiveness for what Sandy considered a rash act, and payment for teasing.

As they settled down in the nearly deserted canteen and Sandy got to work on a pile of his favourite gingersnaps, Bob McInnis told him what he'd learnt the night before.

"Gretna was a huge munitions complex Sandy. They built miles of railway track and, I suppose, what was the equivalent of the conveyer belt factory for armaments. Each part of the assembly was volatile or flammable or both, so they spread the buildings apart and set them amid sand dunes so that if one building blew up the others wouldn't go up in the blast. You can still see where the mounds were built. But the factory buildings are gone."

"Well I knew Gretna was a new town. Like Milton Keynes only earlier; I suppose I might have known why it had been built if I'd thought about it." Sandy dunked and crunched, looking at the enthusiasm on his younger colleague's face.

"It makes some of the stuff I've been reading more interesting, when you can actually go along the roads, and there's this bit where you can smell the ether from the processing plant. Even though all you can see are a few sections of stone and concrete. He was a damn good writer Sandy, and it's a bloody shame that someone topped him."

"Have you had a look at those letters yet? They'll make interesting reading too, I should think. I've only skimmed them so far myself."

"No I haven't got round to it either."

112

Sandy sat back with a satisfied grunt. "So lad, what's your next plan?"

"I put off visiting Barker when I heard Cavendish was going in and out. Didn't want to send either man to ground, but I think he has to be the next string we pull at Sandy. I don't know if the Prof' was murdered for robbery but we seem to be running out of other motives."

"Agreed. Even so it's not like Cavendish to commit GBH. He's normally just a bookies runner and a bit of a fence. Doesn't move in the heavier circles."

"But he had access to the keys, fingerprints are on 'em. Tracy Cavendish wouldn't have known if the man had rummaged through her bag or not. It wouldn't take much to get a copy made, couple of hours max. I'm having his photo circulated in the local 'Mr Minnit's' and key cutting shops. You'd be amazed how many offer the service with no questions asked."

"No I wouldn't, there's fools everywhere." Sandy stood up, brushing crumbs off the front of his white shirt.

"So shall I take Barker now? While you take Cavendish?"

"Yeah that seems fair. Anything on the shoeprints?"

"Not yet, but we're still searching, going through the FSS." The two men walked out of the canteen and round the back way, Sandy poked his head into a small room near the back door. "Oh, good! Care to come visiting, Gareth?"

Gareth raised his head from the mountain of paperwork he was submerging under. "You are a life saver sir. I don't know what I did to offend the Sarge, but I've got all these car maintenance reports to file, and then he wants rosters done for next month."

He pushed up from behind the metal desk, making muscles bulge under his shirt sleeves, turned and picked up his dark jacket and looked at the flak jacket. Sandy saw the look of loathing, "Better wear it lad, we're going to see a friend of yours, Little Dennis. I shouldn't think you'll need it, but you never can tell."

"Bob, do you want a lift or your own transport?"

"I'll hitch a lift to the square Sandy; I can walk back. Morning Gareth." He gave the constable a friendly nod.

"Morning sir."

The three men went out and found a squad car, and the two detectives climbed in the back. "Going to the Professor's, Inspector McInnis?"

"Yes Gareth, but you can drop me near there. I think I'll phone first and see if the electronic forensics has finished printing out his work."

"Don't you get so wrapped up in history you forget what you're doing lad." Sandy permitted himself a small smirk which earned him a gentle thump.

Bob hopped out as the car stopped at a set of lights near the Technical College. "See you later Sandy. I'll see Cavendish next." He slammed the door just in time to allow Gareth to move off with the flow of traffic, then pulled out his mobile and phoned the forensics lab.

"OK, well let me know when you've got anything will you Forester?" He flipped the phone closed and looked about him.

McInnis strolled along the road, enjoying the sun which today had consented to shine. It was actually getting quite warm, he thought, as he watched a few more venturesome souls without jackets strolling along the road.

There was no constable on duty now. After all, what was there left to steal? He pushed the key in the Yale lock and went through into the study. He was hoping that Elizabeth would be in at the Professor's house but the place had a musty smell and echoed to his footsteps.

He looked around absently at the bookcase and then stood still; the safe which the police had closed and hidden again was standing open. He sniffed the air and frowned. That was the last thing he remembered.

5

Sandy Bell chatted quietly to Gareth about the sport on the TV while they drove along the Warwick Road towards Botcherby to visit Mr Barker and Dennis Little. As they drew up he said, "Wait outside the door like the last time we visited, Gareth. If it starts to get a bit crowded out there give a tap on the door and then, if you think we need it, pull in a few troops. But I shouldn't think it'll come to that; Barker doesn't like to dirty his own patch."

"OK Chief." Gareth followed Sandy into the betting shop and stood to attention outside the manager's door with a bland expression on his face, even while his eyes missed none of the action going on around him.

The shop went quiet, except for the television presenter shouting the odds for the greyhound racing. Gareth made mental notes of those who sidled out without placing a bet. Meanwhile Sandy was being welcomed into the very masculine room belonging to Frank Barker. It smelt of cigars and sweat, vaguely reminding Bell of a gym locker room.

"Nice to see you again Inspector Bell."

One well manicured hand offered a leather chair in front of the desk; the other lifted a decanter of whiskey invitingly. Inspector Bell took the seat but shook his head at the drink.

"No thanks Mr Barker. This is semi-official and I'm on duty."

"Now Inspector, I'm a respectable businessman, I am. You've no cause to see me."

"Well now," Bell drawled the words, "it's more your man we're interested in Barker. Providing you can give me an alibi for Monday morning?"

Barker raised an eyebrow, sat down opposite, and straightened his trouser creases. Bell watched the performance. "Mondays is a busy day for me Inspector; there's all the books to attend to after the Saturday sport and the banking. Got to keep an eye on things for the Inland Revenue haven't I?" He smoothed back his non-existent hair while Bell wondered just what fairy tales the tax people got to read. It must send them to sleep.

The two men fell silent, each waiting for the other to speak. Bell noticed that Barker hadn't asked which Monday the alibi was required for, just emphasised that he was busy every Monday. He would love to know what the man was up to the day of the murder but he was convinced that Barker would have an alibi, whether he needed one or not. Eventually the silent battle of who would speak first was lost by Barker. It wasn't always that way; Bell hadn't always got the time to play games.

"What do you think Little Dennis has been up to this time?"

"I didn't say I wanted to speak to you about Dennis," he watched the well-controlled annoyance flit across Barker's face, "but as it happens you're right. What was he doing frightening the school children with that face of his last Monday?"

"I'm not his keeper Inspector. Dennis just runs the odd job for me now and again; I supplement his wages, that's all."

Privately Bell thought Dennis needed a keeper, but he knew better than to say so. "So what little job was Dennis running for you that had him loitering next to the school?"

"I have no idea Inspector; I didn't have any commissions for him last Monday."

"Come on man, you have commissions..." Bell looked him over as he dragged out the word, "every day of the week for Little Dennis."

117

Barker smiled nastily, showing his perfect teeth. "You have to prove that Inspector."

"It's a civil enough question; he could have been posting a letter for you, or picking up your daughter."

"I haven't got a daughter." Barker smiled again.

"And aren't we all grateful for that." Sandy said tongue in cheek. "Alright, so if you don't know what he was doing I'll have a word with him myself."

"He isn't here at the moment."

"Well where can I find him?"

"As I keep saying, I'm not his keeper."

Sandy was vaguely aware of a racket outside the door, but had been ignoring it. He wasn't sure how much more sparing he would have indulged in, if the object of their conversation hadn't burst through the door with Gareth clinging to his arm. It put Bell in mind of a bulldog hanging onto a well-dressed bear.

Both men started to speak, Gareth rather breathlessly to the Inspector. "Sorry Chief." He got a firmer grip of the ham-like muscles under Dennis' rather natty black suit.

"Boss, someone come in."

Inspector Bell swung back and kept his eyes firmly fixed on Barker while the two men arm-wrestled in the doorway. He murmured, "Let him go Constable," but continued to watch the bookmaker.

Temper, impatience, chagrin, all flitted rapidly across the somewhat classic features that Barker had used to infiltrate respectable society, all to be hidden behind a bland front.

"Dennis, Dennis, stop hurting the Constable and come and stand over here. The Inspector is just leaving. I'm sure he's not interested in our private business." He too had ignored the men in the doorway, keeping his eyes fixed on Bell's face.

"But boss..."

"Dennis!" This time the voice held not just faint command but a threat. Dennis loped forward at a twitch of one of the elegant fingers and subsided in front of the empty fireplace. Like, thought Bell, a large and disobedient dog brought to heel by its master's voice.

Gareth stood bristling with equipment, his bulk swollen by the flak jacket and indignation. "Sir?"

Inspector Bell knew he wasn't going to get anymore information at the moment. "Come along Constable. It's rude to listen while employees are being told off by the boss." He smiled nicely at Barker and made a casual exit.

Gareth went to the squad car, opening the door and waiting for Bell to climb in the front seat, then going round and climbing in himself. "Start her up lad; we'll talk in a minute." He gave a casual wave to a lank-haired man standing on the pavement lighting a cigarette and grinned wickedly at the resultant scowl.

"Well that was enlightening."

"I'm sorry Chief." Gareth was annoyed and embarrassed with himself. "He was like a ruddy rugby player moving in for the touch; he just ploughed through me."

"Yes, that's our Dennis for you. Solid muscle, and that includes his head." His mouth twisted wryly. "Don't fret about it Gareth. Sturdier men than you have been flattened by Dennis. Now I wonder who came in where?" He looked at the passing traffic, seeing an ambulance approaching rapidly. "And just what Dennis did about it."

"Where to Chief?"

"Back to the station Gareth, and file me a nice report on the comings and goings; especially the goings, in that shop."

There was a lot of coming and going happening in Inspector McInnis' head too. He was somewhat confused as to the sequence of current events, but couldn't complain about the position of said head. He opened one slightly blurred eye and looked up into a pair of very anxious brown ones.

"We appear to be lying on the floor." He chanced the other eye. "Well I do. You, Miss Fielding, are only sitting on it; why don't you lie down next to me."

Elizabeth felt her cheeks begin to glow, but continued to hold the ice pack to the back of Bob McInnis' head. "I don't think that would be a good idea with these other gentlemen present."

Bob McInnis shifted his eyes to the side and saw a couple of stalwart ambulance men; one of them appeared to be checking out his lower limbs.

"Everything appears to be in working order, sir. Can you tell us your name and where you live?"

Bob McInnis twitched his head slightly and partially sat up, with some reluctance. He'd more than enjoyed resting against the breast behind him, encased in soft blue cashmere, and he was aware enough to appreciate that the heart going like a trip hammer might just be doing so because of him. 'Hmm nice!' he thought.

He directed his attention to the patiently waiting ambulance driver. "Yes of course I can." He returned his attention to Elizabeth and smiled at her.

"Well then, will you tell me your name and address sir?" The ambulance man was beginning to think they better get this one loaded; he'd obviously sustained major damage.

"Eh!"

Elizabeth repositioned the ice pack they'd provided and spoke to the fool next to her. "Bob, the man wants to check your reactions. He needs to know if you've damaged that excellent brain of yours."

McInnis surfaced from whatever rosy world he was living in as the portion of his brain which had been sandbagged finally said 'ouch'. He closed his eyes briefly and put up a hand to the back of his head. "Somebody hit me."

He turned to the two men. "It's alright, I'm not addled." He became as businesslike as it's possible to be sitting on the floor while a pretty girl holds an icepack to your head. He supplied name, rank and number and somewhat testily denied knowing how long he'd been unconscious. "How the hell would I know? I was unconscious!"

"Yes, sir." The senior of the two looked at Elizabeth. "He was out of it when you found him, how long before you rang us?"

"Straight away." She indicated her mobile sitting on the ground next to her open handbag.

"OK, so say seven minutes for us to get here and another," he looked at his watch, "four, that makes eleven. Plus however long before you found him." He turned back to a lightly seething Bob McInnis. "I think you'd better have the free ride sir."

"Well I don't," Bob was rapidly recovering now, "I've got no blurred vision, no nausea, and I'm not concussed. I've just got a blinding headache man." He stood up, staggering slightly, then recovered and went to sit in one of the office chairs. "Thanks for your help but I really don't want to go to hospital."

After some brisk argument they left, very unhappy but unable to change his mind. "Now that they've gone," Bob winced, "have you got any paracetamol on you?"

Elizabeth nodded. "Are you sure you..." she caught his eye. "OK I'll stop nagging. I'll fetch you a glass of water." She left the study and McInnis rang Sandy's mobile. "Sandy. Hi, do you think you can come out to the Prof's house? Someone's coshed me."

He listened to the quick squawk over the line. "Don't panic for God sake. I've been checked over but there's something damn funny going on, and I think we need forensics too." He put down the receiver as Elizabeth came back.

Sandy, when he arrived with Gareth in tow, was distracted enough to lose his caution in front of Elizabeth. "What the hell happened Bob?" He came into the room in what for him was a rush.

"Don't shout man! I feel as though I've got the hangover from hell." McInnis sipped the coffee Elizabeth had also provided, and sat back in her office chair. She also sat drinking coffee. The slightly anxious look on her face had not entirely dispersed; in fact she looked quite relieved to see the older man.

"He won't go to hospital."

Sandy spared her a glance. He'd given his partner the once over and, while a bit paler than usual, he could tell that Bob was more angry than seriously hurt. "He always was thick-skulled, in both senses." His lips twitched.

"Do you want a drink Inspector Bell?" Elizabeth stood up as Sandy sat down in the Professor's office chair at the desk.

"Yes please lass, put a sugar in it." He spoke almost absently. Elizabeth went through to the kitchen.

He took time to look around the study. "Everything untouched?"

"Yeah. The safe was opened as you see; the smell is lighter fuel, and the bottle is over here." Bob sniffed.

Sandy, now the first fright was subsiding, was wondering what was going on himself. "Tell me then lad."

"I came in using the key, walked into the study; the safe was open like you see. I smelt something," Bob put his hand up to the back of his head, "and someone slugged me. I've been thinking about it Sandy. It was a rabbit chop. I felt the warmth of someone's breath just before I fell and I think I can remember the feel of a hand." He gently felt the lump at the base of his skull.

"I haven't moved about. Forensics coming Sandy?"

"Yes, Gareth's watching the door; he'll let us know when they turn up."

Elizabeth came in with a thick blue mug and handed it to Sandy. She sat down in the easy chair, saying nothing for a minute, and then said, "Do you need me to go away Inspector?"

"No lass, I need your statement."

She looked from Bob to Sandy and squared her shoulders. "OK, what do you need to know?"

"Why did you come here today?"

Two flags of colour grew on her cheeks as the men watched but she answered quickly enough. "Twofold, Bob, Inspector McInnis, and I were talking about the research and I wanted to read a bit more, and," she fixed her eyes on Sandy, "I thought the Inspector might be here. I rather wanted to see him."

Sandy didn't ask why; instead he nodded, "So tell me what you found when you got here. In your own words lass."

"I came in using my own key; I thought I heard someone so I called Bob," she bit her lip, "Inspector McInnis' name."

Sandy exchanged a serious look with McInnis but spoke to the girl, "Call him Bob lass, it'll make life easier." Sandy smiled gently at her.

She blushed a bit more, her cheeks by this time rosy; she could feel the sweat on her palms and surreptitiously wiped them on her jeans to the secret amusement of McInnis. "Anyway, I called his name, and continued walking towards the study. When I pushed open the door I saw him lying on the floor."

"Show me how far open the door was and where Bob was?"

Elizabeth rose and went over to the door. She went to pull it. Sandy stopped her with a word. "No, tell me, don't touch the door for a minute."

"It was half open like this," she demonstrated by marking the carpet with her sandal, "and Bob was lying facing towards the bookcase just here." Again she indicated with her foot.

"Ok I've got that. Now did you close the door behind you?"

"No," she hesitated, "no I just dropped to my knees and felt for his pulse, then I got out my mobile and phoned for an ambulance. I stayed with him until they came."

"Could you smell anything?"

She looked puzzled for a moment, sniffed the air and said, "Now you mention it yes, it's like turps, or pear drops, or something," she frowned.

"You didn't turn on the lights, the computer?"

"No, I told you, I came in and knelt next to Bob, I didn't move until the ambulance men got here." Sandy exchanged another look with Bob. The Professor's computer was switched on, emitting a low hum and demanding a password, but unless Elizabeth had walked over she couldn't see his screen, only her own blank one.

"You let them in?"

"No. No they just came in."

"OK that's clear enough. Now who was on the street when you came in, can you remember?"

She shook her head, "I wasn't really noticing Inspector."

Bob McInnis suddenly came back into the conversation. "Elizabeth. Think carefully love. What kind of sound did you hear, and where from in the house."

Sandy shot him a warning look but he ignored it.

Elizabeth sat frowning, "I don't know, it's just that feeling you get when you know you're not alone. I'm sorry Bob."

"That's alright love, don't worry about it. Come and sit down again."

They fell silent, the two men because that was the way they worked together, digesting ideas and absorbing information before they moved on, Elizabeth because she didn't know what to say. She kept shooting anxious glances at McInnis, but he seemed to be recovering rapidly. Then she opened her mouth to speak, and closed it again.

McInnis looked at her, "Yes?"

"The computer was on when I arrived. I thought you'd been using it Bob."

"No, not me."

Bob looked across at the desk where a pipe rested on a little triangle of wood. "The Prof' smoked a pipe Elizabeth?"

"Yes." Elizabeth gave him a puzzled look

"How did he light it?"

"Eh?" She frowned at him.

"Matches, lighter, what?"

"Oh!" She flicked back her hair and smiled. "Oh he used matches, said there was an art to pipe smoking, you had to burn down the match to get rid of the sulphur before you used it."

"Never used a disposable or a pipe lighter?" He nodded at the chunky desk lighter sitting between the computers.

"No," Elizabeth shook her head, "that was a leaving gift from some college or other. He never used it; I don't think it's even got any fuel in it."

Silence descended again. Elizabeth had just supplied herself with a 'get out of jail free card' had she but realised it. The reverie of all three wasn't broken until the entrance of Mark Forester. "Morning sir," Mark was watching his P's and Q's. Inspector Bell had had a word about protocol and procedure that had stung more than a little, that was partly why, but Mark was also a good policeman despite his normal lighthearted ways. Anyone who slugged a copper must be either very stupid or very dangerous. He would make sure there were no mistakes gathering the evidence on this job; he didn't want a mistake of his to let a dangerous, and/or a stupid criminal, go free.

"Alright Bob?" The concern was genuine and showed.

"Yeah, I've had worse hangovers." McInnis smiled grimly.

"Where do you want me to start?"

"Dust the safe, computer, door here." Bob indicated the areas with a sweep of his hand. "I want a check upstairs. Elizabeth." He spoke to the young woman who was obviously beginning to put together facts the police had already tied up. Her expression was growing alarmed.

"Come into the kitchen and show me what you've touched in there." Bob held out a hand. She accepted, gripping his firmly and Mark, watching, mentally shrugged. Looked like he wasn't going to get that date after all.

126

Sandy watched his partner leave and turned back to his other colleague. "I think there was someone hiding upstairs when she came in, we need to check up there too."

"Right Guv."

Mark got out his gloves and started to do his job.

Bob was steady on his feet, the pain-relief seemed to be kicking in and he had a pretty girl holding his hand and showing him she cared; it was almost worth getting hit on the head.

Sandy, meanwhile, was phoning the station to ask for a few PCs to canvas the area and see if any neighbours were in and might have seen anyone leaving the premises. He didn't hold out a lot of hope; most people were at work this time of the day.

He went out into the hall and to the front door.

"Gareth, I've called for a replacement for you. When they arrive I want you and another hefty cop to go and fetch Dennis down to the station for an interview. I want to know if he was the one to slug McInnis. He said 'someone came in' when he saw Barker; maybe he was looking in the safe now we'd all left. I think he'll have disappeared, but you never can tell."

Gareth, his usual sunny smile missing, nodded grimly. "Right Chief."

Sandy felt a smile flit across his face as Bob came back down the corridor.

"I've told Elizabeth we've finished with her for now. I'm going to phone that solicitor and get his permission to take the computers into the station. Just in case. I'll get hard copy of the research to you Elizabeth, if I can." He smiled at the girl as she nodded her understanding at him. "I've got to work. I'll see you later love. Alright?"

The late afternoon sun was filtering through the dust and grime on McInnis' office window when he and Sandy next had an opportunity to talk over the case.

"It's as we thought; nobody much in and those that were saw nothing unusual. Dennis has gone to earth for the moment. He won't stay lost for long, just until Barker's hammered the right story into his head. Forester's almost sure someone had been upstairs since he went up last time. He's sure he shut the bathroom door when he'd finished up there, and it was ajar." He shook his head and then ran both hands over his face, massaging his forehead on the way.

"Nothing on the door of the kitchen, and there ought to have been. I think your young lady had a narrow escape Bob, and so did you."

"Why would anyone risk coming back to the house Sandy? They had to know we'd empty the safe."

"You would think so. If it was Little Dennis, Barker must have sent him, and Dennis might be thick but Barker isn't."

"And why boot up the computer? What's on it that's so important? It's research into the First World War for God's sake! I know: I've looked."

"I don't know Bob, but we're going to have to look again." Sandy sighed, "I wouldn't have said Dennis was computer literate. I wouldn't have said he was literate at all except that he must be to have passed his driving test, and he's one of the best wheels in this county. Can't fault his driving, just his criminal tendencies." He grimaced.

The two men looked at the machines now installed in the office. "How's the head Bob? Do you feel up to looking at a computer screen?"

"Not really Sandy. We still need to interview Cavendish too."

"He'll keep, go home lad and rest your head."

McInnis had gone home. He'd lain in the quiet of his bedroom on the non-squeaky divan and rested his head on the pillow, thinking of how it had felt to rest it against Elizabeth. She definitely had the edge on the pillow.

He'd rung her that evening, thinking that police work had its compensations, one of them being that he already had her phone number. His conscience had given him a little kick for that; wasn't it an abuse of police information? Then he decided he didn't care, and then felt guilty about that as well. He decided that introspective thought was guaranteed to give you a headache, even if you didn't already have one.

Still the silly smile lingered on his face as he thought about the conversation.

"So how's my favourite policeman's head?"

"I'm much better."

"I was talking about Inspector Bell actually."

"Oh well, if you feel like that I'll ask him to give you a call."

"Idiot!"

He thought he detected a bit of love in that brief word. And he was a detective, so he just smiled quietly to himself.

"I was wondering..." He paused at the slow, "Yes..." from the other end of the line and grimaced at the cautious note in her voice.

"Would you come with me to the museum at Eastriggs this Friday?"

"You romantic fool you."

He wrinkled his nose at the tone of voice. "We don't have to go but I would like to see you again?"

"Bob I would love to show you the treasures of Eastriggs; I just hope you won't be too disappointed." Elizabeth was wondering why she was committing herself to a trip round a small museum; she must be mad.

They'd talked for a minute or two more then he'd rung off. Elizabeth had replaced the receiver slowly and looked across the room at her father, a silent but interested listener.

"I gather that was the seeker after justice my dear."

"Indeed it was Dad. As you heard he's invited me to a museum." She pulled a funny face.

"Well he's either interested in the museum, or wants to spend time in your company and thinks he'd better take an interest in things he thinks you might like."

"Hmm, a bit of both perhaps. I like him a lot Dad, he's a bit stiff but I think that's because he's shy."

"Can a policeman be shy I wonder?" He looked fondly at his daughter. "Well I suppose they are as human as the next man or woman."

They exchanged a happy smile and then she challenged him to a game of backgammon and no more was said on the subject until bedtime.

"I liked your policeman too darling." He kissed her and watched the faint blush. "I'll see you in the morning."

The next morning had seen McInnis and Sandy Bell hard at work. On top of the initial murder scene reports they were now reading reports on the second incident in the house. To whit one wrap on the head sustained by an Inspector of police.

"What do you think Sandy? Robbery or something else?"

"If it was robbery then it was the same group as before because that door hasn't been butchered; someone has a key and they're using it. But there again, if it was the same people why come back. The safe's been emptied once, there isn't anything to steal."

"It could have been opportunistic. The notice of the funeral was in the paper and the house would be expected to be empty. But you're right," Bob shook his head, "the lock hadn't been jimmied or finessed that forensics could see."

"So what did they come back for? Which brings us to that computer," he nodded to the machine sitting on a small table in the corner of the room surrounded, like a Conestoga wagon, by boxes of papers from the drawers of the Professor's filling cabinet. "And did they intend to set fire to the place?"

"I tell you Bob I don't know. I don't think that lighter fuel got there by accident. I think it was brought with the intention of starting a fire. So what have we missed? Something someone else didn't want us to see and was prepared to burn if they couldn't take with them?"

"Yeah I got your point yesterday. Peter Neville used matches. Someone brought it alright."

"I've had forensics going over the place again and they weren't happy." McInnis frowned. "We haven't found as much as a stray hair that shouldn't have been there. Tracy Cavendish was a rotten cleaner; she only cleaned the surface where things showed. There are plenty of fingerprints but we can account for them all."

"There has to be something man. Whoever it was, was taking a hell of a risk striking a police officer. They must know that we'd be thicker than fleas on a dog round the place after something like that."

"Well I'm prepared to read all that stuff over there Sandy, but fascinating as it is I just don't see its relevance."

"No lad, me neither." Sandy smiled, "but I have found out what 'Babel' is."

"Oh yes?" Bob cocked his head on one side.

"You just need a small child in your back pocket and you can find out anything about these computers. My nephew is only seven Bob, and he knows more than I'll ever know." Sandy grinned. "Let me impart knowledge." He leaned over to Bob's despised computer.

"You connected to the broadband?"

"I expect so."

"OK, now use the search engine." He suited action to word, "See that bit there?" He clicked on a small icon. "That's 'Babel Fish', it translates stuff for you. The nephew tells me his big sister uses it for her French homework. Which I think is cheating, but I promised not to tell his dad in exchange for the information on how to use it."

McInnis played with the little box for a minute or two. "Here Sandy, give me one of those letters."

"We've got the translation of those."

"Yeah I know, but I want to see how accurate it might be."

He typed busily for a minute or two then clicked the translate from German to English button.

"OK let's see what we've got here."

Hans, dear friend of my heart,

As I told you in my last I am working up north, I can't tell you where my friend, I hate this war that's sets us apart. I understand why you will not fight but I am not so committed to God as you, I just think it wrong to kill men I've never met and have no reason to quarrel with.

I have been working as a plumber wiping lead pipes. There is enough work here to keep me out of the fighting for a good few months; I hope. I have no desire to fight, and there are not many plumbers with the training to do the work I am doing, you know father always said it was a secret of the trade, but I can see no real reason why others shouldn't do it too. This is a huge project. There are lots of girls arriving daily from all over the world, mostly they are still training in preparation for doing jobs that most men would find exhausting, and then they go home and care for their children.

I have to admire them even if what they are doing means men will die. I must not tell you their exact occupation my dearest friend. But I have to admire them. There is one girl in particular. She has been doing the same job down in London and has been brought in to train the others; she works mainly the day shift. So I have been able to take her to a couple of dances. I don't know how she has the energy after the hours she has worked.

Her name is Victoria; she has beautiful long dark hair and the most glorious blue eyes. Because she comes from a different part of the country the other girls tease her about her accent which is slower than our northern ones. But being shift foreman they seem to respect her. She cares for the girls she is in charge of and tells me some of their troubles.

These are many, from having to wear trousers and show their legs, to not being allowed to use hair grips. They all live in wooden hostels which she tells me are cold even though it's now spring; they worry about their men at the front and when this terrible war will end. She is a lovely girl, Hans.

"Phew! He'd got it bad hadn't he," Sandy smiled across at Bob. "I wonder if he could have been shot as a traitor Bob?"

"God knows! He's writing to an enemy in wartime. I've read this bit in the research Sandy; I think the Professor was writing a biography of some sort, maybe his dad had talked to him about the war. I'm going to Eastriggs with Elizabeth on Friday."

He kept his serious eyes on Sandy's face. "I wanted to find out a bit more, he's got me hooked on the story and it seemed a good idea to take the researcher of some of that information with me and, before you say it, I want to spend time with Elizabeth too." He suddenly revealed a wicked smile, "I think I've got it bad too Sandy."

Sandy offered a faint smile but refrained from other comments about Bob's new relationship. "So what's our next move Bob?"

They had sat quietly thinking over the information they'd just looked at; now Sandy stirred in his chair looking at the younger man as he spoke.

"We know the crime was committed by someone skilled in the art of killing, Sandy. The autopsy report makes that clear. Someone who knew just where to put their hands to kill quickly and efficiently. Martial arts, army, hell, you can pick up that sort of info on the TV these days, or the net."

Sandy shook his head, and then scratched an ear. "Well I agree with you in part lad, but knowing something and being able to do it are two different things. You know, theoretically, how to operate that computer," he nodded to the machine in the corner of the office, "but when it comes down to it we're both amateurs compared with your Elizabeth."

Bob grinned quickly, "And how!" Then he shook his own head. "Yeah you're right there Sandy. So somebody who has more than rudimentary knowledge. Cavendish, Madogan, Little Dennis, even Barker, though I've never known him do any of the dirty work before."

"Well we've got DNA from under the fingernails, but we can't force any of them to provide that without just cause. We could ask, but a refusal often offends," he grimaced, "especially when it's me that's being refused."

"What else have we got Bob?" He scratched the offending ear again. "We've got the key, or rather keys, for the safe and the front door. Cavendish had access through his wife and Barker through Cavendish. Madogan hasn't, Elizabeth has." He looked challengingly at his young partner.

"I know Sandy. We'll look again but my gut doesn't go with that."

"No lad, nor does mine."

"There hasn't been any sign of the missing silverware, but then if it's those in the business they would hardly fence such hot stuff. I've got feelers out in all the usual places, second hand shops, pubs, pawn shops, but so far nothing."

"Alright. So if it wasn't a robbery, what was it? That brings us to the research. Now the second attack on my favourite partner's head left us some interesting clues. The safe might have been open but that computer was on too." He stopped and pointed a finger at Bob. "Did you check the filing cabinet?"

"I might have had a bash on the head Sandy, but what makes you think it's my first day on the job?"

"And?"

"Elizabeth and I checked over the stuff. That first day." He felt himself blushing. "OK, so she could have told me anything! She said she couldn't see any of the first source material missing. Stuff that she'd had to send away for, original documents, and photocopies from places," he huffed out a breath, "and dammit that day she wasn't suspected of anything but having a key." He rubbed the back of his neck. "I went through it again yesterday as we were packing it up and it all looked the same."

He held up a hand, "I'll check again. Now what about the lighter fuel. Any prints?"

"Smudged jobs on the side of the can, I'd say it had run out on the hand of whoever used it. But the smudges only indicate driving gloves, those leather ones with the fancy pattern on the fingertips. Forester was wanting to use some fancy experimental thing on the can." Sandy grinned quickly, "I said he could once all available data had been logged. Some professor in Wales has invented something new, I haven't got a clue what he was talking about, he lost me when he started blathering about scanning and Kelvin probes." He raised comical eyebrows at McInnis. "He assured me it wouldn't affect the evidence. We'll catch the murderer eventually Bob, never fear."

But the investigation was stalling and both men knew it; they had worked on all the most likely scenarios, a robbery gone wrong, and certainly things had been stolen, but not everything that could have been taken had been. Opportunists would have taken the expensive CD player, the DVD player, digital cameras, anything that could be quickly and efficiently fenced with no questions asked. Granted they'd cleared the safe but that wasn't the work of an opportunist, but required inside knowledge about the safe's position and the key to open it with.

The Professor had lived a fairly blameless life. So far they hadn't turned up anything that might have given a blackmailer even a toehold in the door of his life. The man smoked a pipe, drank sparingly, had no females visiting, nor men, and didn't encourage the neighbourhood children to knock on the door.

The interviews with fellow academes proved that he was a conscientious member of their society who referenced his work, didn't plagiarise, and had refused a chair when he reached the age where other, less able men, might have accepted. He was well liked, if somewhat reserved.

They had discovered he was a member of the Society of Friends, whatever that was, but hadn't attended any meetings since his accident. One member had stated that he'd been a fairly regular attendee until then. His father had also been a member she stated.

He had been generous with his money and kind to the people he employed. On the face of it then the man had been in the wrong place when someone had wanted to steal his valuables. However those valuables didn't amount to much more than a few pieces of silverware and a thousand or so in banknotes. Or he was poking his nose into something which someone wanted kept quiet. Neither man liked that idea, but they would keep probing the research just in case.

They'd gone their separate ways that afternoon and now it was Friday afternoon and Bob McInnis felt as nervous as a schoolboy as he waited in the front room of the small neat house to take Elizabeth to a museum. He'd even changed his suit and tie to a pair of chinos and a tweed jacket.

"Won't be a minute." She'd whisked out of the room after showing him in and he'd been confronted by a table tottering under the weight of several very hefty tomes and bestrewn with closely typed papers.

He wandered over and cautiously picked up the top page. It quite literally was all Greek to him. He knew enough to recognise the alphabet but couldn't have read a word. When she came back with a light denim jacket that matched her jeans, over her arm, flicking her hair back as she walked in, he started guiltily.

She grinned wickedly. "Don't worry. I won't tell dad you've been looking at his work. I suppose it's being a policeman."

"I'm sorry," Bob looked genuinely remorseful, "being a policeman doesn't give me the licence to pry into your private business, but I couldn't read this if I wanted to."

She grinned, "Nor could I, so stop feeling inferior." She held out a hand and he grasped it and, moving closer, his nostrils were assailed by her newly applied perfume. He felt his senses spin slightly and took a firmer grip on the resolve he'd made that morning to keep things casual for a bit longer.

They headed out and he installed her in his car, pushing in a tape as he drove off down the street. The car was filled with the haunting music of Chopin. "I like him too." It was all he said. Elizabeth smiled happily and relaxed against the seat, prepared to enjoy herself.

They arrived at the museum in Eastriggs in bright sunshine. Bob shed his jacket and slung it over his shoulder by its loop as they headed for the entrance. Both blinked as they entered the rather dark interior and Bob peered across the dust-moted space then headed for the desk and paid the modest entry fee while Elizabeth nodded at the elderly couple who sat behind it.

"Miss Fielding, come to do a bit more research have you? You've only to ask, we'll help if we can." The grey-headed woman was small and dumpling shaped; she sat in a comfortable wicker chair knitting some shapeless object in pale pink.

Elizabeth smiled over, "Thanks, we're just going to stroll around today."

Bob came over and looked down into the brown eyes which looked sad. "I'm sorry, I didn't think. This must remind you of the Professor. We needn't stay; I can do this on my own."

"It's OK Bob; there are lots of places I went to for Peter. Mostly they're good memories of how happy he was when I came back with information. It was just for a moment there..." She held out a hand. "Come on, we need to go round this corner here."

The information for the moment was displayed on large boards, placed to form a corridor around the edges of the room. The outer walls of the room had small glass topped display cases with various items grouped together. Bob got his first look at the triangular 'On War Service' badges the girls wore.

There was one display of rather odd jet jewellery, with a section on brooches made of hair from dead fiancés killed in the trenches. The young couple exchanged a glance and Elizabeth said, "Bit creepy!" and gave a shudder. Bob took the opportunity to sling an arm round her shoulders as he looked more closely. "Yeah, and I think maybe, yeuk!" He smiled down at her and they moved onwards.

They settled to a slow wander, hand in hand. Bob was fascinated by the letters written by the young women who'd worked at the factory, Elizabeth pointing out the stranger little pieces of data. "See this one?" She kept her voice low, "It's about a couple who were arrested as foreigners when they came to seek employment here; they actually came from South Shields in Newcastle but their accent was so broad nobody could understand them. They were arrested as spies."

McInnis, after one astonished and disbelieving glance, read the newspaper article, "Good grief!"

"These are sad," Elizabeth tapped against some articles framed in black. "These young women died during the time the factory was open. They were really brave, and put up with horrible conditions as well. Look this one was a charge-hand; she got all her girls out and got caught just as she was leaving."

McInnis found he was thinking of the letter he'd read a couple of days before. "They sacrificed as much as the soldiers in the trenches didn't they?" He gripped Elizabeth's hand suddenly and swung her around another corner, pulling her startled body against his, then just stood holding her tight, his face buried in the soft raven wing of hair.

"You're becoming rather special to me; did you know that Beth?"

Elizabeth, held firmly against him, breathed deeply and tilted her head back, "I'm beginning to realise that." She moved the hands he'd imprisoned against his chest, and he eased the pressure so that she could spread her palms against his chest wall and feel the beat of his heart. "I think you might be rather special for me too Bob."

He bent forward and placed a butterfly kiss on her nose. "They'll be wondering what we're doing."

"Possibly." She looked up at him, her eyes glowing in the dim light, "I think we'd better concentrate on munitioneers for now Bob."

He nodded, reluctantly letting her go but keeping a firm hold of her hand. They finished looking around the exhibits at a rather quicker pace and went out into the late afternoon sunshine. He led her over to the car, waiting like a lazy dog on the grass outside, "Tea?"

"Actually I'd love a cup of really rich, hot chocolate, with swirls of cream and lots of chocolate sprinkles on top."

"That, Miss Fielding sounds not only decadent but very girly." He paused, "I know just the place to go." He held open the car door to be met by a wave of hot air carrying the smell of hot car with it. "Hmm. Let's get a through draught here shall we?" McInnis went round and opened his door as she slipped off her jacket and flipped it into the back seat before sitting down. He admired the revealed figure enormously.

They spent the rest of the day together and Bob McInnis found he was becoming quite desperate to kiss her. Having vowed to himself that he'd take things slowly he decided he'd better wait for a goodnight kiss. It was worth the wait.

6

"So how did you get on with the museum then Bob?" He hoped his patience would be rewarded so he studiously avoided asking until they'd got through the bulk of the paperwork on the desk.

Sandy had had a busy weekend; his eldest child had finished all her exams and finally persuaded him to allow her to go backpacking with a large group of friends. It hadn't been an easy decision to make. Being a cautious man he'd set up check-in points, phone numbers, and insisted that the itinerary be adhered to at all times, otherwise the project was off.

He didn't suppose he'd stop worrying until she came back home, but that was the price you paid for being a parent he supposed. He put his thoughts aside as he looked at Bob's face and asked the question; here, he thought, was another of his children. Older, but still one of his.

Bob McInnis smiled and sat back in the chair, his smile somewhat sad. "Oh it was very interesting Sandy. I have a much better understanding of what the young woman called Victoria was doing. It was called the 'Devil's Porridge', and the girls worked a conveyer belt mixing the guncotton with nitro-glycerine. Nasty stuff!" He swung his chair and looked out of the window at the bright sunshine, then drew his gaze back in, watching the fall of dust-motes in the disturbed air. It reminded him of the museum and the feel of Elizabeth as she'd stood next to him.

He sat forward putting his clasped hands on the desk in front of him. "I've got an idea what he did too. I've spent a lot of the weekend reading Peter Neville's research. If the Peter of the letter is the one he's writing about, he worked at lead smoothing, joining pipes to basins. Victoria died, according to his research, one of three

141

hundred girls who lost their lives doing that horrible and dangerous job, and that altered the original Peter's attitude. He still didn't want to fight the Germans, but he didn't much care what became of himself either. It's rather melancholy reading Sandy."

"So what did he do?"

"He joined up. I think he thought it was the quickest way of ending his life legitimately. He had barely any training as a soldier; I don't think many of them did really."

"What month did he join up?"

"June. She was one of the first casualties; they hadn't finished commissioning the site even."

Sandy sat quietly absorbing the information, "I wonder how I would have felt."

"Yeah, me too Sandy." Bob moved back in his seat. "We'd better get back to this murder of ours. How do you want to divide the work?"

"I think, if you don't mind, I'd like to interview Cavendish. How do you feel about taking on Madogan?"

"I thought we hadn't got anything on him Sandy."

"Well we have and we haven't; he's a nasty piece of work with the knowledge needed to kill the Prof', and I'd like to frighten him a bit. Maybe he'll clean his act up if he thinks we have our eye on him."

"OK. But how are we going to angle things?"

"Let's just lean on him; false representation, mixing with undesirables, dangerous driving while under the influence."

"Fine." McInnis stood up and shouldered his suit jacket; it was getting warm and he'd rolled up his shirt sleeves. He glanced at his watch. "I'll see if I can track him down now."

He tapped a report he'd been studying when Sandy had come in. "One of the constables thinks he's got a sighting of Cavendish by the way. At a 'Mr Minnit' on the market, the man who works the stall thinks he recognised Cavendish as having had a key cut over a fortnight ago. The man isn't prepared to go into a witness box and swear it was Cavendish. But he thinks it might have been."

"Well why didn't you say so?"

McInnis raised an elegant eyebrow. "I am saying so."

Sandy Bell snorted inelegantly, prodding a finger at McInnis' good silk shirt. "You're in love man, and all over the place with your information."

"No I'm not." McInnis came back with the swift rejoinder even while his cheeks grew hot. "I might find Elizabeth very attractive, but there's been no talk of love between us. I've only known her a fortnight." He sounded both shocked and indignant.

"It doesn't take long, and who needs to talk of what is?" Sandy twisted his lips wryly.

Bob McInnis gave him one startled look and shook his head, but whether in denial or confusion Sandy couldn't tell.

"Give me the report then; it'll maybe give me a bit more clout with Tom Cavendish." They left the office, each to make enquiries about the whereabouts of his own particular quarry.

Sandy Bell ran his party to earth at Frank Barker's betting office. They hadn't pulled the tail entirely yet, though Sandy was inclined to think it was a waste of precious manpower, so it wasn't such a difficult feat. He waited outside, a couple of shops away, studiously ignoring the policeman who was assigned to watch, even as he himself was ignored. When he saw Cavendish leaving he followed quietly until he was sure that Barker wasn't running his own tail.

He moved in then, catching up and speaking in his usual genial fashion, "Hello Cavendish. I'd like a quiet word with you." He examined the man's face as he spoke, thinking the man looked ill.

Cavendish turned, cast him a scared look, then an equally frightened look around, and speeded up his footsteps. "Who are you? I don't want to talk to you; I haven't done anything." It was said truculently.

Bell, keeping pace down the quiet street they'd turned into, smiled a bit grimly, "Well lad, I don't recollect accusing you of anything." He paused. "Yet."

Tom Cavendish walked even faster, heading for his own front door.

"I could of course talk to people about the fact that your wife has been working while you've been claiming social for the pair of you." He paused significantly as Cavendish struggled to open his own door. "Or I could forget all about that if I got the right answers from you."

"My Tracy isn't working."

"Ah! But she has been, hasn't she lad?"

Cavendish finally managed to get his key turned in the lock and the door open. He swung back, an animal at bay, snarling at Bell, "Go away," he hissed.

"Not a chance lad 'til I've had my quiet word."

Cavendish, after another quick survey of the street, whirled round and went through his door; he wasn't quick enough for a copper who'd been expecting the move. Bell followed him inside.

"I told you I don't have anything to say to you."

"Well while you're not saying it you'd better shut the door so that Little Dennis doesn't see you."

Cavendish pushed past him, glancing up and down the street before slamming the door shut. He pushed passed again in the narrow hallway and went into the sitting room, ignoring the policeman. He headed for the kitchen annex, going to the fridge and extracting a can of beer. Sandy Bell raised an eyebrow; it wasn't even half past ten in the morning.

Bell sat down uninvited and waited for the man to stop pacing about the room, going from one window to the other and looking cautiously through the slightly grey nets.

Eventually he was satisfied. "Who the hell are you, and what do you want me for? I ain't done anything wrong."

"Oh! I'm sure we could find something if we had a little look Tom, but we won't look, provided you answer a few questions. Honestly, we coppers are like that."

Tomas Cavendish lost even more colour but he stood back, leaning against the wall so that he could watch up the street. He did his best to look tough, and succeeded in looking like a fractious schoolboy confronted by the headmaster after playing truant. He pulled the tab and took a swig of beer, but said nothing.

"So," Bob smiled faintly, watching the bead of sweat roll down the badly shaven face. "Making a lot on the horses are you? You must be good at picking winners if what my man tells me is true about the sums you bet." He raised his eyebrow again.

"I do alright."

"Do any odd jobs for Barker do you?"

"Who's Barker?"

Bell sighed loudly. "Don't be stupid man; you've been in and out of his office half a dozen times this last week alone. I'll ask again; done any little jobs for him?"

Cavendish opened slightly protuberant eyes wide, making him look like an indignant hake. "An' if I have? It ain't a crime to help a bloke out."

"Get a key cut for him did you?"

Cavendish licked suddenly dry lips. Shook his head, and glanced out the window again.

"Come on man, there's no harm in getting keys cut for someone. Doing them a favour."

"An' if I did?"

"Of course it does depend on where the keys came from?" Bell watched another bead of sweat break free and roll downwards.

"Look I got a key cut for him; I dunno where it came from."

"Hmm!" Bell sniffed the air. "It's a bit close in here, you should get your wife to open the windows, or there's this wonderful stuff you plug in, it gets rid of the smell of nicotine in the air," he paused, "among other things." He watched as the man turned grey.

"OK so I got him a key. It was from our Tracy's bag. He wanted a spare so he could use our house as a *pied-à-terre* sometimes."

Bell nodded, raising an eyebrow at the French. "It's a good story; I should stick to it. You certainly got the key from her, but it wasn't for this house." He stood up and came towards the window going to pull back the netting.

"Here, what you doing?" Cavendish grabbed an arm which he found surprisingly solid under its light weight summer shirt. In fact it was like grabbing a steel bar.

"Just looking up the street, seeing who's about." Bell twitched his arm and Cavendish released him. He leaned against the opposite wall so that anyone looking in would have been able to see him in apparent casual conversation with Tom Cavendish. He could see dark patches growing under the man's arms and smell the fear coming off the man in waves. While he'd expected a little resistance he hadn't expected this degree of fear. He wished he could see into the man's mind.

"You ain't got no proof of nothing."

"I don't know about that. So when did you give him this key, and remember we know already?"

"If you know, why you asking questions?"

"Just like to have our facts confirmed."

Cavendish walked away, dumping the can on the divider between the sitting area and the kitchen, and rummaged in his pocket, coming out with a packet of cigarettes and lighter.

Bell eyed the lighter narrowly for a moment, but it appeared to be one of the disposable kind. He watched as the man lit up, noting the slight shake in the hands. "I ain't answering any more of your questions. You can get out; you haven't got any right to question me."

Bell smiled; it wasn't pleasant to see, like a pike sighting a minnow. "Quite right, I should get yourself a solicitor, or better still change your friends my lad. You're walking a thin line." He turned and sauntered out of the room, quietly opening and closing the front door after himself.

He walked briskly down the street, his sharp eyes looking for signs that Barker was also keeping a watch. He saw no sign of a watcher, but that didn't mean there wasn't one about.

That had been informative, if not conclusive. Cavendish had had a key cut and it seemed more than likely that it belonged to the Professor's front door. Now what had Barker wanted it for? How had he known there was anything worth stealing? Bell pondered this as he mixed with the crowds in the town centre. He'd pull the tail though; it wasn't getting them any extra information.

If Tracy Cavendish had spoken freely to her husband and he had passed the information on, then... but no, Bell thought, it was chicken feed to Barker, the contents of that safe. What else had been in the house that was worth taking? It looked like he needed another talk with that young woman. What had she seen and talked about however innocently to her husband? And what had Barker, for he was sure it was the bookmaker, said or threatened Cavendish with, to have him in such a muck sweat?

While Sandy Bell was extracting information from a petty criminal, McInnis was dealing with an altogether more nasty type. Major Madogan wasn't going to be anywhere near as easy to intimidate.

McInnis had run him to earth in a set of offices in one of the suburbs to the north of the town. Bob noted it was in an area with easy access to the motorway, and to the border road to the ferry routes. It wasn't much of an office, just two rooms rented in what had once been an elegant town house.

"Good morning sir." He kept his voice official and very polite. "I'm DI McInnis, we're just following up on the slight accident you were involved in a fortnight ago."

"Yes. I gave a full statement at the time, Officer. I fail to see why a minor motoring offence should bring you to my offices in the middle of a working day." He hadn't bothered to stand up or offer McInnis a seat when his secretary had shown them into the sparsely furnished room.

Gareth stood at attention, his back to the wall next to a filing cabinet with its top draw open, watching the action carefully. McInnis, after a moment, uninvited, pulled out a hard backed chair on the visitor's side of the heavy metal desk and sat. "Well sir it was hardly minor; the young woman in question could have been killed

148

and you had been drinking while driving." He paused, "And not for the first time."

"I've paid my fines Officer. That woman wasn't hurt and really," his brow rose making a black line across his forehead, "she should have taken more care when crossing. It was, I believe, as much her fault as mine. Don't you agree?"

McInnis mastered an almost overwhelming desire to plant a fist underneath the well-trimmed moustache. How dare this creature refer to Elizabeth as 'that woman'? He kept his mouth closed until he'd calmed somewhat.

"No sir I'm afraid I can't agree. She was pushed into your path, but it was only the fact that the school traffic had slowed you down that saved it from being really nasty. We have you on CCTV, and a speed camera, doing over eighty as you approached the city centre that day."

"I think these speed traps are just money spinners, Officer. The government try to wring every penny out of us. There's no point in having bypasses to keep the traffic moving round the town if they then restrict you from moving." He smiled but it didn't stray into his eyes, just showed off his teeth.

McInnis made a small grimace; he'd heard that argument before. "I understand what you say sir, but the speed restrictions are there for a reason." He leaned back in a relaxed pose, mimicking the Major's position. "However that wasn't what I came to discuss. The young lady that you nearly ran over had discovered a crime that day; anything that happened to her therefore is of interest to us. You'll understand that we have to make enquiries of any contacts she made, I'm sure."

"Well I certainly didn't murder her employer; I'd never seen her before."

149

"I didn't say it was her employer that had been murdered sir." McInnis smiled somewhat silkily.

If he'd hoped to disconcert Madogan he couldn't see any sign of it.

"I read the papers; I'm intelligent enough to put two and two together man. A murder was reported in the part of town where I had the minor accident. I presume there isn't that much crime to keep you occupied if you can chase up such a peripheral person as myself." He sat back satisfied.

McInnis said nothing to this, just carried on with his line of questioning, he didn't think that it was as obvious as all that. "So you didn't know Miss Fielding at all."

"Who?"

"I thought you said you'd read the reports in the paper sir?" It was McInnis' gently questioning voice, the one Gareth had learnt meant he'd got more information than the person being asked had intended to give.

"Oh yes, of course that was her name," the Major smoothed down his moustache, "I'd forgotten."

"Strange sir, that you forgot her name when you were so good at guessing just what crime she'd been involved in." He shrugged lightly as if it didn't really matter. "Anyway sir to get back to my question, you didn't know her?"

"I've just told you I've never seen her before or since."

"And do you normally go round that way when going out to Upperby? Wouldn't it be easier to go down the London Road?"

"I fail to see what business it is of the police how I reach my destination. But I habitually go that way and through onto the ring road. It cuts out the centre of town."

"Right sir," McInnis let a little doubt creep into his voice, "I don't find it any quicker myself. Miss Fielding lives out that way I believe."

"Does she?" The Major sniffed. "It's a small world isn't it Inspector?" He shrugged, making his suit jacket bag slightly and revealing a set of rather hideous trouser suspenders and a string vest which showed through his thin shirt. McInnis blinked and repressed a grin; the man might put on airs but it seemed he was working class for all that. Then he frowned slightly as Madogan moved again, showing part of a leather strap. It seemed the Major was carrying a knife too. Now wasn't the time to challenge him however.

"Well you've been most helpful and informative sir. Thank you for your time." McInnis stood up, gave him a nod and started towards the door; he swung back round. "Oh by the way sir, I believe SOCO found some mud on the underside of your car when they checked it over."

"Well what of it? It's a car; they don't stay clean very long."

"They were just wondering where you'd been to get that particular shade of red. I think there's a bet going on." Bob McInnis smiled genially.

"God knows man, I probably picked it up on the motorway or maybe down St Nicholas Bridge, they've had road works down there for the past three weeks."

"Thank you sir. I'll pass the information on."

Gareth opened the door, sketched a brief salute, and followed the Inspector out very correctly.

Bob McInnis was grinning as he left the building. He and Gareth went to the squad car and once it was moving he said, "Well wasn't that interesting Gareth?"

Gareth drove carefully back onto the main road. "I know you got something, but I missed it."

"He not only knew who Miss Fielding was, he knew who she worked for. His tale of reading the papers was good, but we've deliberately kept her name out of them. Therefore it follows he either did know her before, or he's been checking up on her since."

"Ah." Gareth cocked his head on one side, and then overtook a slow moving lorry as they moved back into the centre of the town. "And that bit about the mud. I know they've been doing the road works down the St Nick area, a right mess they've made." He paused to change down gears. "He must have used that road to know about them, right sir?"

"Yes, and what's more the CCTV was at St Nick's retail park, we've clocked him there four times in the last fortnight, the security guys have been most helpful about that, and we've had vans using vehicle recognition in the area as well."

McInnis smiled happily. "So we know, Gareth, that he's checked up on Miss Fielding's movements since the accident, and possibly before, and that he lied about using the ring road through town. He wasn't normally in that area of town; it could have been a set up after all. We need to check out his alibi for the time of the murder; we just checked to see where he'd been before the accident." McInnis sat back and watched the flow of traffic as they drew near the police station.

"Er! I know we can't use it sir but ..." Gareth looked squarely in McInnis' face then back at the traffic, "I got a peek in the filing cabinet while you were talking like."

"And?" Bob McInnis waited expectantly.

"Well it had those little tabs on the top of the files, and it might not mean anything, but one of the files said Cavendish sir."

"Did it by God! You're right it might just be a coincidence, lots of people called Cavendish, but I don't like coincidences." McInnis looked through the windscreen as they turned into the station yard. "I somehow don't think Tomas Cavendish will have any dealings with a broker, but he might have enough secrets to interest a blackmailer. I wish we had enough grounds to get a look at those files Gareth."

He shook his head, tiredly. "He was carrying a concealed weapon, a knife, of some sort and that might just prove to be illegal, so we can twist his tail a bit more, but not enough for that."

Gareth nodded as they climbed out. McInnis looked across the roof at the young policeman. "He's a nasty customer Gareth, and I want him locked away for all sorts of reasons."

Major Madogan would like to have locked away McInnis too, mainly because he didn't like anyone who spoke in reasonably educated tones and, he felt, looked down on him. He didn't for one minute think that the police had anything against him. They were bumbling idiots in his book, who fumbled their way around crime scenes, occasionally getting it right enough to catch a crook.

He didn't like them looking for all that; it made his customers uneasy to know he'd had visits from the law. His secretary was a pretty thing just out of school and as naive as they come; she had obviously been a bit alarmed by the presence of the constabulary. She typed his letters for the brokerage firm he supposedly ran and didn't poke her fingers into the filing cabinets. This visit could make keeping his privacy a bit more difficult if he didn't act fast.

He called her in to sooth her worried frown away. "Make us a coffee, Susan, the police have distracted me. It was only an enquiry about a minor accident I had the other week, but you know how they go on and on."

153

"Oh Major, you weren't hurt were you?" She had a breathy quality to her voice, which in other circumstances he might have found attractive, but he didn't believe in messing up a good cover story for a bit of skirt.

"No. Just a stupid woman stepping in front of my car. Nobody hurt. Now if you wouldn't mind bringing the coffee, and the notes on the Thompson file?" He looked significantly at her.

"Oh yes, of course sir."

He sat back, satisfied that he'd allayed her curiosity, and waited for her to return. Once he had her occupied with the wholly fictitious Thomson file he could concentrate on the real business of the day. A little spot of blackmail. That copper would have been delighted to be privy to the files currently in the metal cabinet across the room he thought. He frowned across as he saw the drawer slightly opened.

He went across and without shutting it looked at the top, standing next to it as Gareth had. He looked carefully at what was revealed then shook his head. Nothing there for them. Just names, any firm would have names, still... He pulled out his keys and locked the top draw, effectively locking all the drawers of the cabinet. Maybe he would take his more recent activities home and put them in the wall safe there. It was a bit risky; he didn't like keeping evidence in his home. He shrugged, better safe than sorry; he smiled at the bad pun as Susan came back into the room.

Sandy Bell had spent the rest of the day in court so McInnis couldn't verbally pass his findings on, but he did leave a neat note on the desk as he headed out for the night. It was a beautiful summer's evening, and he was going to spend it with a beautiful girl he thought, as he slung his jacket over his shoulder. The crooks could get on with whatever they wanted; he'd deal with them in the morning. He was going to regret that decision.

154

Elizabeth was agreeably surprised to find that Bob McInnis did indeed possess a pair of jeans. She admired the casual way he wore them as he led her to the car. She blushed slightly as he swung round to speak to her while opening the car door. She'd been thinking he had a nice butt.

McInnis was somewhat puzzled by the red cheeks. "Did I do something wrong?"

"No, nothing." She blushed still more under his scrutiny.

He gave her another cautious look, still unsure, waiting until she'd seated herself and then going round to get in and set the car in motion.

"Elizabeth," he spoke slowly, "I don't mean to offend you, but my mother would have my hide if I didn't open the door for you and things. It's the way I was brought up. I know women don't like that sort of thing but I can't help it."

"Stop worrying Bob. I like it. It's pleasant to be cherished. It's not as if you don't acknowledge my worth when it comes to work."

He relaxed slightly, settling to driving.

"Where are we going?"

"I thought you might like a bit of a picnic at Powfoot. The tide will be half out so we can go for a little walk if you want. Is that alright?" It was said a trifle anxiously. McInnis wondered if she thought he was being mean not taking her out for a meal.

"Sounds lovely." Elizabeth Fielding was enjoying being courted; it was a new experience not to be propositioned into bed on the second date, not that she allowed them to get away with that. She discovered over the weekend that the man kissed like a dream, once he'd overcome his shyness. She wasn't quite sure why he was holding back, but it was sort of nice all the same.

When they arrived at the small sleepy village, he drove through, past a row of white cottages reflecting the late evening sunshine off their windows and walls, and parked next to the seashore at the far end. The car park was provided with some rough wooden tables and benches. They got out and Bob walked around the car and held out a hand, "Walk or eat?"

"Oh walk I think Bob." She grasped his hand, feeling the calluses across the top of his palm and bringing his hand up to her face to have a closer look. "What do you do to get these?" She smoothed her thumb over the rough patches.

"Mainly gardening for my mother."

"And these?" She gently touched the hard patches on his fingertips.

"Guitar."

"You are a man of mixed talents aren't you? Do you live with your mother then?" She was a little curious about his living arrangements, wondering if that was why he was being so circumspect.

"Good grief no! We'd end up strangling each other." He heard her faint gasp and swung round.

"Oh God I'm sorry Beth, that was crass of me." He reached out an unsteady hand. "I love my mother dearly, but we both have our own lives to lead." He smoothed down her cheek, then tipped her face up and touched his lips to hers. "It hurts doesn't it, when someone dies. It doesn't matter how close they were to you, every death affects so many lives, that's why I do what I do. Damage control."

He turned and they made their way down the slight incline, away from the car park and onto the rough maram grass which bordered the shoreline. Elizabeth bent and plucked a spray of sea thrift, sniffing the pink blossom before tucking it into the belt of her

156

powder blue dress. The sea smell rippled over them, ruffling their hair, and danced down the shoreline to tease the birds fossiking among the stones with visions of fish.

Elizabeth and Bob continued to walk along the tussocks of grass then, as the tide receded more, made their way onto the small patches of sand the sea had revealed. They were joined by a small and noisy dog who kept them company for a while. His nondescript tail wagged frantically and he barked happily as Bob obligingly threw a piece of drift wood into the water. The dog dropped the wood back at their feet with a silly grin on his face in anticipation of further play, only ceasing when they moved too far away from his home.

Eventually they turned and walked back into the setting sun. Bob was busy with his own thoughts, looking at the deep red of the sun as it spread over the hills, making the muted purples glow. He was happy and thought he understood the truth of Sandy Bell's words; you didn't really need to talk of what was.

Not speaking much, Elizabeth had been following her own train of thought too. She said, "I thought living with your mum was maybe why you hadn't..." She stopped speaking, discovering that she could hardly ask the man why he hadn't tried to sleep with her. Talk about opening your mouth and putting your foot in it; she'd got both hers in up to the kneecaps.

"Why I hadn't what?"

"It doesn't matter."

He stopped and she discovered that, jeans and casual manner notwithstanding, he was still a policeman underneath, his attitude demanded an answer. "No, I think you'd better finish the sentence Beth." Maybe you did need to speak, otherwise people might misunderstand. He grinned, thinking he'd have to have a word with Sandy about that.

She swung away and looked across the estuary towards the English shoreline opposite. "I'd rather not say Bob." She pointed out the path of the old Caledonian railway bridge. "Look you can still see the embankments on the other side of the estuary."

She could feel herself growing warm at the thought of putting the unspeakable into words, and tried diversionary tactics.

"Fascinating, you can tell me its history sometime." He swung the hand he held trying to look at her face. "Shall I guess?" Bob apparently wasn't being diverted.

"I don't think you could." She blushed even more as he turned her gently towards him, keeping her eyes firmly fixed on the pocket insignia of his polo shirt.

"Oh I think I can, I'm a policeman after all." He raised her face with a firm hand so that she was forced to make eye contact. "I haven't slept with you because I'm a bit old fashioned, and I'm not prepared to jeopardise something so important to me. But I'm a man and I wouldn't want you to think I don't want to, because I do. Who wouldn't with a beautiful girl like you in their arms?" He pulled her even closer and proved the point to the satisfaction of them both.

"Oh!" It was the only coherent noise she'd managed to make in the last five minutes.

"I think we'd better have something to eat." He grinned at her, "And I can occupy my hands. Have I answered the question Beth?" He smoothed a hand over her hair and then began walking towards the car, towing her like a pup on a lead.

She waited until they were seated at a picnic bench set above the tide line with substantial submarine baps in front of them and a thermos of chilled fruit juice, before she spoke again. "I was beginning to think maybe you didn't find me...er, like me er... in that way."

158

He grinned happily around the bap, "And have I changed your mind?"

"Oh definitely!"

"Good. Eat your picnic. I've got a bar of your favourite chocolate for afters."

She beamed at him, "I think I love you." It was said half jokingly until she caught sight of his serious face.

"I think I might love you too Elizabeth, so let's take our time and find out shall we?" He stretched out a hand across the table. She smiled a bit shyly, placing her hand in his.

"Yes please."

Someone who hadn't taken their time thinking about relationships was Tracy Cavendish. She'd got on reasonably well with her husband until the last couple of weeks, but now he'd become, she said, impossible.

They'd just had a blazing row and she was sitting on the settee sniffing into a shredded tissue, listening to the echo of the door slamming on his last few words. What was she supposed to do? He'd moped around the house, making the place untidy with his cigarette butts and beer cans. When he spoke it seemed he could only criticise her clothes and her habits. He wouldn't tell her what was wrong, but she could see he was scared of something.

She sniffed some more then dug out her mobile and pressed the key for her mum's number.

Meanwhile Tomas Cavendish was slouching down the street, muttering to himself. He hadn't quite decided where he was going, just so long as it was away from nagging women, he muttered to himself. He'd been so absorbed in his own misery that he'd failed to notice the presence of Dennis drifting onto his horizon until, that is, he felt the arm that went round his shoulders.

"Here what's the game?"

"Mr Barker would like a word wiv use. He told me to fetch you." Dennis' arm was a solid steel bar across his back and Dennis' breath was solid garlic. Cavendish flinched as much from the one as the other.

They marched along in step, like soldiers squaring up on the parade ground. There wasn't much resistance in Tom Cavendish, but it wouldn't have stood a molar's chance in a toffee factory against the sheer brute force of Dennis on an errand.

They went in the back door to the betting shop and Dennis grinned happily at both men as he shut the door after shooing Cavendish into the office.

"I brung him to see you boss, just like you told me. We didn't make no fuss in the street neither." Dennis felt he needed to get back in Barker's favour. His boss had torn strips off him for speaking out the week before, when the coppers had been visiting.

He subsided onto the mat, pulling out a yoyo and playing 'walking the dog', totally absorbed in the occupation as Barker began to talk to the other man.

"Tom, nice of you to visit."

As if, Tom thought, he'd had any choice in the matter. He could still feel the pressure of the big man's arms across his back; it ached slightly. Barker pulled the chair out with his toe and smiled genially. "Sit down Tom. I think we need to have a little chat about things. Would you like a whisky?"

Cavendish nodded and was handed a small shot glass of amber liquid. He clutched the glass with one unsteady hand and eyed the man suspiciously. Barker sat down opposite him behind the desk.

"Now Tom," Barker steepled his hands and rested his elbows on the desk, "this is just curiosity you understand, between friends? I was wondering what you and Inspector Bell found to talk about for, oh, all of half an hour this morning?"

Cavendish raised frightened eyes, then quickly dropped them back to the drink he held in his hand. "He followed me home; I didn't want to talk to him."

"Yes, so Cyril said. Said you tried to shut the door in the man's face. I thought you had better manners than that Tom." He wagged a playful finger under Cavendish's nose. "But having let the man in you seemed to have got quite cosy with him, talking in the bay window like old friends you were."

Cavendish felt the sweat begin to roll down his back in the stuffy room, even though he felt ice cold in the pit of his stomach, and Barker watched the faint stains under his arms growing in the ensuing silence.

"He talked to me. I didn't tell him anything." He took a gulp of the fiery liquid, and coughed, "He wouldn't go away. I told him I didn't know nothin'."

"Now now Tom, don't you know you should always cooperate with the police like a good citizen. They only get curious if you deny things. So what did he tell you then?" Barker dropped his hands to the desk and began to play with a ruler that was lying on the pristine blotting paper in front of him.

Tom kept his eyes fixed on his drink while he muttered, "He was asking about that key. The one to the place our Tracy used to work at. He knew I'd had a copy made." He jumped as the ruler snapped. "I don't know how; and I didn't tell him what I'd had it made for, honest I didn't Mr Barker." He felt sick and he took another gulp of whisky, the glass chinking against his teeth.

"Well that was careless of you Tom, to let the police know what you'd been doing. Still, no harm done if you didn't tell them who it was for. Still," Barker shifted his bulk in his seat and rubbed his balding patched thoughtfully, "you owe me a lot of money Tom and I expect a bit of loyalty, so you need to know I won't tolerate mistakes."

Tom shook his head frantically, "It won't happen again Mr Barker, I'll be very careful."

"What else did the nice Inspector ask you about Tom?"

"He didn't ask me anything else."

"Oh come now, you can't have sat in silence together all that time."

Cavendish shook his head. "He was threatening me. I'd had a joint, and he reckoned he could smell it."

"If you can afford joints we might need to rethink your repayments Tom." It was said with a grin that displayed the fine dentition of Barker's mouth to its best advantage. Cavendish shuddered slightly; those teeth belonged on a safari advert aimed at seeing the wild beasts.

"I only had the one from a mate."

"Hmm, yes, I understand Tom." Barker glanced at Dennis. "Dennis just walk Tom home and make sure he doesn't have any other visitors hanging about will you."

Tom, not following the coded message just given, sagged with relief. "It's OK Mr Barker I can find my own way."

"Oh no, I insist. You seem a little upset Tom. I wouldn't want anyone else to distress you."

Dennis carefully stowed his yoyo in his trouser pocket where it nestled next to a leather cosh. "Right you are Mr Barker." He wandered over to Tom and hoisted the younger and lighter man to his feet, placing an arm around his shoulders again in an irresistible hold and walking him out the back door of the bookies. It was like being hugged by a grizzly bear dressed by 'Moss Bros'.

"I fink we'll take the pretty route, don't you?" Dennis was strolling along the road, headed towards a back lot he knew about, his whole demeanour one of the pleasurable anticipation shown by someone out for a stroll on a summer evening.

Tom, held captive physically, submitted, though not without verbal protest. "I want to go straight home, Dennis." He gave an experimental wriggle that did nothing except prove he wasn't going to get away easily.

The back lot seemed deserted and Cavendish, already nervous, tried to resist again. "I'd rather stick to the streets."

"Oh no, that wouldn't be a good idea. Someone might see us."

Tom Cavendish, reflecting that that was the idea, pulled back to no avail; he was led inexorably towards the far end of the deserted area and through a corrugated fence. Dennis then proceeded to kick his kidneys with the aid of his very stylish biker boots, adding a punch or two to his carotids and solar plexus to prevent further arguments. The beating was scientific and brutal, and Cavendish was left in no doubt, when he woke up on the hospital ward, that he was lucky to be alive and not need a kidney transplant.

Two teenage girls had found him on the back lot, a couple of hours after Dennis' treatment, as they took a shortcut home. They'd called for both police and ambulance services.

"We saw him lying on the ground and I said to Jane that he must be drunk." She'd giggled at her friend, "But she said 'no look at all the blood'. So we called the police 'cos it looked like a crime."

There was righteous concern in the voice but also a good dollop of excitement.

"I thought maybe he was dead." Jane had been just as giggly; the oldish policeman interviewing them didn't make the mistake of thinking they were heartless however, just nervous.

"Was there anyone around? Did you see anyone running away?"

"Oh no he was just lying there." Jane looked to where Cavendish was being loaded onto a stretcher. "He's not dead is he?" She sounded a bit disappointed.

"No, thanks to you girls he'll be alright now. We appreciate all your help. And if you should remember anything else you need to come and report it to us."

The girls had stood around watching the proceedings for a bit longer then, apparently catching sight of the time, scampered away like a couple of rabbits out after dusk.

The police, when they came to interview Cavendish, found him almost mute. He didn't know who'd done it; it had been muggers. He'd been minding his own business when he was set upon, and that's all they could get out of him.

He was scared and more than a little shell shocked by the brutal treatment recently meted out to him by Barker and Dennis Little, but he wasn't going to invite more of the same by talking to the coppers about it.

7

*In Germany the Great War was seen as a test of spirit, of life. The
propaganda of the day saw the war as defending German freedom
against a barbaric enemy; Hans couldn't see it that way. Faced day
by day the results of what he perceived to be a futile war he saw
men returning from the trenches, injured and shell-shocked. Their
disfigurements were on display in the villages and towns and he'd
concluded that he must use his medical training to serve his fellow
men where they needed it most.*

*For three hours now he'd been crouched behind the sandbags,
listening to a symphony of sounds conducted by Death: high-pitched
screams and curses, the tympanic rattle of the machine guns, the
deeper bass of the big guns; then the muted sighs of the dying.*

*He shivered in the late evening rain, his feet soaking in mud
and gore, took a firmer grip on the canvas bag and prayed some
more. He was hanging onto his faith by fingernails bitten and
chewed by the agonies he was listening to. He was no longer sure if
it was rain or tears coursing down his face, and he no longer cared.*

*Hauptmann Brymer, the Captain in charge, wouldn't let the
stretcher bearers go into no man's land until he was sure the sector
was clear of snipers. The Hauptmann had had scouts out, but now
they were back. Hans took up position on command and prepared to
climb up the side of the trench wall. He wore the insignia of the
Society of Friends.*

*He clawed his way over the top and bellied his way slowly
along the ground. He couldn't use a light, and the pitch black land
in front of him was filled with potholes, each filled with nameless
horrors. His hand touched a body and he felt carefully around it. It
was a headless corpse. "Rest my friend in the arms of God, and let*

him grant comfort to your loved ones." He moved on, swallowing bile and fear in equal proportions.

A few yards further he felt himself slipping and ended up in a shell hole filled with rain, and the remains of two bodies that had obviously been there some weeks. He shuddered and scrabbled his way out. He no longer felt like screaming like a girl every time his hand encountered something loathsome; he'd been doing the job for seven weeks on this small section of the Somme, but he couldn't stop the antics of his stomach.

He continued moving, going ever deeper into unclaimed territory and away from the dubious safety of the trenches. Suddenly the whole area was lit by the blinding green light of a star shell. He froze on the ground, hugging it to him, his face buried in the mud and blood that had been fought over for nearly four months now, breathing in its stench.

He waited, praying silently as the light dimmed. At the last moment something moved in the periphery of his eye, a soldier misjudging the timing. There was a quick rat a tat, a high keening sound, and the figure dropped again.

Hans waited until he was sure it was safe and headed towards where he'd seen the body fall. He might be able to help. He didn't care whose side the soldier was fighting on, the injured man was a man in need.

As he approach he heard the harsh rasping sound he'd come to associate with the lung shot. He spoke very quietly, first in German, "Freund ich bin nicht bewaffnet, Ich komme, um den Verleteten zû helfen. Braûchen Sie Hilfe?" then in English, "Friend I am not armed. I am come to help the injured, can I help you?"

The rattle of breath stopped and he sighed, too late, but then he heard a gentle groan and crawled closer. He repeated himself. He didn't want to be shot trying to offer comfort.

"Come ahead friend." He heard the effort to draw breath as the hoarse voice continued. "If indeed that is what you are," another long pause, "if you kill me I shall be as pleased as if you don't."

Hans crawled over the rim of the dirty hole and dropped into a pool of stagnant water, the filthy liquid staining his uniform trousers and leaching through to his skin so that he shuddered slightly, struggling out of the morass and onto a patch of dry earth at its side. "Where are you?" He spoke in English since that had been the language of the other voice.

"Move to...your left. I can see you... against the sky."

Hans felt with his hands, moving his feet slowly until he touched the rough earth sides of the hole. His foot kicked against a body and he grunted quietly; it was lying under some overhanging roots.

"Found Alec have you? ...He was going for help ...we've been here nearly... twenty four hours and that water is a bit disgusting."

Hans ran his hands over the still warm form of Alec peering at the body as his eyes adjusted to the darkness again. It was obvious the man was dead, his chest shiny black and wet in the fitful starlight. He stepped around the corpse and moved on towards the rasping breathing he could hear.

"Where are you hurt?" He knelt beside the author of the voice.

"I was creased and I've lost a foot." The man stopped to draw breath, "Alec was determined to get me back to the line." He stopped again, breathing in short shallow gasps. "He was a good man; Alec...wouldn't leave me behind...which was foolish...'cos I'm done for, lost too much blood."

Hans had by this time managed to raise the man's body. He spoke slowly. "My name is Hans." He saw the face in the next star shell. And relapsed into German. "Peter, Mein Peter." He shook his dark blond hair back out of blue eyes in a violent gesture of

167

negation. "Wir warden ihnen hier raus helfen," it was a cri de coeur;" We'll get you out of here."

Peter took an unwary and deep breath and choked out, "Hans, is it really you? Oh God."

The Englishman began to cry; it was laboured and difficult and muffled against the mud and dirt encrusted uniform of his sworn enemy. Peter clung to his erstwhile playmate with a fierce grip as Hans tried to sooth his frantic gasps for breath.

"Hush, I'll get you to safety. All will be well." Hans rocked the body of his cousin, cradling him. "All will be well, I promise."

They continued to sit holding each other until Peter was calm again. His strength was so little that this didn't take long. "But what are you doing here Peter? You should be back in England making sweet love to your Victoria."

Peter gave a short, harsh bark of humourless laughter, "My Victoria died for this stinking war… I figured I'd join her as quickly as possible…I just didn't know it would hurt so bloody much." He paused, adjusting his body on the hard ground. "Why are you here Hans?"

"Stretcher bearer, there is so little I can do. I hate this war, this senseless killing. I don't understand how men can do this to each other. I wanted to help. I saw them coming back, maimed, half dead in their minds and bodies. I had to do something, you understand my Peter?" Hans gripped the hands of his cousin, asking forgiveness for being born German.

"I understand dear friend." Peter shifted again. "I'm not afraid to die Hans, just afraid to die alone…do you think God will welcome this…black sheep?"

"When the time comes; but you are going to live a long time yet my Peter. See God has sent me to you." They sat talking quietly of their adventures over the past few months; but mostly of their

childhood and the holidays each had enjoyed in the other's homeland.

Peter fell silent eventually, too exhausted by lack of blood and nourishment to sustain any lengthy conversation. Hans sat watching the stars emerging; last night had been an almost moonless night, the sliver lying on its back and providing little help for rescue attempts but some cover for the rescuers. He was hoping they'd seen the last of it so that he might take Peter back to his own lines under cover of the darkness.

He judged the time at almost two when he decided to make the attempt. "Peter."

Peter, who had slipped once more into a fitful doze, stirred.

"Peter. I'm not quite sure of my bearings, which way are your lines? Do you know?"

Peter looked at him silently for a moment, "God knows, but you can't take me... they'd shoot you as a spy as soon as you stuck your head... over the dugout." He relapsed into silence again.

"If I'm carrying you, your uniform will be seen first, they won't shoot me."

"It's not worth risking your life man."

"It's my life."

"Hans, I love you as a brother, you know that... but I'm not going to make it back... either line." He paused for breath and gripped hard on the hands of his cousin. "Just stay until the end would you, then get yourself out of this hell...and back to Germany. And let them know at home." He drew in a shallow breath, "Promise me."

Hans nodded his head, but leant back against the side of the pit. He wasn't leaving without Peter. He'd just wait for the right moment. After a time he heard his cousin's breath growing more

169

shallow and felt for his pulse. It was faint and growing weaker; he didn't dare to delay longer. He'd have to chance it.

He hoisted the now unconscious man on his shoulders and pushed him up onto the ground above the hole, then crawled out himself. He looked around cautiously, trying to judge which direction he'd been travelling in when he'd found Peter. Then, coming to a decision, began to half drag, half pull him along the ground, feeling his own way with extra care. He didn't want to fall into another shell hole with his precious burden.

He'd left it too late; realisation came when they'd travelled less than fifty yards. A huge explosion shook the ground and the pre-dawn bombardment began all around him.

Sandy exploded through the door of the office and Bob McInnis raised his head from the papers he'd been reading to look at him with some astonishment.

"It's time you went home Bob, you've had your head buried in that research half the day." Sandy was dressed in his second best brown suit, the one he wore for court appearances; it was rumpled. He carried his jacket, and the collar of his shirt was undone, his plain brown tie wilted slightly in the heat of the day and his exertions. Bob thought he looked more than a little pissed off.

"Did I do something wrong? We've got to read all this stuff, but if you'd wanted me for something…?"

"It's not you Bob. Bloody kids I caught a couple of weeks ago, kicking seven shades of hell out of an old woman for her pension. They got an ASBO and a slap on the wrist. I ask you what good will that do? What kind of message does it send to our youngsters?" He slumped into the chair facing the desk, giving it a kick in passing to vent his feelings.

"Bloody Antisocial Behaviour Orders, the kids collect them like badges of honour. It doesn't seem to deter them. And one kid's only fourteen. I wish I could scalp him, maybe that would have

170

some effect. The bloody ASBO won't." He subsided and Bob looked at him sympathetically.

"Want to go for a cuppa Sandy?"

"Yeah, might as well. You can bring me up to date with the progress of this murder." The words were hardly out of his mouth when Constable Higgs tapped on the open door.

He looked from one man to the other and decided that he'd rather talk to Bob McInnis for once. Inspector Bell looked as though he could personally commit a murder and Higgs didn't particularly want to be the victim. He cleared his throat nervously.

"Inspector, the murder of the Professor..."

"Yes?"

"Well sir," he hesitated, obviously not sure if his news would be welcome.

"Spit it out man, we're all tired and want to get home tonight."

"It's like this sir, you asked me to look at the photos of the men that I was to show round the school, and one of them has just been hospitalised. Claims he was mugged. I don't know if it's relevant sir, but I recognised his name when it came up from dispatch and thought you might want to know." Higgs stood silently, waiting for some reaction.

"Perhaps Constable, when you tell us the name we might be able to form an opinion." McInnis grimaced.

"Oh, it's Tomas Cavendish sir." He was justifiably pleased at the reception his news got. Both men shot to their feet.

"In the Cumbrian Infirmary is he?"

"Yes sir."

"Good work Constable." Bell patted the man on the shoulder as they surged towards him, putting jackets on as they surged past. He felt he'd been caught in an incoming wave and buffeted against the shoreline.

They started down the corridor and he stood watching their departing backs somewhat sadly, feeling like unwanted flotsam.

McInnis turned around, "Well, what are you waiting for, don't you want to come along?"

"Oh yes sir!" A huge grin spread across Higgs' face and he quick marched his way in their wake out to the parking lot.

"Grab a car lad. You can be driver while we talk things over in the back." Sandy exchanged a fierce grin with Bob McInnis. "We've obviously disturbed something Bob; maybe, just maybe, we might be able so see where this case is going now."

They settled in the back. Sandy fastened his seat belt and leaned back. "I put a little pressure on Cavendish yesterday Bob, nothing very heavy. I might be the cause of him being beaten up, or it just might be muggers, but I really don't believe that."

He told his partner of his short visit the day before. "Cavendish was scared witless Bob. We'll see what the doctor's report says but I'll lay a pound to a penny it's Little Dennis' handiwork."

"You'll not get a taker in me." McInnis shook his head. "It could have been me though; young Gareth glimpsed the name Cavendish in the top draw of Madogan's files. If he thought we were onto Cavendish and wanted him to mind his manners he might have done the beating, he's nasty enough." He continued, filling Sandy Bell in on his interview. "I don't like to think I'm the cause of a man getting a beating Sandy."

"Nor me lad, but we aren't. You can't afford to think like that. If the man hadn't been walking on the shady side of the law in the first place then our having a little word wouldn't have precipitated anything."

While the two detectives went to see if they might gain a little information from the badly beaten Tom Cavendish, another interview was taking place in a different part of the town.

Major Madogan was talking in his most urbane way in the sitting room of a respected member of the public. Neither man had sat down, despite the fact that there were some rather nice leather armchairs set in front of a fireplace filled with golden rod in an antique vase.

172

"I really do think you should reconsider paying me this small sum; I have, after all, expended considerable efforts to find the information out for you. After all, your son's career would suffer considerably if his employers should become aware of his, shall we call it, 'past history and inclinations'?" His moustache bristled as he stretched his lips and smiled in what he believed to be an avuncular manner.

"Since I neither desired nor wanted you to find out the information, I fail to see why I should pay you at all. I also intend to lodge a complaint with the relevant body concerning its failure to maintain security measures over the internet." He sat now, carefully straightening the creases in his pinstriped trouser legs. He didn't invite the Major to sit, nor did he offer him a glass of the nice cognac he was currently pouring for himself.

"The internet is so hard to police isn't it? It's amazing the amount of knowledge that can stray into the public domain if you know how to look for it." It was said in very sympathetic tones and the Major smoothed down his moustache and straightened a regimental tie he had no claim whatsoever to wear, before continuing. "But I really don't think you ought to complain to the authorities. Things might just appear where even a dumb policeman would see it easily."

The older man raised an eyebrow; in his experience policemen were far from dumb. However he held his peace waiting to see what else the objectionable and jumped up man in front of him would say. He recognised the tie; he had one himself, and the right to wear it. Which went to prove that this man hadn't done his homework completely. He wasn't about to pay a blackmailer, no matter how politely the terms were couched, until he was absolutely sure there was no other way.

He decided he needed a bit of thinking time, "There is no way I can raise five K just like that."

"Of course you can." Madogan eyed the seemingly frail old man sitting before him. He preferred to stand; it made a better impression on his clients he thought. Made 'em aware of who was in charge. "I know to a penny what you have in your bank account. You really should use a secure server when you're buying goods over the net." He allowed himself a tiny smirk as the other man's cheeks lost a little colour before he sipped at the brandy in a seemingly casual manner.

"You might know how much I have but you can't know all my commitments Major. I tell you I can't just take that sum out of my bank account." He held up a hand as the other was about to speak. "I might be able to pay you on Friday. Will that do?"

Madogan frowned, pausing. He didn't like delays. But this bird was a bit more composed than he'd expected. "I'll see you in your office Friday morning; otherwise I might need to e-mail the CO of your son's regiment." The Major was shown out and then his host returned and sat leaning back slowly in his chair to think about how he could stop the nasty piece of goods who'd just left.

McInnis and Bell were having as little joy with their prey. They'd been allowed a grudging fifteen minutes by the harassed doctor in charge of the case.

"The man is quite ill, and he's been very lucky. We've got him nicely stabilised overnight and I don't want him too stressed." He disappeared in a swirl of white coat and antiseptic odour.

Tom Cavendish was still prone in his bed on the six bed ward. His face, aside from a few minor scratches and a badly swollen and cut upper lip, was relatively free of marks but his throat was a mottled blue purple, the bruising peeking above the hospital's pale blue gown that he wore. He had a needle in the back of his left hand with tubing running from it to a clear bag feeding him a mixture of saline and potassium. There was also a plastic bag attached to the side of the bed by two metal hooks. This contained a blood stained amber mixture which made the slightly fastidious McInnis shudder a bit.

Tracy Cavendish was by the bedside. She wasn't speaking, just sitting reading a magazine and chewing gum. Her legs were crossed and displayed in a red skirt of miniscule proportions. Tom Cavendish had his head turned away, apparently staring out the window at a clear blue evening sky and the top of a leafy tree.

When Tracy saw them approaching she gave a genuine smile, laying the magazine down on the bed. "Oh hello, I'm glad it's you. I told Tom they'd send someone to catch the b's who done this to him."

"Good evening Mrs Cavendish. I'm glad to catch you, we need to speak to you again, just a few more questions." Bell spoke quietly.

As she spoke Tom turned his head and gave Bell a malevolent look, "I ain't got anything to say to you." His voice was hoarse as he growled out the words; it was obvious to both men that it was an effort for him to speak. He looked at his wife, "An' don't you go talking to 'em either."

"Tom, they're trying to help. Don't you want to catch the muggers?" She stood up, wriggling her bright red leather skirt down her thighs. "I'm going for a coffee while they talk to you; you tell them what they want to know Tom." She leaned over and pressed a kiss to his mouth causing both Bell and McInnis to wince in sympathy, and Cavendish to gasp in pain. She left, smiling perkily at the man in the end bed, who was admiring her legs as she walked towards him.

Causing a distinct rattle, Sandy Bell pulled the green curtains around the bed, motioning Higgs forward. Higgs, who'd been standing guard at the double doorway watching the proceedings, came into the room; Bell spoke quietly to him before disappearing behind the curtain. "Make sure the end bed doesn't listen too hard lad."

Higgs came to attention and put on his fiercest frown, the one he had when he realised another pimple had appeared like Mount Etna among the lower reaches of acne on his face. It had the patient in the end bed rapidly overhauling his conscience and picking up the sporting page of the paper to hide behind.

McInnis was pulling up the plastic chair in vomit green recently vacated by Tracy and was seating himself facing Tom Cavendish. Sandy Bell went to the other side of the bed, preferring to stand rather than risk his limbs to the rickety furniture.

"So who did this to you then Tom?"

Cavendish, with a policeman on either side, directed his eyes to the ceiling and watched the slow turning of a ceiling fan. "Muggers."

"What did they steal from you then?" Bell was patience personified.

"Nuthing, I didn't have anything worth stealing, that's why they beat me up."

"You keep saying they, Tom. How many were there?"

"I dunno they was onto me too fast."

"A strapping young man like you and you didn't get a few blows in to anyone else." McInnis' voice dripped sarcasm as he fell into pattern with Bell.

Still addressing the ceiling Cavendish muttered, "I was taken by surprise."

"I'll bet." Bell's voice was full of spurious sympathy. "What were you doing on that bit of land then?"

"Taking a shortcut."

"Where the hell to man?" McInnis growled the words. He and Bell were good at the nice and nasty cop routine. They didn't expect it to work with Tom Cavendish but it was worth a try.

"I was going home."

"That way? Tell it to the marines lad." Bell spoke gently. "We can give you some protection if you tell us who from."

"I told you, it was muggers." Cavendish closed his eyes, and apparently his ears, refusing to answer any more questions by as much as a twitch of an eyebrow. McInnis exchanged a look with Bell and, as the other nodded, they both stood and left the bedside.

As they left the six bedder Bell carefully drew the curtains back again gathering their young acolyte on the way. Cavendish only acknowledged their leaving by the fact that he turned his head to look out of the second storey window again.

They headed to the nursing station where a youngish nurse, her pale blue scrubs rumpled and her fair, wispy hair coming unshipped from a bun on the top of her head, was leafing through a black file. Bell took the lead, extending a hand and introducing himself, explaining briefly why they were on the ward. "I know he's protected by the privacy act lass, but this is a murder investigation." Bell applied his most fatherly and charming smile.

The staff in charge of the ward melted under his charm. "You know I can't let you do that Inspector." She laid a hand on a file on the desk pulling it more fully into view to reveal the name Cavendish, and then she whisked her scrubs clad figure out from behind the counter and smiled nicely at them. "I've got to give an IVAB. I'll be back in ten minutes." She winked at them and disappeared up the ward carrying a small aluminium tray dish with a wicked looking syringe full of something white and murky resting in it and a small empty vial.

"What the hell's an IVAB?"

177

"I dunno. I don't much care either." Bell was scanning the ward and deciding that the little office behind the counter would suit their purpose best. He scooped up the file and headed towards the door. McInnis followed and Higgs, wondering what he should do, started to follow too.

"Not you lad, you go and keep an eye out for that nice Sister, flirt with her if you have to. That shouldn't be a hard job." He eyed the flush that suffused the young constable's cheeks like a sunrise spreading over a seascape, and smiled thinly.

The two Inspectors huddled in the office, pouring over the notes that the intern had collected and written. Both men were accustomed to reading PM reports so that at least some of the jargon was comprehensible.

"I was right Bob, good job you didn't take the bet, it's typical of Little Dennis' MO. First disable your man by hitting the kidneys, stop him talking by hitting the throat, and then kick the shit out of him."

Bob nodded. He'd been reading as rapidly as Sandy. "IVAB's are antibiotics apparently."

"Focus lad, his kidneys are pretty badly bashed. The man's lucky, like the medic said. Going to have a sore throat for a while, got some nasty bruised ribs." He closed the file and peeked out of the office like a cautious snail looking for blackbirds, then, the coast being clear, emerged fully and set the file down on the desk sighing. "Which is all well and good Bob, but if the man won't admit to anything…" He shrugged.

Bob frowned, "I suppose you're right Sandy, but it rather sticks in my craw."

"We know Dennis is Barker's muscle, but we never have been able to prove it. We've put him away for acting as lookout and wheel-man. But that's piddly shit really."

Sandy gave the come ahead to Higgs and the three of them left the ward, abandoning the smell of hospital for the equally objectionable odour of a hot city street in mid summer, compounded as it was of traffic fumes and humanity with the antiperspirant on its last gasp.

Sandy glanced at his watch as they stood by the car. "Take us back to the station lad, I'm going home to Sarah and a nice tea. It's been a long day and the lawn needs mowing."

Bob nodded his agreement as they climbed in. "This proves that Cavendish is working for Barker, at least."

Sandy cocked an eyebrow. "Has dealings with him anyway, and has crossed him somehow. It might just be that he hasn't paid off his debts fast enough. But I don't think so. Barker likes his clients fit enough to work off their money. You're right there lad." He settled back in his seat, watching the traffic for a minute.

"How's the research going?"

Bob brought his mind back from wherever it was wandering. "I was reading about the Somme, 1916. For some reason I thought it was a short battle: huge casualties but only lasting a couple of days or something."

"Oh aye." Sandy thought about it, head to the side, resting on the door window. "I suppose it's because they always quote the numbers killed on the first day. How long did it last then?"

"About four months, all together. Our Peter describes, presumably his father and this Hans character, meeting up on the front. Hans was in the Society of Friends. I need to find out what they are."

Higgs cheery voice spoke up from the driver's seat. "Oh that's easy sir. Quakers."

The two senior men raised their eyebrows at each other. "Could you elaborate just a trifle on that Higgs?"

Higgs spared them a look in the rear view mirror before looking ahead into the traffic, then back in the mirror. "Quakers, Inspector Bell, are a Christian organisation, they're a non conformist group, the founder member was George Fox. They're pacifists sir." He fixed his eyes on the traffic again.

"That's very interesting Higgs. You're not a member are you?"

"Oh no sir!" Higgs audibly gulped, "not exactly. But my parents are, Inspector."

"So you'd know a bit about them then?" Bell looked at the tide of red creeping up the young neck.

"Yes sir." Higgs was wishing he'd kept his mouth closed. He was waiting to be teased, as some of his mates had done at school.

McInnis, who recognised the symptoms, said, "I'm Catholic myself, but I'm always willing to learn. Come back to the office and fill me in Constable."

Bell was sitting muttering to himself. He spoke to McInnis, "We've come across the Society of Friends before, I'm sure we have. Now what was it?" He shook his head in frustration.

"Well it was Hans that was in the Society during the First World War."

"No..." Sandy drew the word out, "that wasn't it, I haven't been reading the research, you have." He shook his head again, "Nope it's gone."

Silence descended on the trio as each concentrated on their own thoughts. They arrived back at the very dusty station yard to apparent mayhem. As Higgs turned in two youths were making a spirited bid for freedom. Higgs proved that he wasn't a pacifist at all. He pulled on the handbrake, swung out of the car almost before

180

it had stopped, and rugby-tackled one of the young men. They heard him say "and stay down" as he swept the struggling man's feet from under him as that man tried to head butt him and slipped the cuffs on in one fluid movement.

McInnis grinned. "Definitely not pacifist," he muttered to Sandy Bell and then, "we'll have to get him in the Rugby team."

The two men that had brought the boys in, in the squad car, were now busily reading them their rights. Inspector Bell looked from the scuffed trainers, up the torn jeans, to the hoodies in one contemptuous sweep. "Really lads haven't you got any more sense than to add resisting arrest to your charge sheet?"

He turned to Higgs, "Good work lad." He nodded at McInnis, "I'm going home. If I think of that connection I'll ring you Bob, but I don't think there's anymore I can do this evening." He looked up at the blue sky." And it's a beautiful evening for a spot of work in the garden."

McInnis watched as the youths were frog marched off towards booking. "Come and tell me about Quakers, Higgs. Unless you're off duty?"

Higgs looked at his watch, "That's alright sir."

"We'll go to the canteen for a drink then Higgs, and you can speak words of wisdom to me." They strolled into the welcome shade of the station and made their way into the crowded room and the babble of noise rising to greet them along with a strong odour of chips.

Richards, the solicitor, was sitting in a room filled with the scent of mown grass and roses. It was a quiet and peaceful scene, in stark contrast to his mood. He set the single brandy he allowed himself on the side table and pulled a rather nice single diamond ring from his waistcoat pocket. He turned it in the light from the late evening sun, watching as the facets caught the light and gleamed back and forth. He pushed it back into his pocket and picked up the brandy again, thinking.

What the hell was he going to do about Madogan and, for that matter, what the hell had his son been up to now? He sipped then set the glass down and stretched out a hand for the phone, then withdrew it again. No, he'd better wait until he was calmer; rushing into things caused you to make mistakes. He just hoped he hadn't made a serious one.

He stood up, stretching his long limbs and going to stand next to the mantelpiece where a photograph of his son stood in an army uniform. It would be good to see the boy in his old mess; he had several friends who were regulars; they would see the boy was alright. Providing no whiff of scandal came with him.

Richards picked up the photograph, examining the face. It was a handsome face he decided, blond and blue eyed like his mother. But weak about the chin. He shook his head; his wife had been a weak woman too. If she'd only exerted a bit more discipline he was sure the boy would have turned out stronger. It was a pity he'd had to work so hard that he hadn't spent more time with him in the boy's formative years.

He walked back to his seat, picking up the balloon glass and going through to his study where a shoe box of photographs sat on the desk. Yes he'd do a little more study of the family tree, and then tomorrow he'd phone the boy and find out what he'd really been doing. Perhaps just advise him to be careful. Then he'd deal with Madogan.

Higgs had gone. He'd proved a very useful source of information about the Quakers; McInnis filed away the knowledge for future reference. They'd been persecuted for their faith in both Germany and England during the Great War. Stigmatised as cowards for refusing to fight. But, Higgs had informed him, they'd served on all the major fronts, alongside the Red Cross as stretcher bearers, risking their lives to rescue wounded men from no-man's land and the trenches.

McInnis picked up the research he'd been reading when Sandy Bell came in and started to read again.

The explosion had knocked them both backwards and unconscious. Hans was out for only a few seconds. He lay on the ground listening to the breath whistling in and out of his lungs above the crump and thud of the barrage. Then, remembering what he'd been doing, looked round quickly for Peter.

Peter was lying with his leg at a strange angle, out cold apparently. Hans, keeping as low to the ground as possible, wriggled backwards towards their former shell hole dragging the unconscious man behind him. He flopped down into the mud and almost sighed with relief, until a shower of dirt flew over him and coated them both in slime as it fell into the pool in the centre of the hole.

He pulled his cousin as close to the side as possible, crawling over to the departed Alec to remove his tin helmet and bring it back. He put it on Peter. Then took stock of his own safety. He gazed in astonishment down at his torso in the dawn light. The blast had stripped him to his long johns and vest, but his boots remained firmly knotted and looked enormous at the end of white clad legs.

He began to chuckle slightly hysterically at the sight; Peter, coming round, looked at him in astonishment. "What's so funny 'cus'?" It was gasped out.

Hans indicated his sartorial elegance with a muddy hand while the guns boomed around them. Peter managed a faint grin. "You'd better have my jacket." He struggled out of it as he spoke, even while Hans protested.

"I won't need it much longer anyway." It was said with a grimace of pain. "What the hell happened anyway Hans?"

"I was trying for the lines, but it seems I left it too late my friend." He shook his head in annoyance. "What's more I've lost my water bottle." He peeked over the rim as a sudden silence descended on the area; the world held its breath waiting for a signal. "Our side will begin in a minute." He crawled half out, scanning the area he'd just left. "I can see it. If I'm quick, I'll make it between firings."

As Peter shuddered out his name he was over the top and wriggling back towards the water bottle lying on the ground.

Peter, cursing futilely, lay looking at the space where Hans' legs had just disappeared, only to see his cousin's face reappear over the edge and then his body flop back in like a stranded fish. Hans clutched the water bottle and wore a triumphant grin. "Better get ready my Peter." It was all Peter heard as they both hugged the wall again, trying to bury their bodies in the unyielding earth as the barrage from the German lines commenced.

Both men were holding their heads by the time the noise apparently ceased. "God, will the noise never end." Hans winced slightly at the blasphemy but didn't speak as a stray shell exploded almost straight above them. He clapped both hands to his ears, praying his own silent prayers.

He kept his eyes closed waiting for more, but the silence stretched out. He slowly opened his eyes, looking up at rapidly lightening sky. "It's another day my Peter." He turned towards his cousin. But Peter had already seen the dawn and gone to spend his day with God.

Hans sat in the hole all that day, keeping company with two dead Englishmen and a small red admiral butterfly which had as much chance of survival in no man's land as Hans did. About noon the rain came down in cold sleety sweeps and he picked up Peter's discarded jacket and put it on.

He gathered the few possessions in Peter's trouser pockets too, hoping against hope that he might get the chance to return them to his family. He could always ask the Red Cross to deliver them he thought. Finally he removed a silver chain with a couple of rings on them that Peter was wearing around his neck.

Surprisingly he slept for a large part of the afternoon. The fighting had moved along the line and this section seemed to be quite quiet he thought. Then he realised that part of the trouble was his own hearing. He could barely hear his own voice when he spoke. He'd raided Alec's pockets in the late afternoon, discovering a hard biscuit and a square of chocolate. This, with the water from the bottle, had sustained him for a while.

He found himself talking to Peter as if Peter could still hear him, his own voice seeming to come from a long distance away. He told Peter he'd be alright now. That he, Hans, would tell Peter's parents how they met. He lay down shortly after the sunset. His watch had stopped, he wasn't sure when, maybe in the last blast, so he used Peter's, carefully stowing the pocket watch in the jacket pocket.

He was found there sometime after dark by a group of English soldiers. They slithered into the hole with barely a sound, almost feeling their way around. "I tell you I saw one get back in."

The voice was Liverpool, the others shrugged. They worked their way around the crater, examining first Alec then Peter, before coming to Hans.

He, waking suddenly to find himself surrounded by Tommies, had enough wits to keep his mouth closed until he'd figured out what to say.

8

"Are we having our first argument?"

"It would seem so." McInnis' voice was clipped. He'd listened in silence, wise enough in the ways of women to keep quiet until Elizabeth seemed to have run out of steam.

McInnis and Elizabeth were sitting out on the lawn at the back of her father's small house. It was Saturday afternoon, the sun was shining, the sky was a brilliant blue, and the roses perfumed the air. And Elizabeth had just dropped a bombshell; she'd applied for a job in Cambridge.

McInnis, for all he was a policeman, hated conflict in his personal life, which perhaps explained why he'd never allowed himself to get attached to any girl in a serious way before. Now he sat forward in his rattan chair, the better to get his point across. He looked at the pretty picture she made in the hot pink sundress and swallowed; he didn't want to fight, he wanted to enjoy looking at her.

"Look Beth, I do understand where you're coming from, you're an independent person and I respect that. You have a right to that independence. However I agree with your father. Why must you search for a job so quickly?"

"I won't live on charity Bob."

"I hardly think allowing your father to care for you is living on charity."

"Would you live on your mother's pension?"

"The cases are hardly the same; I'm a man." He knew it was the wrong thing to say as soon as the words were out of his mouth.

"Respect, huh!" Elizabeth poked a finger at his soft green shirt; he wasn't wearing a tie today, and the smart pants and shirt were his idea of casual dress apparently. She thought he looked wonderful, and smelled even better, but she wasn't letting him away with such a blatantly sexist remark.

187

Bob McInnis felt the colour rise in his cheeks. "Yes I do respect you. I think you've got a great brain and you have the right to use it." He stopped looking at her, then reached for her hands and gripped them firmly.

"OK, I admit I've got mixed motives here Beth. I don't want you to move down south, I want you near me." He stopped again, then held up a hand as she would have spoken. "I'm selfish, I admit it, but I work here in the borders. Carlisle is my home, my partner is here. I could transfer, but I'd rather not."

Elizabeth returned the pressure of his hands then released herself and stood up. The trouble was Bob McInnis hadn't declared where they were going. Did he intend marriage, or mistress? Should she abandon this job opportunity at Cambridge on the chance that he meant marriage?

She knew her own mind; she loved him, had done for several weeks she suspected, but what about him? She could hardly ask. He'd said he thought he might, but that wasn't the same as coming right out with it. And if he didn't she couldn't bear to stay.

Bob watched her walk across the grass in bare feet to the nearest rose bush, her back held stiffly upright. Why couldn't things just stay as they were for a bit longer until he'd sorted out this case? Then maybe he could decide what he wanted to do about their relationship.

"It's not just the money or the job Bob." Elizabeth plucked a rose, swinging back to speak to him as she came back to her seat. "Part of it's the murder. I've been uneasy since poor Peter was murdered. I suppose it smears you in a way, being in contact with murder. Leaves you less secure, less..." she sought for a word, "trusting, perhaps, of your fellow man."

She sat down and handed him the pink and thorny rose. Bob began to methodically remove the thorns while he listened to her, the pit of his stomach yawing, thinking his Elizabeth was just as prickly at times. He wished he could smooth her down as easily. She was speaking again, and he looked across at her serious face as

188

she continued. "You got hit on the head a couple of weeks ago and you made light of it. But Bob..." she looked him squarely in the face, "I don't know if I can live with the fear of that either. Of something happening to you."

"Ah, I wondered." McInnis handed the stripped rose back and she sniffed the delicate perfume. "I can't change my job love." He said it slowly and sadly. "Do you want me to stop seeing you?" He waited for her answer, knowing that it would tear the heart out of him if she said yes.

"I honestly don't know Bob." She reached out a hand and he put his in it and held hers tightly.

They sat silently thinking their own thoughts. Bob didn't know what to say or do next. Eventually he moved, bringing her hand to his mouth and planting a small kiss on her knuckles. "When do you have to decide on this job?"

"I've got a month. Term's finished at university, and the professor who has offered the job has holidays booked before he wants to start work, but obviously he wants everything settled earlier if possible."

Suddenly Bob stood up, pulling her up with him. He pulled her close and stood holding her, his hands around her waist. "Let's try to sort these problems out one by one. OK? I'm sure we can find some sort of solution." Under his breath he said, "We have to."

"Alright Bob."

"There are several problems here. You want independence," he cocked his head on one side, "you will have that when Professor Neville's Will is settled." He placed a finger on her lips. "Yes I know you don't want it. But he wanted you to have it. And finish his research."

"He didn't have to pay me to do that; I'd do it in his memory."

"Research costs money love, and he knew that." Bob rubbed her arms, then reached up to smooth back the black hair glowing in the sunshine and framing her face.

"Second problem. My job scares you because there's a lot of scary people out there all determined to put a period to my life." He pressed a finger to her lips. "I'll admit some risks, but I could get flattened walking under a bus. However," he replaced the finger with his lips for a brief kiss, "I would like to take you visiting; it might help," he grimaced, "or it might make matters worse."

He waited for her nod and they went indoors, McInnis shivering at the sudden chill of the shaded room. He hoped it wasn't an omen of things to come. He held her hand tightly, not letting go, even while she collected her handbag and sandals, and his pager. Bidding goodbye to her father, whom they found dozing in his chair in front of the empty hearth, a newspaper lying across his chest and his glasses on a bit askew, they went out to Bob's car parked on the hot tarmac in front of the house.

"Where are we going Bob?"

"We're going to visit Sandy Bell and his wife; I have a standing invitation to Saturday tea at their house."

"Well you might have, I haven't."

"Ah! But Sarah's dying to meet you."

"And how do you know that? Been gossiping?" Elizabeth was trying hard to match his mood and Bob was obviously trying to cheer them both up.

"I, young lady, don't gossip. Policemen deal in facts." This was said in the grand manner.

"Yeah I've heard you and Inspector Bell dealing in facts! Like the fact that Carlisle United couldn't possibly lose next season."

Bob flashed her a grin and shot across an intersection, heading to the varied delights of the ring road and the other side of the town. "Seriously darling, Sandy won't mind. I want to talk to him about the research anyway. We haven't exactly scaled down the murder, but other cases have landed on both our desks since, and we need to have a conference about where to go next."

"I'm a little unclear." Elizabeth spoke somewhat hesitantly.

"Yeah."

"Er, how is it Inspector Bell isn't in charge? He's older than you and er, more experienced." She felt herself colouring and raised what she hoped was an enquiring eye as Bob spared her a brief glance.

"Oh! Sandy's in charge really. I'm the junior partner but he lets me think I'm the boss and handle the cases 'so that I can get plenty of experience', he says. Besides, this way I have to fill in all the paperwork." They both laughed at his appalling imitation of Sandy's accent.

"Ah all now becomes clear!"

While they took the short journey north across town another car was heading just as purposefully southwards. Major Madogan had been visiting another of his clients. He was feeling in a good mood and had a thousand pounds in his pocket to help the mood along.

Richards had contacted him the day before and asked him for a slight delay and a meeting at a pub out of town today, as he had a dying client requiring his Will altered. Madogan thought it was a trifle odd, but if the man was willing to pay up he wasn't bothered if the other wanted to do it in a public place. After all the man could hardly claim extortion if he handed the money over in front of witnesses.

The Major's big Range-Rover Sport ate up the distance to the little village of Scotby. He pulled into the side of the main road and looked around at the pub. A typical rustic place, he'd have a pint, get the cash and go. He got out and sauntered towards its welcoming shade.

The pub was faux olde worlde with lots of oak beams and dark corners. It smelled of ale and pies, and contained only two people aside from the barmaid. One was an elderly man, nursing a small whiskey and a large beer, known locally as a 'half and half'. His moustache was slightly frothy, and his eyes watering. The other was a young man nursing a shandy, neatly dressed, for one of his ilk, in trousers and denim jacket.

191

Madogan hesitated on the threshold, peering around in the gloom of the interior for Richards, then entered the room fully to approach the bar. "I'm looking for a man named Richards; he's supposed to be meeting me here?" He raised an eyebrow in query.

The barmaid, a bottle blonde with eyebrows that resembled a couple of vapour trails across her forehead, raised a bored face from the contemplation of her nails and spared him a look. She shook her head and raised her chin, indicating the other customers. "Ain't anybody else here." She waited for him to say something, then said, "You want a drink?"

"No thank you." Madogan cast her a contemptuous look, straightening his light summer jacket and fastening two buttons, turning abruptly on his heel to follow the young man out of the door. He stood thinking in the afternoon sunshine, looking around the small village street.

"Excuse me sir." A youth was approaching him and spoke politely; he wore the teenage uniform of stone washed jeans and t-shirt.

"An old gentleman asked me to keep an eye out for you; he's with my parents. He said would I show you the way."

Madogan gave another glance around but the young man from the bar had disappeared down a back lane and the place seemed deserted, except for a stray scratching on the opposite side of the road. "Very well young man," he gave what he believed was a genial smile, "lead the way."

The youth slouched his way along; his jeans sagged so that the crutch appeared to be somewhere near his kneecaps, and the hems were none existent, consisting as they did of ragged edges. "It's through here sir." He stopped and held out a none too clean hand to indicate a set of partially opened gates.

Madogan found himself at the entrance to a small builder's yard, with high wooden fences on three sides and stacked timber on pallets set evenly against them. The smell of freshly sawn pine was thick on the air, and the high-pitched whine of an electric saw almost deafening as he took a step through the gates.

"Are you sure this is the place?"

"Oh yes this is my parents' yard."

Madogan strode confidently through, then halted and swung round as he heard the saw's whine cease with a few final whirs like a bumblebee coming in to land, and the squeak of the gates shutting behind him, spelling doom to a man with a guilty conscience.

"What's this all about? Come along, or I shall speak to your parents." He glanced around, seeing the saw glinting as it turned slowly in the late sunshine, and another young man approaching from it.

The youth didn't look so young any longer, and the two other young men with him looked distinctly menacing as they operated a pincer movement towards the Major.

He couldn't see their faces clearly for the hoodies they wore covered part of their faces. He swung round trying to get a clear look at at least one of them, but the first youth had now fixed a handkerchief around his face. He flicked open his jacket, his hand straying upwards to the leather holster concealed under his armpit.

"We don't like old farts trying it on." The first of the young men now stood erect, revealing both more age, and size, than the Major had original thought. His eyes glinted an indeterminate blue-grey as friendly as the North Atlantic in a storm. "So just in case you haven't got the message we thought we'd just rough you up a bit." They now encircled him, "Is that alright with you?"

The Major prepared to sell his honour dearly. Against three young men at the peak of fitness he stood as much chance as a pea in a whistle factory. His attempt to pull the knife was foiled before it had been made.

They dumped him on a bench outside the now closed gates when they'd finished, and walked off. He couldn't move; he sat for nearly half an hour trying to get his breath and dabbing at a split lip which kept re-opening every time he snarled at his own thoughts.

He'd been taken for a ride, fooled like a tyro and beaten up and down until his ribs ached like toothache. He vowed vengeance on them, Richards, his son, and anyone else that came into his mind. They hadn't said they were connected to the man but he was the only one who knew he, Madogan, would be in Scotby today.

Eventually he limped back to his car, only to discover that he'd lost his keys. He stood gazing about him hopelessly for a minute or two, and decided they must have fallen out during the fight.

Having to retrace his steps and then finding the gates closed was bad enough; climbing over the fence to rescue them was difficult in his rather battered state. But being held at bay by a large Alsatian while the owner of the yard called the police and accused him of trespassing, finished his day in real style. He was not a happy man.

Madogan had protested his innocence to no avail. It was difficult, if not impossible, to explain how he had come to be in the timber yard. He was finding it equally difficult to explain his rather assaulted appearance without going into details he was reluctant to disclose.

"I thought my keys had fallen from my pocket in here. Look man, three youths dragged me in here, beat me up in your yard, and then slung me out onto the footpath." He was trying to rein in his temper. The owner of the yard was a good ten years younger and ten stone heavier, never mind the slavering dog which appeared to have teeth all the way down to its stomach, and was quite happy to display every one for Madogan's perusal.

"Why should they do that?"

"For God's sake, I don't know. The youth of today do what they bloody well please as far as I can tell, I only came for my keys. Do I look like I want to steal your wood?"

"Well you don't look respectable to me." He'd cast a scathing look over the Major's person and, telling the dog to guard, had fished out his mobile and punched in 999.

194

The police, when they arrived, had been equally unimpressed, especially as no car keys had been discovered in the yard to support his story. The Major, seemingly unable to describe the villains of the peace, or his reasons for being in Scotby as well, they had suggested he might like to tell his story again for the benefit of a stenographer. It was clear that it wasn't so much a suggestion as an order, so that he had, perforce, gone with them.

Elizabeth was enjoying herself immensely; she didn't get the opportunity to spend time with motherly women very often. Indeed she would have resisted this opportunity if Sarah's methods of mothering hadn't been so natural. They'd abandoned the two men in the garden. Bob had come round the back tugging her after him, and she'd seen the older couple sitting out on the lawn. They reminded her of those best grandparent ornaments you got at the seaside she thought and hid her grin.

Sarah had stood up at their quiet entrance, coming over and leading Elizabeth into the welcome shade of the kitchen. "Go and keep Sandy company Bob, while we make a cuppa." And that had been all the introduction she'd had.

McInnis had discovered Sandy lounging in a deck chair with the sports paper laid over his chest. He was in old gardening trousers, a polo shirt, and an old hat pulled low so that two reddened faun's ears was all that could be seen of the top of the older man's face. He appeared a trifle unshaven with the gingery brown hairs glinting on his chin in the sunlight, quivering slightly like cactus hairs in a zephyr, as he emitted small squeaks as he slept. McInnis grinned and sat down in Sarah's recently vacated seat, stealing the rest of the paper from the grass at Sandy's feet.

Sarah had exchanged smiles as she looked up at Elizabeth while she put a straw hat onto a hook on the back door. The last owner had obviously been a donkey by the holes in it thought Elizabeth. "Well and aren't you a bonny lass then?" It had been the opening salvo in a stream of words directed at Elizabeth. "Yon man is hopeless at describing people. Everyone sounds like a police suspect by the time he's finished."

This left Elizabeth wondering exactly how Sandy had described her to his wife. "Well at least you got a description; all Bob said was that I'd like you." She smiled at the small round person in front of her. "I think he was right too."

They looked each other over. Then Elizabeth said, "You really don't mind me coming?" She paused, "You could hardly say, even if you did, could you?"

"Of course I didn't mind, there's always plenty, and Bob doesn't visit half often enough." Sarah led the way through to a spacious and very clean kitchen. The taps sparkled in the late afternoon sunshine, the stainless steel draining board gleamed, and the air was redolent of fresh cake.

Sarah filled the kettle and fastened a gingham apron about her person while she continued to chat about Bob, and how his father had become Sandy's partner, then Sandy had become Bob's.

"I'm just going to pop a few scones in the oven for tea." She set a mug in front of Elizabeth. "Do you drink that while I get the things out." Sarah was a shrewd as well as an intelligent woman. If Bob had left his Elizabeth alone with her it meant he wanted her to say something important. She'd noticed the slight strain around his eyes when they arrived and the subtle degree of tension between the young couple.

"I always like to use a little of Sandy's beer in wholemeal scones, helps them rise and gives them a nice flavour." Sarah's hands moved gently through the flour, mixing fat in while she watched the girl. She allowed the conversation to run along cookery lines until she'd got the tray ready and in the oven, then she sat down herself and, nursing her own cup, said, "So tell me what the problem is between you and Bob my dear?"

Elizabeth took a deep breath and looked at the smiling woman across the table. "Am I that obvious?"

196

"Only to someone who's been there and knows, dear. It's hard to love them and not be able to protect them." Sarah smiled wryly, "The magazines, they go on about the empty nest syndrome and how women can feel free when the children are gone. You're supposed to be free to do what you like." She gave a gurgle of laughter, "What would I want to be free for?" Her face lit up as she heard Sandy's voice outside. "He's awake."

"Yeah!" Elizabeth smiled back, and then sighed, "But it's rather scary, and I don't know if he loves me." In the way of women they decoded the pronouns perfectly well.

"My dear," Sarah reached across and took her hands, "the boy's besotted with you. You're the only girl he's ever brought to tea and the only one he's risked his career for."

"How?" Elizabeth was startled.

Sarah shook her head. "Ask him yourself. I can tell you facts love. Like the hours and the loneliness, and bringing the children up when their father isn't around to help. I can talk about the gut wrenching fear. And yes I still worry for my Sandy." She nodded her head towards the partially open door and the men outside. "But I love him and that's all that matters. Better the years I've had than no years."

Elizabeth returned the pressure of the hands. "Oh! How lovely, thank you." She offered a rather shy smile.

In the garden, Sandy had snorted himself awake and had scratched his head under the hat with his right hand before pushing it back and opening sleepy eyes. He surveyed his partner with a little surprise. "Hello Bob, I thought you had a date with Elizabeth?" He raised an eyebrow as he transferred the hand to his chin and scratched that too. "Should have shaved, always leaves me itchy." He picked up the paper and dropped it on the ground at his feet, pushing himself into a more upright position.

"Oh! Beth's in the kitchen with Sarah. I thought we'd come to tea."

Sandy Bell was no fool either. He cast a glance at the opened back door and then looked back at his partner. "Trouble in paradise lad?" It was a gentle question; Bob knew he didn't have to answer and that Sandy wasn't prying. Nevertheless he hesitated slightly.

First he rubbed his thick brown hair into disorder then he rubbed the hand over his face, then he looked at Sandy. "Not exactly, but we do have a problem. I rather wondered if Sarah could put the woman's point of view and help me out." He rubbed the back of his neck as Sandy continued to look at him silently.

"Want to talk, or leave it to Sarah?"

"She'll fill you in anyway Sandy."

"Now there you're wrong lad. If Sarah thinks it's private, my lass will keep her own counsel." He sat back, relaxed, and waited.

Bob took a breath, unconsciously accepting the paternal role Sandy had assumed, and beginning to talk about his problem.

As the sun was turning the horizon to a fiery glow Sarah called the men in from the garden. Bob found Elizabeth setting the table with a pretty white cloth with embroidered daisies on it. He stole a kiss and received a sweet smile in reply, but they didn't talk then.

Conversation was kept to generalities while they ate the delicious scones and chocolate cake on offer and then, just as they'd reached the full and contented stage over final cups of tea, Bob's pager went off.

He looked across at Sandy, shrugging.

"Use the hall phone. See if we're both needed lad."

Sandy pushed his chair back and stood up at the same time as Bob. "I'll just run the shaver over my chin, in case," he addressed his wife and she twinkled back at him, then transferred her smile to Elizabeth. "Such is life love; we'll wash up and then walk the dog if the men have to go out," she paused, "unless you want me to run you back home." She looked across at Elizabeth, her head on one side, waiting.

"I'd love to walk the dog with you." It was acceptance of all that Sarah had told her about being a policeman's wife. Bob coming back into the room was a little surprised to get a rather stunning kiss from Beth. He stepped back but kept a firm hold of her. "Hmm! That was nice." He lifted his brows, "I have to go love, will you be alright? You can take my car and I'll get a lift with Sandy." He proffered his keys.

"No, I'm going for a walk with Sarah; I'll be here when you get back."

He gave her a rather quizzical look. "I don't know when that will be Beth. Are you sure?"

Beth looked squarely at him. "Yes Bob, I'm very sure."

They stood holding each other, unaware of their audience as they read the unspoken messages each had offered the other. Bob finally sighed deeply and leaned in for another of those searing kisses. "I'll see you later then darling and perhaps you can explain."

Sandy, aside from asking: "Want me too?", hadn't spoken until they were seated in the car speeding towards the town centre in the gathering dusk.

"So what we caught then Bob?"

"We've caught Dennis?"

"Have we Begod!" Sandy gave a low whistle. "Doing anything illegal was he?"

"Oh yeah! It appears your message about watching for stolen goods has got through to the troops Sandy. Seems like Dennis was trying to fence a few pieces of expensive electrical equipment in a pub. The idiot tried to sell one to an off duty constable, who very naturally wondered how he came to have several unboxed specimens in the back seat of his car."

"Hmm, that's Dennis for you." Sandy flashed a grin at Bob McInnis and then hummed quietly to himself, giving a slightly off key rendition of a popular song. As he drew up in the yard Bob finally managed to put a name to it. 'Mad dogs and Englishmen go out in the midday sun'.

Dennis was sitting in interview room one looking gloomily into a mug of brown liquid on the table in front of him. Gareth was standing at ease next to the door, his short shirt sleeves, displaying his muscles in a gently threatening way, his flak jacket opened half way as a concession to the early summer heat.

Sandy and Bob McInnis came in bringing mugs of their own particular poison, nodding at Gareth as they passed him to take seats opposite the disgruntled purveyor of dubious property. Sandy switched on the recorder and gave details of the date, time and persons present before looking at Dennis Little seated in the regulation blue of the prison uniform.

"What were you thinking about Dennis trying to give a constable stolen goods?"

Dennis had been considering his options. He was much happier when he'd been coached with the most likely line of questions and answers. There hadn't been time for any coaching, and Mr Barker was going to be very cross.

He'd decided not to say anything, believing that they couldn't convict him if he didn't admit to anything. But he knew Inspector Bell could be sneaky, so he wasn't sure a policy of masterly silence would help. After a brief glance at the two Inspectors he therefore returned his gaze to his mug and waited.

Bell had also considered his options; a charge of handling stolen goods wasn't going to get more than twenty-four hours in the local lock up before the man was out on bail again. If they could put him away a bit longer maybe Cavendish would talk. Then again now they'd got him maybe they could find out just what Barker had been up to lately.

Bell sipped tea and prepared his opening shot. He and Bob McInnis had agreed that he'd be the better man at handling Dennis Little, as he said, he'd got used to getting inside the man's head. Whereupon McInnis had shuddered, "Personally I wouldn't want to get inside that head Sandy."

The two men therefore sat quietly waiting. As Sandy said later, you could almost see Dennis' one neuron giving a synapse a nervous elbow and suggesting Dennis get himself out of there quick, before they found out what else he'd been up to and he got into even more trouble.

"So Dennis, would you like to make yourself uncomfortable and tell us why you had all that highly transportable equipment in the boot of your car?"

Dennis looked up, encountered the twinkle in Sandy's eye that said his goose was cooked, and transferred his gaze to Bob McInnis. McInnis was the recipient of a very nervous look. "I want to make a phone call."

"But of course you do, Dennis." Sandy turned his head and looked at Gareth standing blank faced in front of the door.

"What were you thinking about Constable not to allow this man his rights? He wants to make a phone call." Gareth turned a fulminating eye on the amused one of his boss.

"Mr Little was offered the opportunity sir. He denied wishing to avail himself of that facility." The air crackled with righteous indignation.

"Now I wonder why you didn't want to phone before Dennis."

Dennis, having watched the by-play, was grinning. Serve the copper right, he hoped he got into trouble. Dennis hadn't quite forgiven Gareth for the dressing down Mr Barker had given him a couple of weeks before. He therefore wasn't thinking carefully when he answered. "Didn't know it was gonna be you Inspector did I?"

"But that's not kind Dennis, I like you. I came in to work especially to talk to you." Dennis, caught between a glowering constable and the friendly face of the Inspector, responded to the smile.

"I need to phone Mr Barker."

"Of course you do, he's your boss after all isn't he?"

"Yeah and I want him to get me a solicitor."

"Och! That's fine Dennis. I'll get the phone for you. But if Mr Barker's not in, that's your phone call gone and you'll have to stay here until tomorrow. Are you sure you don't want to phone a solicitor direct?" The sentence was delivered with apparently real sympathy. "Of course you could always just talk to us and phone whenever you want."

Dennis suspecting a trick, but not seeing where, shook his head. "No I wants to phone now, he'll tell me what to do."

"Very well. But once you've phoned we can't talk to you until he arrives and that could take some time. You could be home before dark if you just offer us an explanation."

Dennis scowled ferociously in thought; he didn't find decision making easy at the best of times, and this wasn't the best of times. "Well alright if you say so Inspector Bell." He said it slowly and cautiously.

Bell was too wise to allow triumph to show. "So Dennis, what's this about goods in your car."

"It was like this Inspector, I wus down the scrap yard and I thought I might make a bit extra, stripping out old stereos and selling them in the pub."

"Well that explains the stereos then Dennis." Sandy cast an eye down pretending to read the list of goods found in the car. "Where did you find the DVDs then?"

"Oh I got them off'n a mate, they wus fire damaged."

"And the Portable TVs were they fire damaged too?"

"Oh yes Inspector Bell. Lotta fire damaged stuff."

"Hmm! And you were just selling them to make a bit of extra cash you say. Did Mr Barker know about it?"

Dennis opened his mouth, then closed it again quickly. His boss didn't like being implicated in anything shady. He had been warned about that. He flexed and cracked his finger joints absently as he struggled to find the best answer and the watching men winced.

"T'weren't nufing to do wiv Mr Barker. I wus just trying to make a little extra on the side."

"Then do you really want him to know that you've been brought in?" Bell was thinking, the longer they could keep Barker in ignorance the more unfiltered information they could get.

"Er, he's me boss." Dennis shot another very nervous look at McInnis, who was frankly puzzled. He'd never had dealings with him, and the thug had no reason to be nervous. Or any more nervous than usual when confronted by the law.

"Can you tell us the name of this mystery man who supplied you with the fire damaged goods then? Just so that we know it was legit'."

"'E was just a bloke I met in a pub."

"Ah! One of those men who appear like rabbits out of a hat, and disappear like Scotch mist. Pull the other one man." McInnis glowered at Dennis, trying to gauge the man's fear and its reason.

"Now, now, Bob, people do sell you things in pubs. Dennis is a fine example of free enterprise." Bell bestowed a look of approval on Dennis, who looked a bit startled. He wasn't used to approval from people in positions of authority.

"Rubbish Sandy, he's just doing what Barker wants him to, and taking the blame and the prison sentence when he's caught doing the man's dirty work."

"Mr Barker's my boss. He says he'll look after me if I do anyfing against the law."

"And just how's he going to do that Dennis?" Sandy asked the question in a bright voice.

"He says he knows a good solicitor." Dennis' brain caught up with his mouth which hung open for a minute, treating the two inspectors to a fine display of gold caps. They watched as a couple of brain cells conferred. "Not that I done anyfing wrong." Dennis' mouth shut again.

"So what do you do for Mr Barker then Dennis?" Sandy slid the question in silkily.

"I run's errands for him, and I..." Dennis scowled. Sandy didn't however take his expression amiss; he knew this indicated deep thought on the part of the other man. "And I fetches things for him, and I looks after people for him." The expression on his face wasn't particularly nice now.

"Like you looked after Tomas Cavendish? Did you do that for Mr Barker?"

"I never laid a finger on him. I only walked him home."

"Did I say you'd done differently Dennis?" Sandy cast a glance at Bob who was making entirely spurious notes, since they had the recorder running. "Just check what Cavendish had to say will you Bob?"

McInnis flipped through some notes and turned to a page of shorthand at random. "No he doesn't say you laid a finger on him Dennis." His tone implied that Cavendish said Dennis had laid other things on him though.

"I deny's it. It weren't me what beat him up Tuesday."

"Who says he was beaten up on Tuesday Dennis?"

"I dunno but it weren't me." Bob's nose twitched; Dennis was beginning to sweat. Dennis believed in deodorant; he believed you needed half a bottle a day for it to be effective and to attract girls. He hadn't quite figured out why it wasn't working yet, but he'd seen the ads on the TV. It was bound to work soon.

Sandy watched Dennis with contrived sympathy for a minute, waiting for him to relax, then threw in a curve ball. "So we can't charge you with the GBH, but these goods you got from a man in a pub, now we know they were stolen Dennis. We can charge you with receiving and selling them. Do you think Mr Barker will look after you for doing something he didn't tell you to do?"

"I tell you I didn't nick them."

"Yeah I heard you Dennis." McInnis looked across at Gareth, a fascinated listener. "Lock him up Constable and if he doesn't like it add resisting to the sheet." Gareth came forward and gripped Dennis firmly round his arm; it was like taking hold of a cobra ready to strike, and Gareth would have been the first to admit he didn't care for snakes.

Sandy looked at the bewildered member of the ungodly. Dennis was still trying to catch up with recent events. "I should go quietly lad; our constable is still upset at the telling off I gave him, and he's on his own ground now."

Dennis Little looked speculatively at Gareth, who did his best to look as though he'd break a few rules if he could.

"I don't suppose you'd like to tell us who "came in" on that occasion and where you were would you Dennis?"

Dennis threw a guilty glance at Bob but shook his head. "I wants to make me phone call. Mr Barker will see I'm alright."

Sandy looked across at Gareth, "Arrange that would you Constable, and then lock him up."

They watched as the baffled man was led away; he wasn't quite sure how the turn of events had led to him being locked up. He wasn't happy, but he showed a touching faith in Barker's power to get him a solicitor and get him off.

Sandy waited until the door closed behind him. He watched Bob as he got up and opened a window. "We can't prove it, but it was definitely Dennis' handiwork that saw Cavendish in the hospital. I'll work on him a bit more after he's been locked up over night, see if we can't get him to admit something for a lighter sentence." McInnis nodded as he came and sat down, leaning back in his chair.

"Why was he so scared of me Sandy? I've never interviewed him before. He doesn't know me and I wasn't exactly being nasty. Besides he was nervous long before I opened my mouth."

"Yeah I noticed. Know what I think Bob?" Sandy ran a hand over his face. "I think he saw you at the Prof's house the day you got that crack on the head. In fact I think he gave it to you, not knowing you were a copper."

"That's a hell of a leap Sandy."

"Yeah, I know," Sandy rubbed his face again, "but I do know him. He's a bit thick is Dennis. He lets others do his thinking for him whenever possible, but he doesn't hit coppers, he knows that's just plain stupid. And he's only just made you as a copper."

"We assumed that whoever hit me knew me for a copper." Bob raised an eyebrow.

"Because no-one else should have had access to the house yet! But would Dennis have worked that out?"

"Depends if he was doing the casing for Barker or off his own bat I suppose."

"Dennis hasn't got the gumption to set fire to the place though Bob." Sandy frowned. "We don't seem to be getting very far." He shrugged, "I'm going home to sleep on it, how about you? It's," he glanced at his watch, "nearly half eight, let's go and rescue your Elizabeth before she eats all the chocolate cake."

They gathered their jackets and walked through the relative quiet of the main office. Sandy had his hand on the swing doors as a burly policeman in his fifties approached. The two Inspectors stepped back to allow him to enter; he was followed by Madogan who was sandwiched by an equally tough looking constable whose bald head made him look even tougher.

"Thank God! A friendly face." Madogan looked at Bob McInnis with something approaching friendliness. He stopped so abruptly that the bald headed one nearly bumped into him.

"Could you tell these goons I'm a respectable businessman Inspector McInnis?"

Bob looked him up and down, taking in the dishevelled appearance of his clothes, the fat lip, and the large contusion on his forehead. "Have you checked him for a knife lads? I've seen it in a leather holster under his left armpit."

Madogan twitched out of the light restraint, turning and scowling blackly at McInnis, "It's legal you fool," he snarled.

The leading constable, with a cautious eye on the Major's hands, frisked him and came out with the knife. "You really should have told us about this sir when we asked you if you had anything on you we should know about."

"You didn't need to know about it." Madogan was going red in the face.

"What's he done then?" Sandy addressed the senior of the two men and ignored the Major's invective and vicious look as he continued to protest his innocence in spite of the evidence to the contrary.

"Suspected B&E sir."

"Breaking and entering and with a concealed weapon, you were looking for trouble weren't you sir." He smiled sardonically. "Have a nice night sir." He tipped an imaginary hat and held the door open for Bob, who sauntered through, hands in pockets, totally ignoring Madogan. Sandy followed. "Phew! Well we know Dennis didn't do that one. I wonder what the other guy looked like and why they fought. Looks like our suspects are piling up in the cells Bob."

9

Bob McInnis had driven Elizabeth home in a bit of a daze. The welcoming kiss had more than met his dreams; he wasn't sure what Sarah had said, but he resolved to buy her the biggest box of chocolates he could find as a thank you.

"So did you save the world for yet another day?" They were sitting close together on the settee in the downstairs room of her father's house. The teapot was nearly empty and Bob had snuck a possessive arm around her waist. Elizabeth leaned back as she asked the question so that she could place a soft kiss on his face. "You need a shave Bob." She rubbed the offending cheek gently.

"Mmm." Bob McInnis turned his head to plant a kiss on the questing hand. He was enjoying his small miracle; that afternoon he'd thought he'd lost her. Strangely it made him think of the research and the character Peter. He could appreciate the man's desire to end things after he'd lost his girl. It went against his own upbringing and beliefs, but he could understand how the man had come to feel that way.

Suddenly he stiffened. "Hell!"

Elizabeth was startled; one minute she'd been enjoying his total attention, the next he was bolt upright on the settee fumbling for his phone in his pocket. "What did I do?" she watched as he searched and found a number.

Bob, recalled to the company he was keeping, transferred the ringing phone to the other ear and leaned over. "You didn't do a thing. I love you." He kissed her briefly and transferred his attention to the phone as it spoke in his ear.

Elizabeth sat, more than a little stunned. It wasn't the declaration of her dreams certainly, and her beloved fool was now concentrating on the telephone to the exclusion of everything else.

"Sandy, I don't know what it signifies but the Peter of the research… he died. He couldn't have been our Peter's father. What's

208

more I've just remembered where we heard about the Society of Friends. Neville attended the meeting house, he was a Quaker, and so was his father. One of the women we interviewed said so."

He listened quietly for a minute. "I'm not sure; I'm going in to read the rest of that research, even if I have to stay up all night." He listened some more, his head to the side and a smile flickering in his eyes, then with a brief, "Bye." snapped the little machine closed and turned to Elizabeth. "Sandy says I'm a fool to be thinking of work when I've got a pretty girl in my arms," he grinned, "and he's right."

The pretty girl in question however had been listening to the phone conversation and now shook her head. They had discussed the research, naturally, but not the latest section. The afternoon had been taken up with their own lives.

"Fill me in on the way darling, I'm coming in with you," she hesitated, "if I can?"

"A girl in a million." Bob stole a kiss to take her breath away, and pulled her up from the settee. "Let's go."

They arrived as the shift was changing. McInnis led Elizabeth through the busy building to his office.

"Wow that's an arrest I'd like to make!" It was said fairly quietly by a ginger haired denizen of the law.

"I heard that Joe." McInnis grinned wolfishly at a passing copper, holding firmly to a blushing Elizabeth as they passed the equally red-faced constable.

He showed her into the relative quiet of his office, shutting the door and the buzz of speculation firmly behind him.

He went round the desk, sitting down and booting up the second computer that now occupied far too much space on the desk. Elizabeth stood, taking in the slightly dusty room and the wilting plant. McInnis watched her for a minute.

"Did you mean it Bob?"

Bob McInnis wasn't a fool either. He might have committed himself in a moment, but it was commitment for a lifetime. "Oh yes! I love you Beth." He smiled the sweet smile she loved and rarely saw, then nodded at the seat normally occupied by Sandy and the pile of paper in front of it. "That's how much I've read so far. Do you want the screen or the hard copy?"

"I'll catch up while you read the screen." Elizabeth sat down, gathering the papers into a neat stack and working through them until she reached the place she'd last been reading.

Bob watched her bend her head to the task and bestowed a loving look on her, then turned his mind to the computer and its data, scrolling down to the relevant passage.

Hans looked at the men surrounding him; he could see them talking but he couldn't understand a word they said. His eyes went from one moving mouth to the next. He realised it wasn't just the words that were strange; they seemed to be arriving through a fog too.

The first soldier to speak had approached him somewhat warily; Hans remained on the ground. He offered no resistance when they pulled him roughly up onto his feet and addressed another string of words to him.

"Can you no understand me man, what's tha' name?"

Hans shook his head.

"He's out o' it Tommy. Look at his heid. He's had a clout on it fit t' addle his brain."

"Aye." The second soldier, addressed as Tommy, bent in his pack and pulled out a field dressing. He too approached warily, "A'll just tie thee heid oop man, alraight?"

Hans watched them, his eyes darting from one grimy face to another. Then as the soldier with the field dressing approached closer he relaxed slightly; field dressings he understood. The dressing was applied none too gently; Hans hadn't realised he was wounded until the bandage was pulled tight, then a searing pain shot across his eyes and he collapsed down to the ground again, out cold.

He came round to find he was surrounded by soldiers. They wore an odd mixture of uniforms. He lay still, trying to work out where he was. He certainly wasn't in a field dressing station, of that he was very sure. The smell was still that of the battlefield.

He surreptitiously felt the ground next to him. He was on a rough blanket placed directly on the earth; he could feel the cold seeping through, along with a faint throbbing. The timber uprights had been roughly hewed, and the lighting was supplied by candles stuck into the walls, and a couple of oil lamps. Ammunition boxes were being used as tables and chairs, and several large howitzer rounds were neatly stacked against the far wall.

A poilu, spots of red showing through the dirt and mud of his French private's uniform, came over at the slight groan that escaped as he moved. He was addressed in French; he knew a little of the language but found he could hardly hear the speaker.

"Voules-vous de l'eau?" Hans was raised slightly and a water bottle was offered. He drank deeply of the slightly brackish fluid. "Quel est votre nomme Soldat?"

Hans shook his head; he touched his ears and shook his head again.

The Frenchman laid him gently down and went over to a group of soldiers standing watching. Hans watched them talking but couldn't make out the words. One of them broke away and came across. Addressing him in German he asked, "Wie ist ihr Name? Ihre Einheit?"

Hans looked at the man blankly. What was a German doing in company with a Frenchman, and why had a group of English soldiers brought him to them? Visions of torture passed across his

211

mind in a mad and macabre dance, inducing an almost bowel watering panic.

Another of the group came over; he'd spoken to the German in that language then knelt down beside Hans. "Look mate we don't care what country you come from, we just want to help, OK?" Hans looked at him, patiently waiting to see what he would do next. He had neither energy, not inclination, to react, both being sapped by the head injury and grief as he remembered what had happened to Peter.

"Now take it easy mate. I'm just going to look in your pocket." He stretched out a hand and took hold of the lapel of his own jacket and mimed taking something out and looking at it, and then putting it back, then gently took hold of Hans borrowed jacket.

Hans watched him, resigned to his fate. He could see no immediate threat to his life but, in truth, at that moment would have welcomed a period to it. His head was throbbing viciously and he felt sick.

Even as he thought it he struggled to rise and relieve his stomach. The English soldier must have realised something of the cause of his sudden movement because he quickly moved a tin bowl with some bloody bandages under Hans' nose and helped him to sit while he threw up the water so recently enjoyed.

He released Hans, who leaned back on his elbow watching the Englishman. He then opened Hans' jacket and took out the papers and dog tags he found there. Hans looked at Peter's wallet and the red and green discs. He wasn't sure what would happen next; he'd got an Englishman's possessions on him and he was a German.

"He's English, Border regiment." The soldier had spoken from his kneeling position next to Hans; Hans heard his voice reasonably from that close. "His name's Peter Neville. I don't think he can hear us. Happen the blast's done for his ears, poor sod."

212

Hans sagged back onto the thin grey blanket, stunned at their conclusions and too frightened to deny them.

"Lookee lad, can you hear us a bit?" The Englishman was speaking to him again. Hans nodded cautiously.

He tried to speak the pure English his mother had insisted upon ever since he'd been born. He heard the soft echo of her voice. "You might have a German father my son, but you owe allegiance to God and England too." Later she'd told him it was good for them both; she missed hearing her native tongue spoken, and conversing with her son in that language was one of the delights of her life.

"Where am I?" The others looked relieved when he spoke. He thought his own voice sounded strange; but no stranger, he supposed, than those Englishmen around him.

"Northerner are ye lad. I'm Corporal Johnson, late of His Majesty's British army. These bonnie lads gathered me up a sennight ago." He held up his left hand where a stump protruded from his ratty jacket. "They fixed me up and now I'm fixing others up the same. You've nowt to fear." He watched as Hans' eyes looked beyond him to the group of mixed soldiery. "Dinna fret, I'll explain by and by. Rest a bit and then we'll talk some more."

Hans was allowed to sleep again after that. After their fashion the soldiers had been kind to him, feeding him a curious broth of bully beef to start with. When he'd managed to sit up without the world spinning like a merry go round, a proper sandwich of German brockworst had been thrust at him by the German soldier who'd first spoken to him. Hans had eaten it gratefully.

The French had even offered him a Gaulois from a packet so dirty and battered Vercingetorix could barely be distinguished on the blue front. He'd refused and had caught the look of relief on the soldier's face; evidently cigarettes were a cherished commodity. However his refusal had cemented the idea that he was an

Englishman. He heard them saying only the English could be so picky at such a time.

He hadn't spoken much for the first three days, frightened of giving away just who and what he was. They seemed to be friendly enough. They supplied him with a pair of British army trousers, though where from he didn't know, and hadn't dared to ask. They were blood soaked down one leg but he was grateful for their warmth. From snatches of conversation they worried a little about being found out of their own uniforms and shot as spies.

He thought it was a minor worry when they were obviously fraternising with the enemy, but he wasn't going to talk and risk anything himself until he'd had a chance to find out a bit more.

On the third evening he'd woken from a fitful doze to find the Englishman with the strange accent beside him. "Hello lad, remember me?"

Hans nodded.

"Is the hearing any better?"

"A bit, you come from a long way off."

Corporal Johnson bent his head in acknowledgement, then raised his voice a bit. "If you're lucky it'll recover all the way. Speaking loud enough am I?"

Hans nodded again. "Where are we?"

"Well if you'd got your hearing you'd know, you'd hear the big guns going. You're still on the Somme lad. This is a German fox hole. The pumps are keeping it dry just now, but we daren't run them all the time. That entrance over there leads to a section of trench but it's deserted just now." He shrugged. "We found a couple of poor buggers dying in it, and one confused German out of his mind."

"We're aye deserters here lad. Some of us were rescued like you and me, some of 'em just had enough and walked away from the guns, some of them like that poor bludy German are so addled in their mind they don't know if it's Christmas or Tuesday." Hans watched his lips as the Corporal spoke, hearing most of the words even if some of them were strange to him.

"Now lad," the soldier continued, "there's a route out of here if tha' wants to take it." He shrugged again. "'Am still undecided, mysen. The lads will take ye to yer own lines if that's yer fancy, or out o' t' country and back to blighty if that's what y'd rather do?" He shrugged again. "If ye go home ye might be sent back here to fight again, if ye go to the lines they might shoot ye for a deserter, or just reunite ye with yer regiment. It depends. A'll leave yer to think on it." He stood up, looking down at the seated Hans. "Don't take too long thinking aye, we mun move out soon, there's a unit of Germans headed back to this sector."

Hans spent the rest of the evening leaning back against a mud wall, watching the men around him efficiently packing up everything transportable and useful in sight. He could stay behind in the trench and the Germans would find him. He could go back to Germany; he wouldn't have to fight, they wouldn't force him too. He could leave this mad house and go back to being a medic there. He looked down at the British khakis he wore; they might shoot and ask questions later though.

He didn't think he could admit he wasn't English so they'd think it funny him wanting to stay where he was; they might turn nasty. The trouble was these men thought he was English; they would deliver him to the English lines. The English might shoot him as a spy or, worse, imprison him. He barely suppressed a shudder at the thought.

If he went to England wouldn't he be shot anyway? Or enlisted? Peter had said they were calling up every man they could. He had heard the Society of Friends had hidden a few men after the

215

government had imprisoned some conscientious objectors on Dartmoor. Maybe they would hide him; he'd go to his mother's people in England and see.

His decision made Hans pushed himself up so that he half stood; this close to the wall there was only room for a half grown midget. His eyes searched and found Corporal Johnson on the far side of the widish den. He moved across slightly unsteadily so that he could stand upright and speak to the senior man. "I would like to go home."

"Fine lad, I'll talk to the lads." And that had been that. He'd been shipped back via a small fishing village on the coast, and landed by some Belgium peasants on a deserted stretch of beach he'd later found out was the Yorkshire coast. Corporal Johnson and a taciturn private named Draycott had accompanied him.

"They'll happen think you're in ma' unit lad when they see ma' stump, and that way mebbe there'll be few questions asked."

McInnis breathed deeply. "My God, the man was taking a hell of a chance." He looked across at Elizabeth. "How far have you got?"

"He's just discovered 'Peter' in the trench."

"I'll go and fetch us both a cuppa while you get to where I am." Bob came round the desk and in passing dropped a kiss on her ebony hair. "I won't be long. OK?"

"Fine." Elizabeth spoke almost absently as she turned back to the pages in front of her.

McInnis decided not to take her attitude the wrong way, and quietly left the room on his self imposed errand.

When he returned with two pottery mugs which steamed as he set them down on the desk she was sitting in his chair behind the desk. "Hey, you have to pay for that privilege."

"What privilege?" Elizabeth looked up at him and caught sight of his grin as he advanced around the desk.

"Didn't you know it was enforceable by law, anyone sitting in a police officer's seat has to give said policeman a kiss?"

"Oh yeah! Says you!" She wrinkled her nose at him as he arrived at her side, and was then pulled upright and soundly kissed for her inelegant comments.

He turned his attention to the screen, noting where she'd scrolled to. "Finish that bit and then we'll drink our tea and read the rest together."

He sat down, pulling her onto his lap and cuddling her as she scrolled down the rest of the page. "You need your cardigan, you're cold."

"Oh is that why you've got your arms around me?"

"Could be." He held her lightly, waiting for her to finish reading.

"Want to find out what happens next?" He'd heard her indrawn breath and saw she'd reached the same place in the narrative as he had.

"You bet!"

They bent their heads and began to read again, Elizabeth doing the honours with the mouse as they followed the story.

The trip across the moors in the company of the Corporal and Private had been a bit dreamlike to Hans. Johnson repeatedly and naturally called him Peter. At first he was slow to answer to that name, indeed he found himself looking around once or twice to find Peter, only to realise he, himself, was being addressed.

He supposed that Corporal Johnson had put it down to his faulty hearing, thank God. They had gone to a relative of the Corporal's who had found them some other clothes, then the Private had disappeared for a couple of weeks, only to return suddenly and as closed mouthed as the proverbial clam. Hans was still very weak from the head wound and a doctor, who had come to check on Johnson's stump, had examined him as well and pronounced him unfit to return to the front.

Travel papers had come from somewhere; he hadn't questioned their appearance, just been grateful. He had lodged with the Johnsons on their upland sheep farm for several weeks, recovering his strength and helping wherever he could. It seemed to him that the English were struggling as hard to maintain their land as the German peasants were.

Eventually a day had come in late November when the Corporal had taken him for a stroll to the sheep pens and spoken to him seriously. "Lookee lad we've got a letter from the Doctor for you. Thou are't known for a fellow soldier of mine so tha' can stay here if tha' wants or go to yr ain folk. Yr fit to travel now and it's nigh to Christmas."

Hans had nodded, thinking. He was as safe as he would be until this war ended, hidden away on this remote farm. But these good people deserved to know the truth. He'd waited to speak until they had had supper that evening and were gathered around the big open fireplace.

He sat on a small three legged stool, hands dangling between his legs, and inhaled deeply of the wood smoke and pungent oil lamp fumes, gathering courage. "I must thank you. You have been so good to me that I feel it right to tell you the truth, and trust you to do what you think right by your consciences." He watched them nod.

The aunt and uncle of Johnson were old. Or maybe just worn out, their faces nut brown and seamed as walnuts as the oil lamp shadowed and flickered over their faces. Corporal Johnson continued looking at him, his half serious, half sad, face fixed upon Hans.

218

"I am German." He waited for their reactions in fear and trepidation, fixing his eyes on the leaping flames of the wood fire and praying fervently for their understanding.

"Aye lad we know." The uncle had spoken, his speech slow and careful as if speaking was an exercise he indulged in infrequently. "Tha' babbled a bit i' German our Fred said, but it were bit's o' the Bible."

Hans sat with his hands between his legs. What did he say now? He was their enemy and they had fed and clothed him, concealed him and lied for him.

Fred Johnson spoke after a lengthy pause. "It were on the boat tha' understand, tha' kept asking 'Peter' if he were alraight." He paused again, "Happen y' could tell us tha' story if tha' wants." He stopped again, exchanging a look with the older couple. "But tha' needn't, we'll none betray thee. And a meant what a said, tha' can stay here till this madness ends. Tha's a good man."

The soft voice of the Aunt spoke, "What would be your name then?"

Hans looked at her, seeing the gentle smile and the kindness in her eyes. "My name is Hans Erkel, Peter was my cousin. He was an Englishman. I didn't know what to do." He stopped, impossible to explain the conditions that obtained on the western front to those who'd never seen it. He glanced slightly desperately between Fred Johnson sitting on the age blackened settle on the other side of the hearth, and at the silent Draycott sitting at the wooden table in the centre of the room.

"Nay lad dinna fret. Na', dost tha want to go to thy English relatives?"

It came to an abrupt end at that point. They looked at the screen in frustration.

"That's as far as Peter had got apparently."

"Damn!" The comment was heartfelt and Bob shifted slightly in his chair, readjusting Elizabeth's weight over his thighs. "Can you work out how it would have finished from the research?"

"I don't know Bob. I know the Professor was investigating across in the Cumberland fells. A hamlet called Stone Pot, wherever that might be."

"I know the Quakers sheltered some conscientious objectors during the war. I've to thank Higgs for that information." Bob grunted.

"The Society of Friends didn't lie, but they nevertheless kept people safe until the end of the war." Elizabeth smiled, shifting round so that she could look at his face better. "And from the research I've done on the First World War I have more than a little sympathy for them."

Bob shook his head. "A lawbreaker, that's who I've fallen for."

Elizabeth stood up, straightening her skirt as Bob reluctantly let her go and looked at his watch.

"It's nearly one o'clock. Your father will be worried about you; we ought to have rung him." Bob looked at her, feeling more than a little guilty.

"I'm a big girl now Bob, I can stay out until the wee small hours if I want to."

Bob eyed her slightly untidy appearance. "Yes, but he might think I... you...we..." He stopped, going slightly red.

Elizabeth found his embarrassment rather sweet but didn't quite know how to tell him that her father probably thought they were already sleeping together. "Don't worry so Bob." She laid a gentle hand on his cheek, "I love you too."

He smiled into her eyes and then said, "Come on I'll run you home. I'll talk to Sandy on Monday morning; I think this might give us a motive." He scooped up her cream cardigan and placed it round her shoulders, then took her hand as they went out of the office and down the stairs.

"I don't see how Bob. If it was his father Peter was talking about, and reading that story tonight I think that likely, and his father was really a German, so what? It wasn't Peter that did anything wrong."

"Well I suppose his father was technically an illegal immigrant."

"But his father is long dead. I just don't see how it can help us Bob."

"Nor do I darling, but I've got to look at every odd fact I find." He paused as they reached his car and he opened it for her. "If I can swing it with the solicitor Beth, will you come and work on the research in the office, see if you can find out what he was going to write? Officially, until probate you can't, but you'd be under police supervision." He grinned. "Me!"

"Yes alright Bob." She flashed him a smile as he shut her door and watched him walk round the bonnet and get in. "Why? Aren't I a suspect any longer Bob?"

Bob McInnis flashed her a smile as they drove down to the roundabout and circled it to head to the southern area of the town. "Who says you're not?"

"You'd hardly ask me to help if I was."

"Quite right my poppet." He drove past the twin, squat towers of the Citadel at the railway station and turned down the London Road. He glanced over, noted the frustration on her face and grinned, and then turned his attention back to the traffic.

"OK. Why am I no longer a suspect?" It was said with a huge sigh.

"Because you told Sandy and me how to light a pipe properly." He grinned again as he heard her muttered comment. It wasn't fitting for a lady to use words like that.

He felt the punch on his shoulder as he swung the car onto St Nicholas Bridge. "Alright," he sighed deeply and with a great deal of exaggeration. "Some people with their degrees!" It was a measure of how far they'd come that he could tease her, instead of worrying

221

about her degree. "You told us that the Professor always used matches to light his pipe. Therefore the can of lighter fuel we found had to have been brought to the house." He halted at the lights and looked across at the frowning girl sitting next to him.

"Now, if you'd brought it for the purpose of arson, you'd have said the Prof' used a lighter, which would have explained the presence of the can. But since," he pushed the gear lever down and moved the car forward, "you told us different, when you could have offered an explanation for it had you brought it, you didn't bring it. And if you didn't you aren't trying to conceal any research from us." He shot the car through another set of lights on amber and headed into the suburbs.

"It seemed obvious that the research was the target that day; nothing else was taken and we've been through that house a dozen times now. There isn't anything worth stealing that's worth the risk of hitting a copper around the head and antagonising the whole police force." He stretched out his hand and gripped hers for a moment. "But I didn't believe you were guilty a long time before that."

"Is that what Sarah meant when she said you'd risked your career for me."

"Ah!" Elizabeth felt the wave of embarrassment as Bob removed his hand and focused fixedly on the windscreen.

"Bob, I wasn't prying." Elizabeth's voice was quiet.

"No I don't suppose you were darling, and if I wanted Sarah to help I couldn't expect her not to mention things if I didn't tell her not to." This rather convoluted sentence brought the smile back to Elizabeth's face as nothing else would have done. Her Bob was always careful to say what he thought.

"Sandy wasn't too keen on me asking you for a date, in fact he thought it was a bit unethical."

"I'm glad you asked anyway Bob."

"So am I darling." Bob reached out a hand and grasped hers, drawing it to his mouth for a brief kiss before relaxing into his seat and concentrating on his driving again.

Bob wasn't quite so relaxed on Monday morning when Sandy sought him out. He was sitting at his desk drinking warm coffee and scribbling one-handed on a form.

"You didn't call back, so I take it the research is a wash out?" Sandy brought his own mug with him and came to sit down opposite the younger man.

"Well not exactly Sandy. I don't know if it helps but I'm sure the answer lies in this research." He set down the mug and brushed hair off his forehead.

"Tell me then lad, and I'll see if I can bring my age and experience to your aid." Sandy watched Bob's lips twitch wryly, and then settled back in his chair to give his undivided attention to the story that Bob had read on Saturday night.

"So what you're saying is that the Professor had a slightly off-white father who's been dead for twenty years. The Professor is telling this story, presumably for publication, and someone doesn't want him to." Sandy rubbed a finger under his nose, then picked up his empty mug and looked into it with a rather disgusted expression before setting it down again.

"Nope, I don't get it Bob. What could anyone be afraid of, unless it's a Pacifist Quaker suddenly turned savage at the thought he was going to reveal they'd hidden his dad all those years ago." Sandy looked, and sounded, mildly sarcastic.

"Well it's more of a bloody motive than we've had up to press." Bob was tired and frustrated. He'd spent the night chewing over all the facts again and this was the best he'd managed to come up with. "It's a pity the poor chap was murdered before he finished the book."

"It's a pity the poor chap was murdered at all Bob." Sandy looked at him with mild reproach.

"Yeah I know Sandy. My gut says the answer for that murder lies here." He rested his hand on the hard copy lying at the side of his desk.

"Well if someone didn't want this book published we need to find out who." He held up a hand as Bob would have spoken. "Let's get some more tea lad, I think better with a biscuit in my hand."

They scraped back their chairs and strolled out together, hands in trouser pockets and shirt sleeves rolled up as the June heat filtered through the building. As they eased their way along the busy corridor to the canteen Sandy looked across at his partner. "Sorted that little problem out with Elizabeth have you?"

"Oh! I intend to give your Sarah a big..." He stopped to hold open the door for a WPC.

"A big what?" Sandy eyed him suspiciously.

"A big box of chocolates what else, she's a miracle worker Sandy. Elizabeth didn't tell me all they talked about, but I don't care as long as she'll have me."

"Fool." Sandy spoke affectionately as he pushed the door of the canteen open on a hubbub of noise and the smell of burning. He sniffed and winced slightly, "Looks like Dennis got burnt toast for breakfast again."

Bob glanced over as they queued for their mugs of tea, "I thought his solicitor would have got him out before now."

"Nah, remanded for further enquiries." Sandy grinned evilly, "But where does he fit in your theory Bob? If he was looking for something it was at Barker's instigation." He raised a quizzical eyebrow.

"I haven't come up with a single connection between Barker and Neville, except for the probable B and E of Little Dennis." McInnis scowled into his inoffensive brew, dumped the mug on the table, and slumped down into a plastic chair.

"Never known Barker deal in blackmail, not his style at all."

"I dunno Sandy, this one's got me running around chasing my own tail. The only good thing about it I can find is Beth." His voice unconsciously softened and Sandy opened his mouth to gently tease, and then closed it again. His Sarah hadn't told him much either but he remembered the uncertainties and delights of their courtship and decided not to spoil Bob's pleasure with idle comments.

"What do you want me to do for you then lad?" Sandy, methodically dunking ginger nuts, looked across the slightly sticky table at his colleague.

"Can you phone that solicitor... Richards? I want permission for Beth to look at all the research, on a formal basis. Including the genealogy stuff which strictly speaking isn't part of the research proper." He paused a minute, thinking and absently stirring his tea, "I want to try to find out what other information Peter Neville had got and where he was going with it." He scratched his head while he gazed off into a corner in an abstracted manner. He spoke slowly, still looking into the near distance.

"We think Cavendish gave a key to Barker, maybe for opportunistic theft, or maybe because Tracy Cavendish told her husband something and he passed it on and Barker thought it was worth the risk of getting a key to steal it. Valuables or information, it could be either." He paused, bringing his gaze back to Sandy Bell patiently sipping tea and watching him.

"Mrs Cavendish is coming in today." Sandy nodded at a passing constable then continued, "Says she doesn't care what her Tom says, she wants the people who beat him up, locked up. Now we're almost sure that was Dennis. But I can maybe slip a few questions in about what she saw in the Prof's house and talked about to her husband."

"Just maybe there's a connection there we don't know about yet."

"What else?"

"I know it's ridiculous, knowing what I've found out about the Society of Friends but I have to tie that knot off too."

"Yeah, I should take young Higgs with you on that, he might be able to ease you into the community and see who knew what about the Professor." Sandy spoke matter of factly; he didn't think it would prove of any use but he agreed that they'd have to check it out anyway.

"Anything else?"

"If Madogan has got anything on Cavendish maybe that's how Barker became involved." He looked thoughtfully at Sandy Bell. "Do you know if he was charged on Saturday night Sandy?"

"I'll find out. We might be able to get a look at Madogan's files if he was, it's a bit..." Sandy waggled his hand, "but I'll find out whose in charge and see if I can't pull professional courtesy Bob."

"Right Sandy, that should be enough to keep us occupied today. I tell you Sandy, I'm tired of this case. It looks so simple and we're no nearer now than when we found the body. I must be missing something, but I'm damned if I can see what." McInnis shook his head, rubbing over a freshly shaven cheek. "I'll go and find Higgs and see if I can steal him from whatever duty he's currently doing. He's a nice lad and a mine of information once he forgets you're a senior officer."

10

The sun was streaming into the office when Sandy got back. A desk cluttered with papers, files and a computer screen that stubbornly refused, despite all the hype, to solve his crimes for him, glinted back at him. He flopped down onto his seat, which squeaked slightly in protest, and loosened a tie which had been worn at half mast so much it was now the normal default position.

He leaned back with his eyes closed, trying to see what they had missed; slowly he reviewed the case. A man had been strangled. They were looking for a murderer; never mind all the other stuff just yet, the motives, the means, and the opportunity, he just needed to get a picture in his mind of the murderer.

Sandy pulled a pad towards him. Now. He chewed the pen for a second, and then started to write, working his way down the page. The murderer had inside knowledge of how to kill quickly and effectively. He'd cased the house but not well, since Elizabeth Fielding arriving wasn't expected. He hadn't a lot of compassion, but not many murderers had. Sandy chewed his pen a bit more. Murder wasn't the only objective since someone, possibly the murderer, had returned at least once to search the place again.

"Now lad, think." Sandy sat back a minute, staring at his family group blue-tacked to the side of the computer. "What does that give us? It gives us a very determined killer with something they believe needs hiding from the police or someone else. But someone who isn't entirely free to check things out before they act. So someone who was," he mentally put speech marks round the word in his mind, "'respectable', not a real criminal, and a person with other commitments.

"Someone like me in fact. Damn! I committed it and forgot to tell myself." He nodded at his wife, "Now wait, let's look at the other bits as applied to our suspects. There's Barker. Means, yes, he's thorough enough in a fight if he wanted the dirty end of the job.

Motive, maybe theft, but I've yet to discover what the poor old boy had worth stealing. Opportunity, no, he never leaves that bloody office of his, he always sends someone else, and he always has an alibi. So we cross him off the list, for this job anyway." Sandy did so with a flourish. Then turned the page and wrote 'Cavendish', then chewed his pen a bit more.

"Means. Nah, I don't think he has the guts. He certainly hasn't got any training we've been able to discover. Plenty of opportunity there. The man works when he feels like it, and he could have cased the joint with no trouble, but he had so much information from his wife he'd never have made the mistake of turning up when Elizabeth was due on scene. And his wife did give him an alibi. I mistrust alibis.

"Motive, Hmm!" Sandy rubbed his nose. "Well I suppose, Tracy Cavendish could have told him about something worth stealing, and if he's as deeply in debt to Barker as I think, he might have seen it as a chance to recoup his losses. So why hasn't he? He obviously still owes Barker big time. Weel," he scratched his head, "I'll talk to the wife, but unlikely." He placed a question mark against Cavendish's name.

"Madogan. Well he's a nasty enough piece of work, has the right training but Bob says the alibi for that morning checked out, and the boy would have checked and double checked, and we haven't found a motive there at all, only a connection to Elizabeth that's pretty thin." Sandy scratched his ear and applied his teeth to the end of his pen again then said, "Which brings us to Elizabeth herself."

Sandy carefully laid down the pen and sat back with the notebook in his hand. "Nah, there's motive: money, there's opportunity: she was there. The Prof' trusted her so she could get close enough to do it but Bob loves her and he's no fool, so cross her off." He moved the pen through thin air. "Now what did I say just then?" He frowned in concentration, wishing he'd written things down. "He trusted her, mmm!"

Sandy grabbed for the phone. "Put me through to Jonesy will you Fiona." He picked up the pen and turned it over and over while he waited for the ME to answer. Then, hearing the lilting Welsh tones, transferred the phone to the other ear and spoke into the phone while his pen moved across the sheet of paper.

While Sandy Bell was grappling with a man whose thoughts were filtered through the language of Welsh, Bob McInnis was coping with a different form of language. "So you say both Professor Neville and his father attended on a regular basis." He looked at the tall elegant woman in front of him. She sported a set of pearls he was sure were the genuine article, her hair had the same translucent glow and colour, and her voice the same quiet understated elegance.

Miss Anderson smiled and inclined her head. Bob was having trouble with the concept of a church that had no leaders. Higgs had said she was the nearest to one of the leaders they hadn't got, but to a good catholic boy with the fear of the parish priest in his memory banks, it was odd to say the least.

Higgs sat, or rather perched, on a chair at his side, sipping tea from an elegant bone china mug. It was, Bob conceded, very nice tea; and the room had the kind of peace he associated with the parish church. It smelt of the roses displayed on the table, with a slight undertone of beeswax rather than incense. Nevertheless it had a, Bob searched his mind, hesitating over holy as inappropriate for a sitting room, but couldn't come up with a better word for the feel of the place.

"They were both very deeply committed to Christ Inspector. We do rejoice that they are in heaven. However the manner of Peter's death was a shock to the whole meeting. Several of the Friends visited Professor Neville after his accident and he was always delighted to receive them but he found it difficult to attend the meeting house. I believe he was in pain most of the time though he didn't complain about it." She drank tea and set her own mug down on a small coaster on the mahogany table.

"Now as to the fact that Peter's father was a German, yes we knew, he prayed in German occasionally I believe. I myself have only a dim recollection of him when I was younger. Peter was very like him. His father married into one of our families, a lovely girl from the fell country." She paused, thinking, "I can put you in touch with our London office if you wish, they might be able to tell you her family, I'm afraid I don't know them. She'd died before I was born. I think giving birth, however I'm not sure about that."

Higgs carefully set his mug down. "Aunt Addie?"

Bob cast a quick surprised glance across but held his peace.

"Yes Ian."

"Would the records show who the Prof' was hidden with in the First World War?"

"I doubt it. They might show which meeting house he attended and the families who attended with him." She shook her head as he opened his mouth. "Wait, let me think."

"You should be able to track down both families, Peter's father and his mother's, via the London office. They could also give you the names of the German branch but I'm not sure how far back they go. The Germans don't keep records in the same way that we do." She sighed, "Two world wars have destroyed much of that information."

She looked at Bob, "Would you like another mug of tea Inspector?"

"No, but," Bob smiled suddenly, lightening his whole face, "tell me what kind it was; I know someone who would really enjoy it." He thought of Sarah Bell; she did like her cup of tea.

"Oh! I'll give you a packet before you go. Now I wonder, these questions, I know you're trying to find Peter's murderer but I don't quite see their relevance, and anyway Peter would have all the notes. I'm sure he spoke to old Isaac months ago about it. Peter was studying his family tree."

Bob McInnis sat up very straight. "You say Peter, Professor Neville, has all this information anyway."

"Oh yes I'm sure he would have it. Isaac would have sent him to the London office too. He's getting on is Isaac, but his brain is sharp enough."

This from a woman who Bob estimated must be somewhere in her late seventies. He suppressed the smile. "Could you tell me roughly when he spoke to Mr Isaac?"

"Isaac Armstrong and it would be about six months ago, give or take." She thought for a minute gazing off into a corner. "Yes I believe it was just before the Christmas holidays."

Bob stood up. "You've been most helpful Miss Anderson."

Miss Anderson rose; Bob conceded that her means of getting from vertical to horizontal couldn't be described in such inelegant terms as standing up. "I'll just fetch you that tea Inspector."

She drifted out of the room and the two policemen looked at each other. "Aunt Addie, Higgs?"

"Courtesy title Inspector." He looked a bit embarrassed.

Miss Anderson floated back in, her chiffon dress swirling slightly. "Here you are Inspector, and I've written down Isaac's phone number and the number for the London office too. It's been a pleasure meeting you, and it's been very nice to see Ian growing into such a fine young man." She looked at the blushing boy and smiled, "We miss you at meeting." It was said softly and she touched his arm gently, then directed her attention back to Bob. "I'll pray that you find the answer soon Inspector."

As they left Bob McInnis was surprised to find the world still bustling around outside her door. He looked up at the clear blue afternoon sky. "She's a peaceful woman Higgs."

"Yes sir."

"I need to phone the London office and Mr Armstrong. But I suspect the Professor's notes will have the information, as Miss Anderson says." He opened the car door. "I'll drive Higgs. I want to think and I think better when I'm driving."

231

Ian Higgs obediently got into the passenger seat, adjusting the seat belt around his flak jacket, and putting his hat on to his curly hair. "Where are we going sir?"

"You're going back to the station. I'm going to find Inspector Bell. I want to ask him a few questions, and then I'm going to find Miss Fielding and ask her some." He grinned, and then settled down to his driving.

Sandy Bell, when he tracked him down in the station, was returning from his interview with Tracy Cavendish. He had a large mug of tea in one hand and a white paper bag in the other. Bob approached quietly behind him.

"What you got there Sandy?"

Sandy's hand jerked slightly and slopped tea over his fingers, causing him to swear mildly at his partner as he swung around to face him.

"Oh it's you," he eyed Bob, "you're looking very chipper. What have you discovered?"

"I've discovered you with a cream doughnut."

"Shh! I was hoping to sneak it past the squad room."

"Why? They know you eat 'em."

"Yeah and they tell the secretaries, who complain I get grease on the files."

"Well you do." Bob obligingly held open the door of Sandy's office and followed the older man into the room.

"So what else have you found out Bob?"

"Me, I've had a lovely cup of tea with a..." he searched his mind, "a gentlewoman you might call her. She was really helpful and I think might just have nudged me onto the right track, if I can find the right information in that towering pile of research in my room." He sat down opposite Sandy at the desk and watched the Scotsman removing the clear foil from the doughnut with all the care of a man undressing a woman.

"Well I'm glad you enjoyed yourself," Sandy spoke absently as he took a bite and savoured the cake.

232

"So have I got permission to show all the research to Elizabeth?"

Sandy swallowed and washed the mouthful down with tea. "Well you have Bob, but that solicitor wasn't best pleased about it. Went on at some length about the probate and the party of the first, to God knows how many other parts, having rights in the law. Wanted to know when we would be returning it to his office to await said probate."

He savoured another bite. "However," he said a trifle thickly, "I persuaded him that it was in the best interests of all parties to solve the murder so that we could get the estate wound up. Probate would then be administered that much more quickly." He shrugged and finished the doughnut, pulling a clean handkerchief from his pocket and wiping his fingers.

"Now what have you discovered my son."

"I discovered that Peter Neville was researching his ancestors."

Sandy raised an eyebrow. "We knew that didn't we, that's what the blasted book is about."

"Yes Sandy." Bob looked at him patiently. "What we now know is that his father was a German, an illegal immigrant to this country all his life, who married a good Quaker girl. They had one son, our Peter, who was obviously a successful scholar and respected pillar of the community." He held up a hand as Sandy would have spoken, "What we need to find out is who else he was researching."

McInnis pulled out his notebook. "Miss Anderson, the gentlewoman that Higgs took me to see, she told me he was looking into his family tree. I think that's what we need to do. I'd like to contact Fraulien Smitt again, and I've been thinking Sandy, about motive and we haven't got one, not yet, maybe we've been looking in the wrong place."

Sandy sat back with his mug, his head on one side as he looked at the gleam in Bob's eye. "Yeah, I'd come to the same conclusion

Bob, but let me fill you in on Tracy Cavendish's interview first, and then we can take Tomas Cavendish off the list of suspects."

He finished off the tea and sat forward, resting his forearms on the desk and blinking slightly as a shaft of sun shot through the cloud cover and poked an inquisitive ray into the room. "Mrs Cavendish has got a tongue hinged in the middle, and she can't resist flirting with men. It doesn't matter how old they are."

Bob detected a tinge of embarrassment and grinned. "Glad you did the interview."

"Oh go boil your head." Sandy grinned back. "Anyway we started off nice and gentle talking about the mugging," Sandy put the word in inverted commas in the air. "She wants whoever did it caught and strung up before the county court. She might flirt Bob, but I think she genuinely loves that layabout husband of hers.

"I don't think she'd know half the things he's dabbling in. Thinks he just needs a helping hand and someone to give him a decent job, and then everything will be lovely in the garden. Thinks he's too good for manual labour." Sandy wrinkled his snub of a nose as if he'd detected a nasty smell.

"We went through the Monday of the murder, and she still alibi's him. I don't think she even realised that's what she was doing. I think," Sandy frowned, "I think she thought we were looking for an alibi for her. She became a little defensive for a while there."

"Once I got her talking about the Professor's house she was really chatty. Told me all about where he kept his stereo, and the 78's he let her play sometimes when she was cleaning. He was a jazz fanatic!" Sandy now sounded incredulous. "They must be worth a few pounds and there's nothing in the notes about them. Told me she'd forgotten all about them until I started talking to her. And yes Bob, she had told Tomas Cavendish. They used to go dancing when they were teenagers, old time stuff." He grinned, "Who'd have thought it."

"Now what you might not know Bob, is that Barker is also a jazz fanatic."

Bob whistled, "So Barker has got a motive after all."

"Motive yes, but I was thinking this morning…"

"Did it hurt much?"

"Cheek!" Sandy gave a kick at Bob's long legs stretched under the communal desk. "I was thinking," he gave a false glare at Bob, "about the means of murder. It was manual strangulation. Someone put their hands around Peter Neville's throat and squeezed against the carotids. I checked with Jonesy to see if a brainwave I'd just had fitted the facts. Whoever did it, did it from the front Bob, and the old man might have put up a fight at the finish but not to begin with. The signs don't indicate that kind of struggle."

McInnis frowned fiercely, "Neville would hardly have allowed a stranger like Dennis Little, or Barker, to get that close without making a fuss. Even in his wheelchair, we know he could stand a bit, and manoeuvre about. Elizabeth told me he was quite proud of how much independence he was beginning to achieve, even showed off to her a bit."

The two men sat scowling for a minute or two. "I wish the blasted woman had remembered those 78's when we took her through the house Sandy. It would be really helpful to know if they're still in the house."

"Well, put that aside for a minute Bob. What I'm getting at is this, he knew his murderer." Bob looked at him sharply.

"Yes I thought of her Bob, I have to do my job lad." He shook his head gently. "I don't believe Elizabeth Fielding has the necessary training, even if it was in her nature, to kill Peter Neville. But I do think we've missed someone Bob. Someone he knew and trusted. Maybe trusted with a key?" He raised an eyebrow.

There was a brisk tap on the door and Gareth stepped through at Sandy's invitation.

"Sir, one of the lads sent this file for you. Something to do with a B & E."

"Oh thanks Gareth." Gareth nodded at McInnis and set it on the desk. "Mark Forester says he might have a bit of forensic evidence that he thinks might really interest you. He said he'd be back about five and would you mind very much waiting for him sir. He has to be in court or he'd have spoken to you earlier." Gareth flashed a smile.

Sandy nodded, "Gareth, you helped with the search out at the Professor's house?"

"Yes sir."

"Notice any old 78's laying around."

Gareth scowled in thought.

"Those old fashioned plastic records, the kind you got before CDs."

"Oh those." The sunny smile returned. "Yes sir some in the front room in a big cupboard thing with a record player."

Sandy glanced at his watch. "Fine, does Forester want Bob too?"

"Didn't say sir."

Bob shrugged. "I've got a hot date with a beautiful woman. If Forester has something earth shattering you can give me a ring on the mobile, Sandy. I didn't get to sleep until nearly two this morning. I figure the force owes me a few hours off for good behaviour."

"If you didn't get to sleep until two it wasn't good behaviour you were indulging in!"

Gareth nearly choked in his effort not to laugh as Bob turned brick red. Sandy had no such inhibitions, throwing back his head to enjoy the joke the better. "Away with you lad, and give my love to Elizabeth."

Bob glared at both policemen then stood up. "OK the beer's on me next time. I walked into that one." He grinned at both of them and left the room.

McInnis went to pick Elizabeth up at home; he found he'd missed her badly the day before. He'd spent Sunday at his mother's house mowing her lawns and turning over part of the vegetable patch. His sister had been visiting too but even her company hadn't stopped some of the longing he'd experienced for Elizabeth.

He wasn't quite ready to introduce Elizabeth to his sister, or his mother. Not that he was worried about how either would react to a girl who was potential wife material. His mother had told him often enough that if he wasn't going into the priesthood it was about time he gave her some more grandchildren to spoil. He loved his independent mother very much, but she did harp on about grandchildren a lot, and it wasn't a subject he'd quite got the nerve to talk to Elizabeth about. He hadn't known her a month yet.

He kept putting off the inevitable meeting; he didn't want to rush things and spoil it. If Elizabeth said she wanted her career or, worse, no children, he didn't quite trust his mother not to say the wrong thing. But he did want children with Beth.

She was waiting for him in a bright scarlet number that made her legs stretch all the way down to the mile high heels. "God you look sexy!" He blurted the words out as she came down the path towards him.

"Well thank you kind sir. You said dress up a bit."

"Yes but now I'm not sure I want to share you with anyone else."

"Oh no, I didn't get myself encased in this dress to not go out." Elizabeth gave him a cheeky grin and put both hands on his shoulders over the garden gate, smiling wickedly into his face.

"It's just as well the gate's between us; you're enough to incite a riot Beth." He leaned in and they shared a kissed which left them both wanting more.

"OK," he stepped back breathing deeply and held open the gate, "I will take you out, but only because if I don't, heaven knows what baser instincts might take over."

Elizabeth walked through and headed to his car, Bob held open the door and tucked her in, sliding a hand across a revealing thigh as he handed her the seatbelt. She glanced up and encountered a very male and very predatory look in his eye, and hastily glanced away, busying herself with the fastening. It seemed her beloved fool was as other men at times.

"So what are we celebrating then?" She'd waited until they were both safely fastened in and Bob's hands where fully occupied with the steering wheel.

"We are celebrating my birthday. Which event took place in this town thirty-four years ago yesterday, but looking at you I have all the urges of a fourteen year old on his first date." Bob grinned wickedly, shooting her a look loaded with lust.

"Oh! Bob why didn't you say so?"

"I thought I just did."

"Not your baser urges! I know about that. About your birthday." Elizabeth reached across and touched the hand nearest her resting on the wheel. "I could have got you a present at least."

Sobering for a minute Bob glanced across, "You're the best present I could want." Then his lips twitched, "I promise not to unwrap you though."

"Oh how disappointing!" Elizabeth shook her head mock sadly. Her Bob was in a slightly wicked mood tonight it would seem.

Bob flashed another grin then swung the car expertly round a corner. "Yet."

She sat quiet for a minute smiling to herself. Then glanced across, "Well I'm glad I get to eat first." She tried for a sober tone and succeeded rather too well.

Bob shot her another look. "I'm joking Beth."

"I know you are darling, but it's rather breathtaking to be desired."

He raised an eyebrow, "And if I wasn't joking?"

"I'd still be glad I get to eat first." It was said softly but he couldn't mistake the message.

"Dear God I love you Beth!" He pulled into a car park and yanked the handbrake on abruptly. He leaned across for another searing kiss which was returned in full measure, then sat back as her stomach gave a small growl. "I'm too old to neck in a car park," he grasped her hand, "OK food first, kissing later. That's a promise."

Mark Forester was keeping his promise too; he strolled into Sandy Bell's office at five thirty that evening. He knew his man well enough to bring mugs of tea for both of them.

Sandy watched him dump them on the table and pull a file out from under his arm. He stood looking at Sandy until that man said, "Well sit down for God's sake man, what you got for me?"

Mark pulled out the chair on the opposite side of the desk and sat down with a quiet sigh.

"Rough day in court was it?"

"I tell you, you collect all the evidence and then some 'lawyer'..." he all but spat the word, "tries to prove you diddled with it. Why the hell would I? What would I gain by putting some scum, who I've never heard of, off the street in clink?"

"I dunno lad, but we all have to work for our living." His look was sympathetic and Forester unconsciously relaxed; he'd been a bit wary since Inspector Bell had pointed out that he was, as a Detective Sergeant still on his way up the ladder. Bell was nearer the top and might know a bit more. It had been the silkily soft tones that had had Forester cringing.

"Drink your tea lad and tell me what you've found."

"It might not be relevant Inspector but that mugging last week, the Cavendish case." He waited for Bell's nod, "Well the ground was pretty hard, it's been a couple of warm weeks. But I managed to lift a partial boot print from the waste ground. We wouldn't normally have bothered for a mugging like that, but the teenagers that found Cavendish got all excited, talked like it was a CSI show." He looked a bit ashamed. "So I got the kit out and did a bit of looking around and, as I say, found the print. I was lucky really; it was in some dog's ... well some faeces sir."

Sandy nodded encouragingly again, burying his head in his mug to hide the grin.

"Anyway," Mark took a gulp of his own tea, "I didn't think it would come to much but I ran it anyway for some like matches through the new FIT system. And I got not one, but two." He looked across at Bell shaking his head in wonder. "It was a match to one in that murder the other week."

Bell, who had been lounging back, sat up and Forester was flatteringly aware that he'd got the senior man's full attention.

"Which murder? What's FIT? And let's have things a bit more orderly lad."

Forester opened the slim file he'd brought into the room. "This is the forensics on the boot print I found in the upstairs box room of Professor Peter Neville on the day of his murder." He tapped the paper with a slim finger. "The steps went in, crossed to the window, and came out of the room. There were smudges on the windowsill, but whoever made them wore gloves and it was hopeless trying to get anything from them." Forester placed the paper in front of Bell then pulled out another sheet of paper.

"This is the same room, but there was a second set of prints, same pattern though, over to the window and back out. They scuffed over the first set but they were definitely made at separate times."

"When did you take them?"

"That was the day Inspector McInnis got clobbered sir."

"You didn't tell me then." Bell sounded testy.

"I thought you knew about them. You sent me up to do them, so I thought you knew." Mark shivered in his own boots as he looked at Bell's face.

Sandy Bell folded his lips to prevent the comments he was thinking, slipping out while he thought about that day. He could remember sending the man up because they thought someone had been there. Elizabeth had heard something and the ambulance men had 'just walked in'. It argued the case for persons unknown being around.

Forester watched him cautiously for a minute but Bell didn't say anymore, just looked pointedly at the open file in front of him. "This is the boot print from the Cavendish mugging last week, it's a partial as you can see, but they are a match sir. FIT is the new national database for footprints, 'Footwear Intelligence Technology', sir."

"Which does what exactly Mark?" Sandy smiled slightly, setting his empty mug and his irritation down; the boy wasn't a mind reader after all was he? He should have asked earlier if anything had been found.

"Well it puts the crime scene foot and shoeprints, and the manufacturer's information together, and if you enter your details it can link them with other offences."

"Ok I understand that bit." Sandy nodded, "Now can I prove my criminal wore those boots? Or can he swear he bought them from Oxfam the week before and get away with it?"

Mark Forester grinned as he set his own mug down. "Oh yeah I can prove it, it's called the Cinderella analysis." He appreciated a man who was as quick on the uptake as Inspector Bell. "If you can give me the boot and the foot that went in it, I can prove the guy was wearing it."

Sandy stood up. "Come with me lad. We might just put that statement to the test."

11

"Ever read 'A Study in Scarlet' Bob? It's a Sherlock Holmes story and he claimed that tracing footsteps was an important, but neglected, art." Sandy grinned widely at his bemused partner as that man came into his office the next morning.

"Can't say I have Sandy. Is it on your list of recommended reading?"

"Wouldn't do any harm." Sandy beamed like a lighthouse and Bob wondered what was coming next.

"I've got Gareth, and one of his big pals, out this very minute picking up Dennis Little. We might not have solved this murder yet, but I think we might get that thick thug on grievous bodily harm after all."

"You're never telling me Cavendish pointed the finger are you?"

"No. Dennis did."

"Dennis! Well I knew the man wasn't all that bright but…"

"Oh not deliberately. He just wasn't watching where he put his feet."

Bob pulled out the chair and sat down. "Alright I'll buy it. Tell your tale Sandy."

Sandy grinned again. "We didn't manage to locate Dennis last night, but I'm not too worried, he's not fool enough to stray far when he's on police bail. Remember Forester had something to tell us last night?"

"Mmm."

"It seems he's been collecting footprints. Dennis left a partial at the scene of the mugging."

"Been a bit dry for that."

"Not if you put your size thirteens in dog faeces." Sandy said it primly and then gave a grunt of laughter. "You should have seen Forester hesitating over the word 'shit'. He was playing clever bastards to a couple of teenagers or we might not even have got it Bob."

He rubbed a hand over his face and Bob heard the faint rasp that said his razor was in need of cleaning again. "Forester was SOCO for the mugging and the girls were all oh's and ah's. So, as I read it, he put on a bit of a show for them. Doing the crawl around and gathering cigarette butts, and as I say he took the boot print."

"He should have done it anyway."

"What, for a mugging! You know we don't have the resources to do that all the time Bob."

Bob shrugged but conceded that the money for forensics wasn't unlimited.

"Anyway he ran the print since he'd gone to the trouble of getting it and was astonished to get not one match but two."

"Bloody Hell!" The normally polite McInnis was surprised into the expletive: "Two other matches! Where?"

"Just so my lad. Now we knew that mugging had Dennis Little's MO all over it, so we can get him and his boots checked and maybe tie the thing to him. But those boot prints also appear in the box room of Professor Peter Neville's house." He paused for effect and was pleased by the look of incredulity on McInnis' face. "Ain't that something?"

Bob McInnis sat staring at Sandy, and then Sandy swore he could almost see the cogs begin to turn. "Hang on, two sets of prints."

Sandy scratched his head, his brown hair standing up with the treatment, "Ah yes. Well that was my fault a bit Bob. If you remember Elizabeth said she thought she heard you moving the day you got the bash on the head and came in to find you out cold in the study. I wondered who she'd heard and I sent Mark Forester upstairs. He thought I knew someone had been up there so he didn't report he'd found anything. What he found was more boot prints, and now we believe we know who left them."

"So are we saying Little Dennis murdered the Prof' and gave me the rabbit chop then?"

Sandy scratched the back of his head this time. "Logically yes, trouble is I just don't think Dennis has the wits to do it, and I can't see Professor Neville allowing him that close. Why would Dennis kill him? Threaten him, yes. I'd keep quiet if someone like Dennis threatened me and I was as vulnerable as the Prof'. The point is he didn't need to kill him, and it just isn't Dennis' MO. GBH, petty larceny, wheel man yes. Murder no."

"He doesn't strike me as having the brains for intrigue and murder certainly, and we've yet to discover what he did with the stuff from the safe if he stole it." Bob shook his head. "Still it gives us a lever. Are we going to charge him Sandy?"

Bell shook his head. "We might Bob, but I don't think we've got to the bottom of this affair yet."

The two men sat silent for a few minutes sifting through the evidence they had so far.

"If it was just theft Sandy, and I agree with you Dennis hasn't the brains for more than that, why would he try to burn the research. That lighter fuel was definitely introduced into the crime scene for some purpose, and the logical one is arson?"

"If Dennis was there to steal jazz records for Barker why didn't he take them? Gareth saw those 78's. He wouldn't be able to resist lifting a few items for his own use either Bob, and Peter Neville still had a full wallet and a good watch."

"Maybe Dennis was too squeamish to lift them from a corpse."

Sandy frowned, giving the suggestion only a tiny bit of thought. "No, Dennis has all the finer feelings of a crocodile opening its underwater larder. A dead body wouldn't faze him."

"So what we're saying is, if Dennis murdered Neville he should have taken the goodies away with him. And if he didn't why didn't he?"

Sandy chewed his lip, worrying at a bit of dry skin, "Elizabeth came in before he had a chance."

244

"No, that doesn't follow Sandy. The body was warm I'll grant you," Bob sniffed, he could recall the feel of the dead man's skin if he put his mind to it, but he wasn't going there, he thought, "but it wasn't that fresh."

"Ah, so she surprised him and he nipped upstairs then crept out again when she was busy phoning and looking at German children's books on that shelf," Sandy leaned forward, "so he could have done it Bob." He sighed, "I just can't convince myself of it though. It just doesn't feel right."

"And we still don't know why he'd try to get rid of the research either. Why come back Sandy? OK, maybe Elizabeth surprised him." Bob felt the light sweat pop out at the thought of Elizabeth surprising Dennis. She could have ended up a corpse too. "So he comes back when he thinks the place is empty to finish lifting whatever it was. Would he use arson to cover his presence, rather than to get rid of the research as we assumed?"

"Seems a bit over the top for Dennis." Sandy shook his head. "He knows about fingerprints and he always wears gloves. I'm not sure he's very bright about the other forensic stuff we can catch criminals with," Sandy grimaced, "unless he's an avid fan of CSI too. Wouldn't that be just our luck?"

"Well he left his boot prints so he doesn't know that much." It was said with a great deal of satisfaction and Bob pushed his chair back on the words. "I've got a pile of files sitting on my desk Sandy. Let me know when he shows up; this is one interview I don't want to miss."

Sandy still sat but he lounged back and swivelled the chair as he looked at the younger man. "Ah yes, how did the hot date go?"

Bob's face lit up. "Mind your own business." He turned and headed towards the door.

"Bob," Sandy's soft voice came across the room, "I'm glad we've got Dennis as suspect number one."

"So am I Sandy." Bob didn't turn, but Sandy heard his faint chuckle as he went out.

Elizabeth was shopping. She had enjoyed her evening enormously; not only was Bob McInnis a handsome man whom she was proud to go out with, but he was also a gentleman. He treated her as if she was the most precious and important thing on his mind and, what's more, she loved him.

She'd risen early this morning despite her late night, determined to get him a birthday present that would tell him that. The trouble was she hadn't found what she was looking for. She'd examined silver pens and notecases. She'd toyed with a chunky bracelet but didn't think he'd wear it. Nor the ring that, she felt, was a bit too obvious just yet.

She'd retreated from the bustle of the tourist-laden streets outside to the relative quiet of the Cathedral cloisters and settled into the café. It had low arched ceilings and the smell of coffee. The muted sound of cups and spoons and contented conversation should have been soothing after the crowds outside, but she was sitting drinking coffee and frowning fiercely into her mug nevertheless.

The voice when it spoke in her ear for a second time was a little impatient. "You are Beth aren't you?"

Elizabeth looked up in surprise; the young woman addressing her was a complete stranger. She frowned in an effort at recall. "I'm sorry, do I know you?"

"No but I've seen your photo. I'm Bob's sister, Mary." She watched the pink colour steal into Beth's cheeks. "We're close, but he doesn't tell tales out of school." She touched the chair opposite, "Can I sit down?"

"Oh, yes, of course." Elizabeth was wondering where Bob had got a photo of her.

"I'm so pleased to have met you. I have to go home tomorrow. I only came up for Bob's birthday." The other woman, now Elizabeth had a chance to really look at her, had the same brown eyes and straight nose as Bob. She set a couple of carrier bags next to the chair and her coffee cup in front of her.

246

"Look I didn't mean to intrude, it's just Bob is so happy. He hasn't been this happy since before our father died. I couldn't help wondering at the cause. Truly he didn't say much, just that he'd met a girl, and he showed me a photo of you." She grinned, "To be honest it wasn't very flattering and rather unnerved me. You were in full academicals."

"Good grief where did he get that?"

"Off the net he said."

Elizabeth burst into giggles. "Poor man! He hates the computer; we had those class photos taken for the college book. He must have sweated trying to download that." She stopped as Mary smiled across at her.

"He does, doesn't he, so I figured it must be serious." There was just a hint of a question. Then Mary shook her head, "I'm sorry. I love my brother, but I've no right to intrude in your personal life, but I spotted you sitting there and couldn't resist coming over."

"That's alright." Elizabeth took a deep breath, "I love him too, in fact I'm in love with him." She blushed a bit and took refuge in her coffee cup.

"Well I hope you've told him, and I'm delighted." Elizabeth, looking at her, saw that she really was delighted; she had the same sweet smile Bob had and it was washing over Elizabeth.

"To tell the truth I was trying to get him a birthday present but I'm a bit lost for ideas."

"Well you could always give him a decent photo instead of that portrait he's got in his wallet." The two girls grinned in a conspiratorial manner and then nodded at each other, "Can't live with them, and can't live without them!"

The object of their affection was doing battle with the internet yet again. Nothing as personal as a picture of his girl was being searched for on the net. Having been directed by Fraulien Smitt to a well-known genealogical site, and having her permission to access her site for the family tree, he was now desperately trying to make some sense of the material in front of him.

"Yeuk! No wonder it's called a tree." McInnis frowned at the screen, trying to see all the information at once. If he tried to get too much of the tree on the screen the print was so small he couldn't see any names, and when he made the print bigger he lost half the information. He pushed back his chair in disgust, glaring at the offending machine.

"I need Elizabeth for this job; she'd have it all on paper in two minutes flat." He looked across to the boxes of research and quailed at the thought of diving into them.

He swung idly in his chair, toying with the cash in his pockets while he wondered what to do. He hadn't arranged to meet her today because he didn't want to rush things, but it was becoming very hard not to want to see her every day. If he rang her he would have the perfect excuse. He glared at the screen again.

Stretching out a hand he lifted the receiver and dialled her home number. The quiet tones of Noel Fielding answered him.

"I'm sorry Bob she's gone shopping to the centre of the town."

"That's alright Mr Fielding it wasn't important. I've just got a minor computer problem."

"Shall I get her to ring you back?"

"No." Bob shook his head at the receiver, "I'll see if she answers her mobile since she's in town anyway."

"Fine. Goodbye." Bob heard the receiver being replaced and set his back on the rest. Would it look too pushy if he rang the mobile? He was still second guessing himself when the phone rang again.

"Hi, McInnis."

"Hi yourself Bob. Can you spare half an hour to eat lunch with your sister before I have to go home and pack?"

"Mary, hello love," Bob's voice softened, "I'm sorry love. I'm waiting to do an important interview."

"Oh, are you sure Bob? I've got a nice present I want to give you."

248

McInnis glanced at his watch. He didn't really have time, but he would like to see Mary before she went south again. "OK, twenty minutes Mary, no longer love, and have the sandwiches ready. Where do you want to meet?"

"How about Bitts Park?"

"Great."

He grabbed his jacket and headed out, fishing his mobile from his pocket on the way. "Sandy?"

"Yeah."

"I'm nipping out for a quick bite. I'll be at the end of my mobile, don't start without me. OK?"

"Fine, bring me a tuna roll."

Bob pulled a face as he wended his way rapidly through the corridors of the station and out into the hot and dusty street. He called into a small deli on his way and waited a frustrating five minutes to buy Sandy's tuna roll before walking very rapidly towards the park under the city castle's looming walls.

He was scanning the park entrance as he approached the gates, so that he spotted both girls before he came up to them. He'd had time to adjust his face from the look of horror that had flitted over it when he'd first seen them together. "What a nice surprise, how did you two meet up then?"

Mary, accustomed to her brother, didn't take the cool tones in the wrong way. Her baby brother was scared he was about to be teased as only a big sister could. "I saw Beth having a coffee and introduced myself."

Elizabeth wasn't quite as attuned to Bob's habits and was wondering if she should have allowed herself to be persuaded to meet him for lunch. She didn't want to rush the guy. She surreptitiously watched his face as he talked to Mary, wondering if he was cross with her.

And then he smiled at her. That smiled revealed a lot that Bob wasn't prepared to put into words yet. "Hello love, I was just wondering if I could ring you. I've got a bit of a computer problem with the Prof's research."

Mary, an interested bystander, looked at the couple before her; she'd deliberately engineered this meeting; she wanted to know if this was her future sister-in-law or not. Now she was mentally reviewing her wardrobe and wondering if she dare buy a new dress, or if she'd be too pregnant by the wedding date. She hadn't told Bob about the new baby yet either.

"So where's my present then." Bob walked between the girls, linking arms with them both as he strolled into the park.

"Well I was going to tell you on Sunday but I never got round to it."

"What that nephew number six is on the way?"

"Bob!"

"Well I am a policeman Mary, and I can spot the signs by now."

Mary pouted as he grinned at her. They found a bench under the shade of some sycamores and settled down to eating, and general talk about Mary's family. She noticed that he shared not just sandwiches but looks with Elizabeth and was content with her diagnosis.

As they gathered the wrappings up she said, "I wanted to drive up before I got too big, Bob. Baby's due at Christmas. But now I really must be going. It's a long haul back down to Aldershot. I'm staying with Joyce overnight, so don't start telling me it's too long a drive 'in my condition'." Elizabeth noticed she had the same mobile and slightly comical eyebrow as Bob when she was quizzing you.

She got up, brushing the crumbs off the long blue summer skirt which had disguised her condition completely from Elizabeth. "I've got the car over in the castle car park. I'll leave you two to enjoy the rest of this glorious day." She bent over and kissed her brother on the cheeks, giving him a suddenly fierce hug which surprised him. "Get on with it Bob; I don't want to look like a barrage balloon in my wedding frock." It was whispered in his ear and then Mary

250

stepped back and hugged Elizabeth. "I'll see you next time I'm up; it's been lovely meeting you."

She skipped away and the pair watched her all but dancing down the path to the gates, "You'd never think she was a respectable married woman would you?" Bob turned to Elizabeth, grinning. "Now I never did get my answer and I have to get back, can you spare an hour to rescue me from technology? I've got all the paperwork to say you can look at the research." His lips twitched, knowing that he'd have let her look anyway.

"Why yes, I suppose I might rescue you, providing you gave me a cup of tea." She looked at the empty juice bottle in her hand, "It just doesn't quench your thirst like a cuppa."

"Well I suppose I might run to a mug of tea, but I was thinking of paying you in kisses."

As he took the offered hand they exchanged a look which a boy scout minus his two sticks would have treasured and they walked back through the early afternoon traffic towards the station, smiling like fools.

"So what can't you work out? It's the research I suppose."

"Actually no, I got onto one of those genealogy sites with the family trees, and truth to tell I can't seem to trace the right bit of family? He brushed his hair back, "I keep going backwards instead of sideways. Fraulien Smitt's been working on the eighteenth century German side."

They entered the relative cool of the building hand in hand and Bob took her through the gate leading to the back offices, past small windowless interview rooms. The smell of deodorant and over boiled coffee wafted down a corridor towards them. McInnis sniffed, wrinkling his nose. "Oh how I love the summer..." he paused for effect, "outside."

Elizabeth was laughing up at him when a door they were approaching swung open and a large and red-faced sergeant emerged. His regulation boots reflected his gleaming bald head, the hair on his arms bristled and he appeared to be wired; a white coil of wire ran up from some nether region emerging at his collar to end in an earpiece. He shot McInnis a look, then swung round and blocked their path.

"Just step this way sir and we'll get the forms written up and signed, then you can collect your property and go for now."

McInnis kept a tight hold of Elizabeth's hand as the person addressed emerged. He was prepared to shove her behind him if necessary; criminals had been known to make a break for it even from the inner precincts of the station. However, Elizabeth watched, as first astonishment, then a quickly masked, fierce pleasure crossed his face.

Bob nodded at the bristling and indignant moustache of Madogan. The look he got in return would have seared paint. Madogan, after a comprehensive look of contempt for Bob, transferred his eyes to Elizabeth.

"Miss Fielding." He inclined his head. "Stepped under any cars lately?"

Elizabeth looked surprised; the accident had been so minor and subsequent happenings so great that she had a struggle to recall just what he referred to and who he was. She looked at him blankly, "I'm sorry?"

"You're in dubious company, Miss Fielding. I would think you'd know better." Madogan shrugged, looking at the pair of clasped hands of the young couple. "Well don't keep me hanging around Constable; I've got more important things to do with my time than wait around for some PC Plod to two finger his way through a statement."

The three striper thus addressed looked him up and down but vouchsafed no comment; he held out a hand gesturing the way as Major Madogan walked down the corridor away from the other three. The sergeant glanced back and exchanged a wicked look with Bob and a shrug that said, "Ignorant Bastard" without him opening his mouth.

Bob watched the men walk away and then gave an exaggerated shiver, "Nasty piece of goods." He lifted the hand he clasped and kissed it, then continued in their wake turning into his office and shutting the door behind him.

Elizabeth saw apparently the same piles of paperwork filling to overflowing his desk. The plant in the window, she noticed, looked even more like something the kids would like to kick their feet through come the autumn, testifying to the fact that Bob hadn't watered it since her last visit.

She opened her mouth to say something to that effect, only to have Bob moving her against the door and giving her a kiss that blew any thoughts up and had them landing in small incomprehensible pieces on the rug at her feet.

"Payment in advance from the dubious company." Bob stood looking at her, grinning slightly.

"Actually I probably don't deserve payment; I think there's a family tree among all the research."

Bob groaned theatrically. "Exacting payment under false pretences, that's a serious offence Miss Fielding. I'm a policeman and I know what I'm talking about here."

"I thought all proper policemen wore uniforms."

"I find it difficult to be proper when you're around Elizabeth, and I don't wear a uniform."

"Yeuk! A naked policeman! No wonder you can't be proper."

She giggled like a school child at the expression on his face. "You, young lady, had better sit down and behave yourself. Here," he gestured to the piles of boxes flanking the wall, "make a start on this lot while I give Sandy his butties. I'll be back in a minute."

Elizabeth watched him leaving with a smile on her face. As the door closed quietly she went across to the cardboard boxes and pulled the interleaved lid open. The police had just emptied the drawers into the boxes without much thought as to what was relevant to what. Her smile faded as she gazed at the jumbled paperwork. "Proper policeman indeed!" She sniffed, then sneezed as the dust rising from the box tickled her nose. "This could take some time."

She was methodically sorting pieces of paper into piles when Bob returned. However he didn't stay, merely sticking his head around the door. "Beth I've got to go, I've got an interview. Will you be OK?"

She figured it was a rhetorical question as his head disappeared again and she heard him shout down the corridor, "OK Sandy I'm coming." He looked back at her, "I'll be back, enjoy yourself." The door closed and she was once again left amid a sea of papers washing over the floor towards his desk.

"Enjoy myself." It was muffled by the sides of the box she was peering into. "Guy sure knows how to show a girl a good time."

She settled down to sort and collate. Some of the material she had collected herself. She emptied the first box then piled the various pamphlets from museums and flyers picked up at tourist information offices, back into it. "Now what I need here is to figure out Peter's system."

She spread the papers, sorting meticulously those she thought directly related to the book he'd been writing, and those she hadn't seen which related to his family tree. The birth, death and marriage certificates went into yet another pile along with a meagre handful of sepia prints of gravestones and, apparently, baptismal records.

The family genealogy she set aside, delving into the historical papers. These she divided into material she could see the Professor had used to colour and flavour the story she'd read so far. There were photocopies and work obviously printed from the net and e-mails from various learned bodies. Eventually she sat back with a sigh.

"Right Bob, I don't know about your family tree, I want to know what happened next with Hans, but first," she stood up, stretching her back and wincing at the twinges, "I want that cuppa and I need the loo."

She cautiously made her way back to the main desk through the labyrinth of corridors. A friendly young constable directed her to the toilets and an equally friendly sergeant asked her who she was and what she was doing when she emerged a few minutes later.

"My name is Elizabeth Fielding; I'm helping Detective Inspector McInnis with his enquiries."

"Oh!" The sergeant looked a little less friendly, like a guard dog coming to alert.

Elizabeth eyeing him, gave a nervous smile. "That came out wrong. I'm assisting him with some evidence. Oh dear that still doesn't sound right." She rubbed her fingers down her skirt, looking at the suddenly hard eyed man in front of her. "Look Bob, Inspector McInnis, asked me to read some papers for him and help him put them in the right order, only then he had to go somewhere with Inspector Bell and he sort of left me in his office." She shrugged, "I wanted the loo and a cuppa but I'm sure you can check with him."

"Hmm, yes Miss. If you'd like to wait over there I'm sure we can get you a drink of tea. I'll just check with the Inspector."

Elizabeth, metaphorically hearing the cell door shut, went and sat down on a rather uncomfortable looking bench and gazed about at the constabulary passing to and fro. The sergeant went across to a desk and picked up the phone, keeping a weather eye on her.

After a brief conversation he came back, once again a friendly man. "Right Miss Fielding, if you'd like to follow me I'll get you that drink. Inspector McInnis sends his apologies." He grinned to himself as he walked in front of her. The Inspector had first exploded in his ear for interrupting the interrogation, then sworn as he realised what he'd done to Elizabeth. The sergeant was owed a drink now and he'd make sure he collected it he thought.

Elizabeth, fortified with strong tea and indignation, headed back with a police escort to Bob's office with murmured thanks. Bob would be paying her more than a drink of tea, abandoning her this way. She soon forgot her indignation however as she started to unravel the research. She'd found some handwritten notes and rough drafts of the continuing saga.

Hans had settled down into the life of a shepherd fairly easily. His uncle and aunt, even while they were devastated by the news of their son's death, had welcomed him into their home. They had sent a guarded message back to Germany to his parents via the Red Cross. Hans had at first been devastated too as he realised he couldn't contact them himself, but consoled himself with the thought that the war couldn't last forever. His hearing gradually returned, never as good as new but certainly enough for him to maintain a reasonable conversation.

They had found him employment in the Cumbrian fells with one of the members of the society, a taciturn but devout farmer who had a club foot and thus had avoided the battle to be forced to fight.

He'd found his services as a healer in demand, working with the animals of the farms around. Elizabeth puzzled over this but concluded that rules about looking after animals weren't as strict in the early part of the twentieth century. Many of the farms were denuded of men, the work devolving upon the women folk and children. Many of the horses used in the ploughing and sowing had gone to war, making the work even harder and heavier so a man, any man, was more than welcome.

The fell folk must have realised after a while that he wasn't English but no-one had said anything. They were a dour folk and minded their own business. He realised few of them agreed with a war that took their menfolk and left them to cope, while demanding they supply the front with meat for a pittance.

Elizabeth, struggling with Peter's small and curling handwriting, grinned to herself. She'd met farmers such as he described, and in her opinion they still paid as little heed to contemporary events outside their farm nearly a hundred years later.

The rough notes had got her that far. Now she laid them aside, looking at a printout of deserters' names. The group associated with them was known as 'Shot at Dawn'. They seemed to be advocating pardons for those who'd deserted due to shell shock. She could get behind that idea she thought.

She frowned over the list for a while, then, thinking about the story, looked for some familiar name, standing up and going over to the desk to leaf through the papers that Bob and she had read on Saturday night. "Johnson, that was the Corporal's name but he wasn't a deserter." She laid down the papers; Peter didn't name the other man he came back with did he? She scanned the papers again but found she was turning pages, unable to spot the scene where he was mentioned. "Oh this is hopeless."

She sighed, sitting down in Bob's chair and swinging gently as he had done a few hours earlier. Bob's computer was blank and she nudged the mouse and watched as the family tree he'd been studying swam back into view, the tiny print making it appear that there was a pattern on the screen.

"Oh dear, Bob, no wonder you're having problems understanding the data." She refreshed the screen, clicking and scrolling to bring the later part of the family tree into view.

It wasn't Bob McInnis that was having problems with the current data in interview room three however, it was Dennis Little.

"Now Dennis, Constable ap Rhys has read you your rights hasn't he?" Sandy Bell looked at the ugly and confused face in front of him. "You did understand them didn't you? You are being charged with breaking and entering and murder in the first degree of Professor Peter Neville at his home four weeks ago."

Dennis nodded.

"Let the record show the defendant nodded his head." McInnis sat taking backup notes at the side of the table. They had discussed who would take the interview and, even though it was Bob's case, he felt Sandy might get more from Dennis. Now considering the way the man was watching him write things down with a terrified expression on his face, he concluded they had been right in that decision.

"Now," said Sandy, "we've got a couple of warrants here Dennis; one is to examine your boots and take an imprint of your bare feet, the other is for a sample of your DNA. Since we're charging you with murder we don't need the warrant but it's there anyway." He showed the papers to the man in front of him. "We've sent for a court appointed solicitor for you, since you haven't been able to name one for yourself, and we won't be proceeding further until he arrives. OK?"

He waited again for the stunned man to reply. Dennis licked lips gone dry and looked from one face to the other. "I didn't murder no-one Inspector, honest I didn't." He shook his bullet head, his face screwed up like a piece of waste paper.

Bell held up a hand. "Dennis your solicitor isn't present. I must caution you again that anything you say can be used against you." Bell looked at him with a certain degree of pity. The poor sap was beyond fear into the calm waters of terror, treading water literally to save his life.

"Yes Guv, but I didn't kill no-one. Who'm I supposed to have killed? I don't know no Professors? Mr Barker wouldn't never forgive me ifn I killed no-one, especially a Professor." Bob reflected that Dennis apparently feared Barker worse than the police.

"Professor Neville lived in Victoria Place, the place you are accused of 'entering with intent to steal'."

"I didn't kill him." He looked into Bell's eyes, honesty radiating from every pore. "He was talking to the other guy when I left." Dennis looked marginally relieved, not realising for a minute that he'd confessed to B and E.

Sandy's lips twisted wryly despite the seriousness of the situation, the tap on the door and the urbane and cool tones of Richards the solicitor broke the silence. "I'm council on call."

Dennis swung round, looking the man over then looked back at Bell. "'Ere what's the idea fastening some murder on me. 'E was there when I done that job, an' when I went back, the guy was alive when I left. 'E knows that."

The ensuing silence resembled the beginning of the world before God spoke.

Gareth, the first to recover, moved smartly in front of the door; thus preventing Richards from leaving. Sandy Bell actually felt his jaw drop, and Bob's face had a wet sponge of incredulity wiped over his features to leave them ready for the next emotion, that of astonishment.

"I think you'd better explain that statement Dennis." McInnis spoke to the thug seated at the table but kept his eyes fixed on Richards, whose normally pale face now resembled a bowl of cold porridge, grey and old.

Bell looked across at Richards. "Would you like to sit down Mr Richards?"

"I'm not sure that I ought to Inspector; this man obviously thinks I'm guilty of some misdemeanour and I wouldn't want to pervert the course of justice by being present at his interview."

"Oh I think you'd better stay sir. After all Mr Little needs a lawyer and you are available. It would be better if we cleared this up now."

McInnis watched Richards watching Dennis. He thought Richards looked like a cat watching a bird; poor Dennis was obviously going to be sacrificed for lunch. "Now Dennis I think you'd better tell us why you think Mr Richards can supply you with an alibi."

Dennis looked at the three men in turn, licking his lips again. He'd just worked out that his alibi was also the witness against him, but better a charge of grand theft than murder. "Someone give me the key to the house." He spoke slowly, working the story out in his head. "So I takes the key he gives me and goes earlyish like. I wuz told the old geezer that lived there," Dennis started to speed up, "didn't get up all that early and he wuz in a wheelchair, so I wuz to go in and get some stuff, records." He paused, looking between Bell and McInnis, waiting for their nod.

"Anyway I got in OK and I went quiet like upstairs, but I couldn't see what I had to get there, so I goes into the big room downstairs and I was looking around when the doorbell goes." McInnis could imagine his horror; a quick B and E in a nearly deserted house had turned into a busy thoroughfare.

"Well when I hears the doorbell I nipped out smartish, and I was heading for the back door but couldn't get past the room next door; I could hear that wheelchair whirring in there." He cocked his head on one side, "If you follows."

McInnis brought the floor plan into his mind. "Yes," he could see Dennis' problem, he'd have to pass the study door to get out the back door. He nodded encouragingly.

Dennis nodded back; satisfied his story was good so far. "So I went back upstairs to wait, and I looked out the little window at the front and I sees him, waiting to get in." Dennis triumphantly came to the end of his recital as he pointed a stubby finger at Richards.

Richards raised an eyebrow; he had remained standing by the door and seemed to have regained some of his colour. "That accusation sounds very like slander to me young man. I wasn't anywhere near Professor Neville's house that morning."

Sandy exchanged a look with Bob.

"This interview is suspended while a new solicitor is found for Mr Dennis Little."

Dennis, trying to catch up with things, spoke up. "He was there. I recognised his voice; he was talking to the old geezer."

"Dennis, I've suspended the interview. If you are satisfied with these warrants I'd like to put them into effect while we wait for a new solicitor."

Dennis might not be bright, but looking from one man to the other he realised the focus of attention had shifted for some reason. "Look I admits I broke in but I didn't murder no-one."

"Yes, we got that Dennis." Bell sighed at the broken record. "Go with Constable ap Rhys; are you willing to allow us to take DNA?"

Dennis cocked his head on one side, "Like on the TV?"

"Yes, like on the TV."

"Cor!" Rather than being frightened, Dennis seemed quite entranced by the idea.

"I should wait for a solicitor young man."

"Nah, wait until I tell Mr Barker you took my DNA!" Dennis stood up with a fluid movement for all his size. "You tell 'em mister; you were talking to him when I left. I couldn't have murdered no Professor."

He walked towards the door and Gareth opened it and ushered him out, closing it firmly behind them.

"Come and sit down Mr Richards."

"I really don't think that is necessary Inspector Bell. It's clearly a case of mistaken identity."

The door opened as he spoke and another constable entered. He looked like a refugee from the police rugby team; his biceps rippled under his white summer shirt like a breeze across a smooth pond. He closed the door and stood sentinel, his face impassive.

"Now Mr Richards. There's just one thing wrong with mistaken identity. We hadn't got around to briefing you on the case. So how did you know it was Professor Neville's house and murder we were talking about?"

"Well, good God! There haven't been that many murders in Carlisle over the past few weeks." Richards came slowly over and sat down, dropping his briefcase on the floor. "Really Inspector, I'm not a fool." He smiled in a rather patronising manner which made Bob's hands involuntarily clench into fists.

"No sir, you're not a fool. So you know that we must investigate Mr Little's story fully." Sandy was also lightly seething, "I must ask you to wait here, sir, while we finish taking his statement with an independent solicitor."

"You're not actually going to take the word of that oaf against mine are you?"

"Dennis might be slow sir, but if he's willing to take the rap for larceny rather than keeping quiet and risk murder, then there must be some truth in his story somewhere."

"Very well Inspector, but you're making a big mistake."

Sandy pushed back his chair and stood up at the same time as McInnis. Both men nodded to the solicitor and the constable and left the room, closing the door softly behind them. "My God Bob, what can of worms are we dealing with here?"

"I dunno Sandy, but let's get a solicitor for Dennis ASAP. I'm just going to see that Beth's alright then I'll be right back." He headed down the corridor while Sandy went in the opposite direction.

He found his beloved sitting in his chair gazing at the computer screen with a deep frown on her face. "I'm sorry darling; I should have let the Duty Sergeant know you were here."

"Don't worry about it Bob." Elizabeth spoke absently, "look Bob I think I've sorted out your family tree for you." She glanced up at him. "Peter had got masses of information on the German side, and that makes sense when his father was one." She prodded a folder of papers on the side of his desk. "There's all this information about where people are buried; he's even got photos of tombstones." She grimaced.

She looked fully at him now, "But there's not a lot for the modern stuff. And I'm not surprised the Fraulien has gaps. I don't suppose she knew about the switch in the First World War."

"No I don't suppose she did." Bob came further into the room; he hadn't expected a rapturous welcome, but Elizabeth seemed to be almost ignoring him. "Look I really am sorry Beth."

Beth gave him her full attention, "Stop worrying Bob, you have to do your work." She stood up, coming round the desk and holding out her hands, "I'll keep going at this but I thought you'd got your murderer." She shuddered slightly as if a cold wind had touched her skin.

Bob took the offered hands and leaned in for a kiss. "I've got two minutes; show me what you've got so far."

They came back to the desk and stood looking at the screen. Elizabeth moved the mouse from one side, clicking and picking up the bar at the bottom to bring a new section into view. "These are Peter's great grandparents." She moved the cursor on the screen again. "They had eight children but only four survived to adulthood, which is par for the course in those days. Now," she scrolled down a bit more, "the four that survived were three daughters and a Peter." She sighed, "I hate when family names crop up over and over. It makes it so confusing."

"Now the son married out. That is he didn't marry a Quaker girl; they had our Peter of World War One and he died. The next daughter married a German called Erkel. They had Hans who was actually the first Peter's cousin. Is that clear?"

Bob nodded, "I'm with you so far."

"They also had a daughter who married a Herr Smitt. Parents of our Fraulien Smitt."

"Aha! So that's where she comes in. She'd be Hans..." he screwed up his face a minute, "niece. And our Peter's second cousin. Right?" It was said a trifle doubtfully.

"Mmm. Now we come to the third and eldest daughter. She married a Mr Hemmingway."

"What like in Ernest Hemmingway?"

"Well I haven't found any connection to him, but the same name certainly. He had two daughters, Sarah and Sylvia." She wrinkled her nose over the names. "Now this is where it gets a bit complicated. Hans, as Peter, married one of the daughters."

"So he married his..." Bob looked into the air, "cousin? No, second cousin."

"Right."

"Well that interesting. Didn't they need a dispensation for that?"

"I have no idea Bob, they aren't Catholics." Elizabeth sounded a bit exasperated.

"Well it's fascinating, but we think it was a robbery gone wrong that led to your Professor's death." He pushed away from the desk.

"Wait, I haven't finished. The other daughter, she married the deserter."

"What deserter?" Bob shook his head, puzzled by mention of deserters. "I thought you said Hans married..."

"The deserter that came back with Corporal Johnson and Hans. Draycott his name was, they became brothers-in-law as well as brothers-in-arms."

"Well I'll be blowed! That's a fantastic bit of research darling."

"And there's more."

Bob sat down on his chair and looked at her expectantly, impatience forgotten.

"The Draycott's had a daughter and she married a Mr Richards, who has one son," she grinned. "That means my Peter had living relatives besides Fraulien Smitt and they ought to get a share of his Will. Isn't that great Bob?" Elizabeth kept the smile on her face; she thought it was wonderful. "I feel like one of those terrible companions in an old novel who's coerced the doddery old man to change his Will in their favour, and now I can give it to the relatives it belongs to." She gradually lost her smile, "Bob?"

McInnis sat with a blank look on his face.

"Bob. Don't you think it's good?"

"Hush darling, I think I've got nearly all the pieces now." He noticed her worried look. "It's alright. Stay here darling, you've been wonderful." He stood up and dropped a kiss on her forehead. "If you need a drink or anything just go and ask, but don't go home yet please. I've got a case to solve but I'll be back." He moved past the desk, oblivious to the fact that he'd dislodged several files in his hurry to leave the room.

Elizabeth watched him leave and sighed; then bent to gather up the work in progress and shove it back onto the desk.

Bob meanwhile was walking rapidly down the corridor towards Sandy Bell's lair. He pushed open the door and entered the room, so precipitately that Sandy nearly dropped the bundle of papers he'd just gripped under his chin, while his hands searched for more on the desk.

"Sandy I think I've got the answer. But I don't know how we can prove it."

Sandy allowed the pile of papers to avalanche down onto the desk again as he looked at Bob's face. "I'm an old man. I can't take too many shocks in a day lad. So this had better be good."

Bob filled him in on the information Beth had just supplied. "It's all in the research Sandy. It can't have been jazz records. Gareth said they were still there when he looked."

"If they were in the research Bob, why didn't the man take them the second time he visited?"

"Maybe he reads even less than we think Sandy?"

"Nah that won't work, Barker must have told him what to bring back." Sandy gathered the variety of files and document folders lying on his desk again. "I'll see if he can recognise the type any way."

Dennis was sitting in a dejected silence in yet another interview room. Mark Forester had been in and swabbed the inside of his cheek. It had taken a few seconds and then he'd gone away again. Dennis was frankly disappointed; he'd expected something more dramatic. He kept looking at Gareth saying, "Is that it?" in a rather pathetic voice.

"DS Forester will be back in a minute; he wants to check your feet."

"I got a corn."

Gareth hid the smile. He actually felt a bit sorry for Dennis, even though he knew what he'd done to Cavendish. "Er, no, Mr Little, he wants you to walk on a sheet of paper in your bare feet."

"Well he'll see my corn then. It's these boots; I only got them last winter."

Gareth shook his head, grateful when Forester came back into the room.

"Right Mr Little. You are cooperating of your own free will?"

"Yus." Dennis looked at the roll of paper that Forester laid on the floor down the centre of the room.

"If you could take off your boots and socks," he paused while the big man tidily set aside the lace-less boots, carefully tucking the socks into each boot in turn.

"See! You can see my corn. I bin to the chemist and they give me some plasters, but they didn't work." Dennis held out the offending foot for Mark to look at.

"Ah yes. Well maybe you should see a podiatrist?" He busied himself opening a flat tin with an inkpad inside and vigorously applying a roller, like an energetic cook attacking pastry.

Dennis was frowning, "Ain't that sumfin what frows furniture about? How would that help me feet?"

"Er…" The two men exchanged a look, drowning in misplaced words and letters of the alphabet.

Gareth looked at the still frowning man. He didn't appear to be mad, but you never can tell. "I'm not sure I follow you Mr Little."

Bell, followed by McInnis, opened the door at this inauspicious moment; Sandy glanced from one face to the other, wondering at the silence.

"Inspector Bell why have I got to see a ghost thing about my corn?"

Bell looked helplessly at the three other members of the force.

"I suggested that Mr Little see a podiatrist sir, for the corn on his foot. I think he misunderstood me."

Bell shook his head. "What are you doing setting up as a doctor now? I thought you were taking his footprint." His face looked grim to Forester. Bob, more attuned, knew his superior was desperately trying not to laugh.

"Er yes sir." Forester swung around, glaring at the puzzled thief. "If I could just put ink on your feet sir? And then if you would walk along the white paper for me one way, and run back the other."

Dennis eyed him for a minute. "Well alright, but I don't want to get ink on me socks."

Gareth found his lips twitching uncontrollably and had to cough vigorously. "I'll er... I'll go and get a wet cloth for you Mr Little, and see if your new solicitor has arrived." He sidled out of the room like a crab avoiding a hungry seagull's eye, shutting the door with a slight bang as he left, the noise not quite concealing to Bob's ears the roar of laughter.

"Dennis."

Dennis, whose mind, such as it was, had gone off for a quiet stroll and a quick fag, returned, nipping out the fag and putting it behind a metaphorical ear in an embarrassed manner, "Yes Inspector Bell."

Sandy indicated the white paper and Forester standing with the inky roller.

"Oh! Yes Inspector."

Dennis had tickly feet; it made the whole process into more of a London stage farce than it had been already. He giggled, making those in the room struggle to suppress their grins, but eventually the job was finished.

"It'll take a couple of hours to get the results back Inspector. I did most of the prelim' work yesterday."

"Fine Mark. And you'll check the other thing for me?"

Gareth entered with a handful of paper towels, some of them obviously wet, and a very young man following on his heels.

Bell and McInnis watched Mark nod and retreat, and waited for Dennis Little to finish wiping his feet with the towels and putting his boots and socks back on.

Dennis had handed the new, slightly bemused, solicitor the towels he'd just used and Gareth threw the towels he, in turn, had received from the young solicitor, into a metal bin next to the door and resumed his position next to it. He had come back with a stern face but Bell, facing him, could see little quivers of amusement passing over his large frame like a mighty oak stirred by a zephyr. However, when they began the questioning again, he became stern in earnest.

"Now Dennis, you have admitted breaking into the house in Victoria Place."

"Yes, that other guy was there too."

"Let's just stick to what you were doing for now. You were looking for some stuff; records you said. How did you know what they would look like? Were they forms or certificates or what?"

Dennis scratched his head, loosening a minor avalanche of dandruff onto the regulation blue suit supplied by the police. "They was just records in cases."

"Well what size cases were they?" Sandy and Bob had tried to work out how Dennis, who considered the Beano as intellectual reading, would know what Barker wanted him to steal.

Now he turned to the pile, "Show us what kind of case lad!" He pointed to the pile.

"Weren't nufin like them. It was just an ordinary record case, wiv a picture of a black man on the front, wiv a trumpet."

Enlightment dawned across the face of the two watching coppers. A positive sunrise of colours grew on Sandy's face as he once more suppressed his hilarity. "Ah! Yes I see. Musical records."

"That's what I said guv… records." Dennis gazed at the two silent men.

Seeing that Sandy had apparently been struck with aphasia, Bob took over. "So the first time you went to steal some records, and couldn't find them. Is that correct?"

Dennis nodded.

"And while you were searching someone arrived and you hid upstairs while Professor Neville let them in and took them into the study."

"Yes I told you. It was that other solicitor and he come in and went into the study. And what's more," Dennis warmed to his theme; "he's a solicitor so he can't tell porkies," he ended on a triumphant note.

Bob waved the interruption aside. "So tell us what happened next."

"I crept down and waited until they shut the door. Only they didn't, it was a bit open and that solicitor was speaking, and he had his back to me, talking to the bookshelf." Dennis looked a bit puzzled for a minute. "Anyway I crept down and took a chance and went out the front door. The other man had a nice voice too." He nodded his head as if to agree with himself.

"What did the other man say Dennis?" Bell was back in control.

"I dunno. Somefink about keys I think. I couldn't hear proper."

"Now, you went back again didn't you?"

"I shouldn't answer that Mr Little. It's rather a leading question." The solicitor was a young man so new to his trade his leather briefcase squeaked.

"Sorright. I already told Inspector Bell I seen the other solicitor there again." Dennis looked at the legal representative. "If you admit it an they has the statement, it ain't no good not admitting it again." He spoke in the kindly tones of an elder brother informing a younger miscreant of his rights. The solicitor opened his mouth and closed it again. Dennis turned back to Bell.

"Well Mr B., he asked me to go again. He said as how the funeral of the Professor had been and so I should look around cos the house would be empty." He frowned fiercely. "Never known him be wrong before, it were like Pica bloody dilly."

Bell noted the fact that he'd just implicated Barker but refrained from comment, patiently reeling him back in again.

"So you went for the records after the funeral?"

"Yeah, only first I goes to see what he was looking at on that shelf and sees the safe. Only when I looks it was empty." Dennis sounded as mournful as a fog horn in the dead of night.

"How did you know there was a safe Dennis? It was behind books?"

"Weren't! There weren't no books. It was open. You could see that when you went in the room." Dennis looked from one man to the other, "I ain't daft; I ain't ever been in the safe cracking trade. Why would I try to open a safe what was closed?" he shrugged.

It was unanswerable. Bob McInnis looked at the ugly face, trying to read if the man was telling the truth. He shrugged in turn, "So what did you do then?"

"I looks for the records. They was in the other room all the time." His voice took on a note of wonder. "I needn't have come back if that other bloke hadn't interrupted me."

"And then?"

"Eh!"

"What did you do after you found the records?"

"I bundled 'em up, and I was just gonna go when the key turned in the lock. So I goes upstairs again to see who it was. But I couldn't, there weren't anyone there."

"That's because whoever it was must have already come in Dennis."

"Oh yeah! I wondered about that." Dennis was pleased to get an answer to his problem.

Bob waited a moment, "So what did you do then?"

Dennis dislodged another snowstorm. "I waited a bit, something fell, and then it went all quiet. So I peeked out the window again and that solicitor was walking away. So I figured it was safe to go down. Only it wasn't." He was feeling aggrieved and it showed. "Someone else come in. It was a female, I heard her call out. You can't trust females not to squeal so I hung on a bit and watched from the top of the stairs and she went into the study." Dennis wagged a finger, "Pica bloody dilly I tells you."

270

Sandy took over; he could see Bob turning a bit white as he connected the dots, "So how did you get away Dennis?" It was said in a conversational manner.

"Oh! I creeps down and she's sitting on the floor holding..." He suddenly stopped, peering at McInnis, "It were you. I thought it was, only then I thought I musta been wrong. Why would you lay on the floor when there's some perfectly good beds upstairs?" It was Grasshopper seeking enlightenment of the Master.

Sandy cast a glance at his younger colleague noting that Bob was regaining a bit of colour. "The Inspector had been knocked out."

"Oh! Right... so you wasn't..."

"No he wasn't Dennis. So what happened then?"

"Well I couldn't get the records away so I went out the front door and went and told..." Sandy saw him bite his tongue, "someone that someone come in."

Sandy nodded. "So you didn't actually steal anything from the house Dennis?"

"I told you Pica bloody dilly. I couldn't get nufin."

"Thank you. Now you understand we will be charging you with breaking and entering with intent to steal Dennis."

"I didn't murder anyone though. I told you straight."

"At the moment Dennis we are dropping the charge of murder." Sandy watched as the huge shoulders sagged like an inflatable doll with the air going out.

"We will be charging you with other things Dennis." It was said almost gently.

"So long as it isn't murder."

"No it won't be murder. Now we have to go and do another interview. Would you like a mug of tea and something to eat?" Sandy glanced at the silently watching solicitor who still wore a bemused expression. "Perhaps you and this solicitor can talk about how you might plead."

"OK." Dennis smiled; it was a torturous experiment in the movement of muscles. "Can I have corn beef sandwiches Inspector Bell? I likes the way they makes them here, wiv brown sauce."

"I'll see what I can do Dennis."

The two Inspectors got up and left the room quietly, taking Constable Gareth ap Rhys with them. "Leave them to have a chat Gareth, and see what you can do about the sandwiches. Poor bloody sap. I know he's vicious but..." Sandy's mobile eyebrows drew together.

He turned to Bob, "So do you want fortifying with sandwiches before we tackle Mr Richards."

"Mug of tea later Sandy, that's all. Let's get this over with."

They walked down the cool and slightly dusty corridor of late afternoon, going to trap Richards into admitting murder, and not caring, knowing that the solicitor would have condemned an innocent man to prison. All this happening because Little Dennis wasn't a very bright specimen of humanity but one of whom he could take advantage.

The Desk Sergeant came up with a sheaf of flimsies. "Got your warrant executed and here's the army records. Son's a bit of an odd one too. And DS Forester sent this," he handed over papers.

"Bring three mugs of tea please Sergeant, in about half an hour." The Desk Sergeant gave a quick salute and disappeared.

The detectives entered the interview room in single file and went to sit down.

Sandy turned to Richards. "Do you wish to have a solicitor present sir?"

"I must protest Inspector. I have been held here for over two hours without reason, and now you ask me if I need a solicitor! Are you charging me with anything?" Richards raised his eyebrows.

Bob McInnis set the recording machine going. He began to read out the rights. Richards listened to him with a puzzled expression on his face. "Of course I understand my rights man." He heaved a theatrical sigh, "I repeat, what are you proposing to charge me with?"

"We are going to charge you with the murder of Peter Neville, your cousin, four weeks ago sir." It was a bold step, and a chancy one, but McInnis knew in his gut he'd got it right. "You can have legal representation whenever you would like it sir. But we have a witness who puts you at the scene of the crime."

"What, that stupid oaf?"

"Just so sir. Would you like a solicitor present?"

"No I wouldn't! Do you think I want half the bar laughing at me because some policeman believes what a criminal tells them about me."

"Am I to understand you waive your right to representation sir?"

McInnis wanted to be very sure that this was done by the book.

"Yes." Richards sat back, crossing his arms, and looked impassively at the two men.

"Very well sir. Now..." McInnis consulted some notes. "We have used a warrant to search your house sir."

"You had no right." Richards' fists clenched. "What grounds did you have?"

"I repeat sir we searched your house with a duly executed warrant. The grounds are set out here," he tapped the paper. "You are under suspicion of murder, you were seen at the crime scene, and you had opportunity as the victim trusted you. You stand to inherit a large sum of money as one of the remaining relatives of the deceased if you care to contest the Will. You have the necessary training from your days in the army." McInnis ticked off the points on his fingers. He watched the smug expression growing on the man's face.

"We have a box of photos which I know were in the house after the murder, and the contents of the Professor's safe. These have all been found in your possession, and finally we have your DNA under Professor Neville's fingernails."

Richards looked stunned, then rallied. "How can you be sure? You haven't taken mine. Nor would you get a warrant to on those flimsy grounds; there certainly hasn't been time to compare any samples you might illegally have taken from my home." He looked at them like the bully in the playground having extorted the dinner money once again.

"Well strictly speaking sir, having charged you with murder, we don't need a warrant for your DNA. But, we didn't have to get it sir; we just needed to see if the DNA under his nails had sufficient alleles to match the DNA chart that the Professor had received from Fraulien Smitt, another of your relatives. This Familial DNA link connects you with the DNA obtained from the fingernail scrapings. You see sir there aren't that many of you left alive. Fraulien Smitt, you and your son are the only surviving members of this branch with the right DNA and you bear the correct XX and XY chromosomes to be a match."

Bob McInnis inwardly smiled to himself. He must thank Forester; he hadn't a clue what he'd just said, he was quoting verbatim but it seemed to have flattened the old man in front of them.

"Would you tell us why sir?"

Richards slumped in the chair. Suddenly he looked like the old man he really was. "I did it for my son."

Sandy and Bob waited quietly, five slow minutes ticked by. "Sir?" McInnis broke the silence. He watched Richards lift his head which had slowly slumped forward onto his chest.

"My son. Do you know what it's like to father a freak Inspector? I got him in the Army, with some of my old buddies. They would have looked after him. But no, he didn't want that. He wanted to stand on his own feet he said. He'd make his own way!" Richards, his face red, clenched his fists. "I could have got him some help. I'm sure it's just a physical thing."

The two watchers frowned. "What is sir?" Bell looked concerned.

274

"This fancying men. He didn't have to, he could have got himself a nice girl, but no he's just like his mother was, weak. I blame it on that sect she came from; I made sure I didn't have anything to do with them as soon as I could. It weakens men and women. Look at Neville, weak."

"Oh!" It was breathed out as McInnis realised what the problem had been.

"I checked you know?" Richards became almost conversational, "I checked back through the family, it wasn't the Richards' side, and Peter Neville wanted to tell the boy he was alright. He wanted to help him. As if it wasn't bad enough that Neville's father had brought a deserter into the family." He paused again, "That was enough to keep my son in the ranks. But I stopped him telling." His face took on a rather cunning look. He looked from one policeman to the other. "Wouldn't you have protected your child? It was the only way don't you see? I couldn't let him publish and spoil it for my son."

McInnis continued to watch him carefully; once the gates were open it seemed there was no stopping the flood of words. Richards had taken over Peter Neville's account two years previously but it had been only six month ago that he'd received a phone call asking him to come round. The Professor had told him they were related, and how pleased he was to find another relative. He'd wanted to meet Paul, the son, but Richards had put it off. He didn't want his son mixing with pacifists.

Professor Neville had trusted him, given him a key to the front door and the safe; allowed him access to all the charts so that they could both work on the family tree. "He was so proud of that tree, with its foreigners and deserters and cowards." He looked at McInnis, "Why, why would any man be proud of that? I burnt it. I knew where he kept it and I took it home and I burnt it."

McInnis didn't attempt a reply; the bigot in front of him continued to rant. "So I went round early. He wanted me to arrange a meeting. I couldn't do that, you must see I couldn't. But he kept on and on, so I had to shut him up."

"You strangled him sir?"

"Yes." Richards tirade halted, the sluice gates closed again. "I killed him and now my son will never get into the wardroom."

Bell had questioned and cross-questioned for a further hour, but the story didn't change. Richards even apologised for hitting McInnis. "You shouldn't have come back. I didn't want you finding the papers. Why couldn't you have accepted it as a robbery and been satisfied?"

"Is that why you took the things from the safe sir?"

"Yes. Of course it was."

They'd formally charged him and placed him in the cells awaiting the arraignment, and the two men had gone back to Bob's office.

"We'll start on the paperwork tomorrow Bob. We've got all the facts now. It just needs pulling together, and the man's confessed."

"I wonder if he'd have confessed if Dennis hadn't seen him and said so."

"Probably not. He doesn't strike me as the kind to shoulder the blame. I feel sorry for his son. It's not as if the army kicks you out for being a homosexual these days; they aren't allowed to for one thing."

"I'll deal with Dennis Little's paperwork tonight before I go home. Are we going to let him out on police bail Sandy?"

Sandy shook his head. "Best not, let's keep him cosy in the cells and hope Forester can come up with the goods on the GBH."

"I doubt we'll get Cavendish to prefer charges."

"Maybe not, but it's worth a try. Dennis is thick and a thug and he needs a lesson in manners." Sandy twisted his lips, "He doesn't deserve to go down for a murder he didn't commit though."

They turned down the corridor leading to their rooms. "I'm going to marry her Sandy."

"Of course you are lad." Sandy looked at him as they walked along the corridor. "You always were."

"Do you mind if I take the day off Thursday? I want to buy a ring."

Sandy slapped him on the back, "Only if I can be best man Bob."

They exchanged secret grins as they went into his office. Then Sandy grimaced as the younger couple exchanged a look that would have fried eggs on the pavement.

"Hello darling." Bob looked at the pretty picture she made in the evening sunshine. "I've got one or two things to tidy up and then I can go."

Sandy looked at them both. "Take this boy home Elizabeth; I've got better things to do with my time than look at the pair of you."

"What about the paperwork?"

"Away with you man."

The men exchanged a glance that conveyed a lot of things then, "Elizabeth," Bob held out his hand, "I've got the day off Thursday; shall we celebrate?"

She smiled back and the oblivious pair wandered from the room and Sandy watched them go. He stood absently gazing at the paperwork, and sighed as he looked at the crowded desk in Bob McInnis's office. He must be mad to let the boy go and saddle himself with all the paperwork for the arrest of Dennis Little.

He saw that someone, presumably Elizabeth, had neatly stacked the research. Not only the stuff from the boxes, but the vital genealogical information as well. It was obviously a printout and he didn't think Bob had had time to print all this stuff out. He gathered it up and revealed the file Gareth ap Rhys had brought in on Madogan. Hmm! He supposed he'd better look at that too; he tucked it under his arm with the rest of the paperwork.

Meanwhile Elizabeth was tucked up in Bob's car. He kept grinning and she glanced across. "So you're happy to have caught your man. Can you tell me, or shouldn't I ask?"

Bob looked at her and then in the driving mirror. "Let's grab a meal and I'll fill you in on events as far as I can. You found the key to this case so you deserve to know who did it."

"Well you shot off without letting me know what I'd said to you to bring things together, and I've been sitting in your office for the past two hours, so you'd better tell me something." She did her best to sound cross but she really hadn't got the heart for it; the man was so pleased it seemed nothing could dent his happiness.

"Sorry love." But he didn't look contrite either.

They found a quiet pub on the outskirts of the town and, after ordering, Bob settled back to tell her about Richards and his son.

"So it was Peter's solicitor all the time. No wonder he didn't want us to look at the research." Elizabeth frowned, working out events from her side of the information. Then offered a bright smile. "I left it all stacked on your desk. You need some new black ink for the printer. Oh, and while I remember, you knocked a file down in your hurry to arrest Mr Richards. I didn't read it, I just stuffed it all back in. Honest," she worried on her bottom lip.

"That's OK. I trust you, I said so." Bob had held her hand and waited for the arrival of the waiter with no impatience at all.

However Wednesday was filled with impatience. Thursday was never going to arrive as far as Bob was concerned. He'd spent the day knee deep in paperwork. They'd finally managed to get a look at Richards' files; the man had asked for several other things to be taken into consideration, including the fact that he'd arranged for Madogan to be beaten up.

When the motive of blackmail was mentioned Sandy was jubilant. "Now we can lock that bastard Madogan up Bob. Him and his psychopathic tendencies!"

They had got warrants for the office and home, but the Major was proving somewhat more elusive. The blackmail information on

278

several prominent persons in the town was providing Sandy with a headache that dimmed his jubilation a bit. But not that much.

When five o' clock arrived they both called it a day. "We've still got a lot of depositions from witnesses to sort out, and a whole slew of interviews to arrange, Bob. But I think we both deserve an early finish with the hours we've put in these last few weeks." Sandy rubbed a hand over his face and stacked the paperwork on the desk. He'd moved into Bob's office on a temporary basis and was considering whether it wouldn't be a good move on a more permanent one. "Away, home lad and enjoy your day off. The weather is promising to be beautiful tomorrow."

Bob McInnis had arranged to meet Beth at Hammond's Pond. It was a tree filled park near Beth's home, and there was a small boating lake. Bob wanted to propose on the lake. He thought that way he could keep Beth captive until she gave in and said yes. He wasn't totally confident she would, despite the way she'd melted in his arms the night before, she was a very independent young woman.

He dressed casually in jeans and t-shirt; the sun shone, and as he approached the gates he could hear in the background the aviary full of chirping birds. He fingered the small box in his trouser pocket, turning it round and round. It had a comforting solidity that gave him a small measure of confidence.

As he strolled along the road towards the entrance he offered a grin to the small child in the pushchair who was waving a stuffed rabbit at him. Now that would be an added bonus, he could see Beth doing that. He smiled happily at the mum as she strolled along pointing things out to her child.

He was somewhat surprised to see an ambulance at the gates until he caught sight of the football strip clad teenager talking to the ambulance driver. Blast! He'd thought the place would be nice and quiet on a weekday but there was obviously a match on. He casually examined the strip; it looked like a couple of the local schools.

There was a policeman on duty at the gate too. He nodded at Bob as the latter strolled through.

He made his way, grimacing, through a small crowd of people. There were several more police uniforms in evidence; it looked like he'd have to find another place to propose. He was casting about in his mind where to go. He was thinking that maybe Gretna would be appropriate. He saw the serious face of Sandy Bell approaching him from among the anonymous group. "Oh Lord Sandy, don't say my day off has ended already?" He pulled a comical face.

"No lad," Sandy towed him away from the group. There was no easy way. Sandy had had enough experience to know that. "It's Beth lad, she's been injured." He caught Bob as he literally staggered from the shock.

"The ambulance men are with her now lad." Sandy held his arm until he was sure he had his attention. "It's alright Bob, they're dealing with her."

Bob ignored him. "Take me to her."

Beth was lying on the grass on a stretcher. Her clothes were soaked; the sun sparkled in the wet hair around her unmarked face. Bob dropped to his knees and cradled the still figure while Sandy spoke with soft vehemence to the police around them.

Ambulance men continued to insert needles, fix and put up bags of saline, fasten on an oxygen mask and cover her in aertex blankets. Somewhat hampered by the man holding their patient, but they refrained from comment. There was a man who might commit murder they felt.

Sandy looked down at the couple on the grass.

Bob was stroking the hair back from Beth's face when her hand came fluttering upwards and her eyes opened. "Hi!" It was whispered out through the mask.

He carefully moved it out of the way for a minute, "Hi yourself."

"Don't cry love," was offered in softened tones.

280

Bob brushed away a stray tear, "Who me?" He leaned over to place the gentlest of kisses on her lips before replacing the mask. "I'm a proper policeman I am. We don't cry."

"Sez you!" Beth had to take a deep breath to speak, but she got the words out. "I love you."

"I love you too."

"Let us get her on the ambulance, sir, and then you can sit with her."

McInnis reluctantly moved aside while they dealt with her, speaking softly to Sandy, "What happened?"

"Don't know lad, couple of the football team spotted her on their way to the game and called the ambulance. I was down at the desk when the call came through for the ambulance and police, and came over because the description matched Beth. You'd told me that you planned to be here today." Sandy looked apologetically at the younger man. "I think she must have slipped and fallen into the pond, cracked her head and gashed herself."

"OK Sandy." Bob had been watching operations, now he gripped the other man's hand for a second. "Thanks for being here. I'm going with her now."

Sandy returned the brief grip and stood back as Bob went over to the stretcher and walked at her side to the ambulance, holding her hand while she was being loaded into it.

"This is another fine mess you've got yourself into." He sat down, stroking the hand that was attached to the monitors, watching her looking at him. "This isn't the vehicle I was going to get you into today." He glanced around as the ambulance man slammed the doors and, for a brief moment, they were alone. "But I've got this little present for you, and I thought I could shanghai you onto a rowing boat till you took it."

She continued to look but the briefest of smiles bloomed on her face, "Tisn't my birthday today."

They were interrupted briefly by the paramedic checking her recordings then he turned his back on them, and McInnis seized the chance to kiss her palm.

The medic swung back holding a chart. "Right Miss, you take it easy, nice dose of antibiotics and some bed rest and you'll be fine." The man filled in some figures on his chart.

"What's your name love?" He looked at McInnis for the reply.

McInnis looked across at him, then at Elizabeth holding her gaze, "Her name's Elizabeth Fielding, but she's going to change it very, very shortly to McInnis." He paused, "Aren't you love?" There was just a trace of worry in his face and voice.

"Yes." It might have been muffled by the mask, but it was a definite affirmative. Elizabeth nodded carefully.

"Right Miss." The medic was oblivious to the marriage proposal that had just been enacted under his official nose, but he did know the pair in front of him were in love. It didn't take a trained observer to see that.